Ketch Colt

by
J.D. Harkleroad

PublishAmerica
Baltimore

© 2005 by J.D. Harkleroad.
All rights reserved. No part of this book may be reproduced, stored in a retrieval system or transmitted in any form or by any means without the prior written permission of the publishers, except by a reviewer who may quote brief passages in a review to be printed in a newspaper, magazine or journal.

First printing

ISBN: 1-4137-7486-5
PUBLISHED BY PUBLISHAMERICA, LLLP
www.publishamerica.com
Baltimore

Printed in the United States of America

For
Dwayne and Big Thunder,
The other 2 "H's" in
The Rafter 3H Connected

"...whatsoever you do, do all to the glory of God."
— I Corinthians 10:31

Acknowledgments for technical and other assistance:

Jerry A. O'Callaghan, Bureau of Land Management, U.S. Dept. of the Interior; Howard A. Heit, M.D.; Haywood Nelms, Gunsmith; J'Wayne McArthur, horsebreaker and poet; Ronnie Brinkerhoff, friend and sounding board; Mira Loy and Bob Ott.

A special note of appreciation to Jennifer Hendershot, a superlative editor whom I have come to regard as a friend — thanks for all your help and encouragement.

Other books by J.D. Harkleroad:

Horse Thief Trail

Blood Atonement

Prologue

*"Ain't no hoss that can't be rode;
ain't no rider that can't be throwed."*

The second rider in as many minutes ate corral dirt. The loafers hanging around Peady's stable hooted a few appropriate insults as the bucked-off rider scrabbled under the bottom rail, away from the rearing stud.

Ketch, sitting on the top rail, said nothing, but allowed a grin to curl his lips.

As Woody Vaught dusted off his britches, he turned his fury and humiliation on Ketch. "What the hell's so funny? You're such a hotshot, buster, you ride the crazy sonofabitch!"

Ketch's grin broadened. "I bust broncs for money, not bragging rights."

Woody grimaced. That part about "money" chafed an already bruised ego. As Slash R foreman, busting his backside day and night, he earned less in a month than Ketch did in a week, just busting one herd for the old man.

He said to Ketch, "You ride this locoed widow-maker and I'll stand you to drinks for a week down to Katie's and an hour in her bed."

"Huh-uh." Ketch shook his head. "I'm a married man now, remember? But I could always use a few extra dollars. Pass the hat, and if you come up with enough to make a broken bone or two worthwhile, I'll give you a show."

"You're on, but only if you ride that devil to a standstill."

The loungers took up a collection and Peady counted it out loud. "Eleven and six bits. What say, Ketch?"

Nueces Pecado yelled, "Hey, I'll break that *diablo desenfrenado* for half that."

Ketch's expression changed…contempt for Nueces and a flash of pity for the horse that the *mestizo* was leading. "Your bronc get in a fight with a puma, Nueces?" Ketch pointed his chin at the scarred flanks of the animal. Every man there knew damn well that Nueces' sharpened Chihuahua spurs had done the damage.

Ketch turned to Peady. "I'll ride your bronc, Mr. Peady. He's too fine an animal to have bear-tracks carved in its hide by a gutless bronc*fighter* not good enough to ride out fair a horse that's better than he is."

His uncharacteristically long speech surprised the other loungers into silence, except for Woody Vaught. "Don't pay Ketch no mind, Nueces. He thinks his shit don't stink like everyone else's."

Ketch grinned at the pair, a mocking half twist of his lips that could rile a man faster than a frog's tongue could catch a fly. While Woody damned Ketch to hell and back, Ketch slid down from the rail into the corral with the snorting, head-tossing stud.

He approached the stud, hands down at his sides, speaking softly. The animal stopped twitching and capering, but its neck humped, ears pointed forward, forelegs braced, ready to charge or run.

The stud did neither.

Ketch planted himself directly in front of the stallion. He spoke softly and let the horse smell him before he raised his hand and ran it over the animal's eyes. Continuing his soft patter, Ketch traced an oval, gently rubbing the recesses above the eyes. The horse visibly relaxed and Ketch took up the off rein with his other hand.

Staying within the horse's peripheral vision, Ketch eased forward until his and the horse's left shoulders touched. His left hand anchored the off rein between the third and little fingers, with thumb and first two fingers gripping the near rein along with a clump of mane. He drew the horse's head close, slipped the ball of his foot into the near stirrup. Hat tugged down tight, Ketch grabbed the horn with his right hand and sprang up into the saddle as the horse lunged forward.

The ride was on!

The black swapped ends, landed stiff-legged, bounded back up in the air again, twisting its body left, then right, as if trying to touch the ground with one shoulder or the other, exposing its belly to the sun.

The son-of-a-gun was a sunfisher.

Ketch had tried to anticipate its moves, but the black hadn't shown this strategy on the two very brief rides preceding his. Caught off guard, Ketch lost a stirrup as the stud twisted in mid-air parallel to the ground. The watchers yelled warnings, thinking it would land on its side with Ketch pinned underneath. They let out a collective sigh as the stud righted and shifted into a more predictable series of spine-jarring buckjumps.

Ketch tightened his legs on the horse's barrel and toed back into the lost stirrup. Just as Ketch picked up the stud's new bucking rhythm, the beast flung its front hooves up, clawing for the sky. He rose too high, overbalanced into a fallback.

Ketch's heart jumped a beat. *A sure-enough widow-maker stunt, if he ever saw one!*

But Ketch's sixth sense with horses clicked in. Gripping the reins, he kicked free of the stirrups and saddle just before the bronc landed on its back.

As the horse completed a half roll and came up onto its knees, Ketch grabbed its ear and twisted. The pain distracted the bronc long enough for Ketch to leap back into the saddle. Toes groped for stirrups as the animal surged to its feet.

Prodding with quirt and blunted rowels, working the reins, Ketch forced the animal into an erratic stiff-legged humping trot, then into a run...'round and 'round and 'round the corral until finally the stud stopped dead, exhausted and quivering.

Ketch dismounted and began walking the stallion around the breaking pen, once more talking softly, petting gently. Although no one else could tell, Ketch's legs were quivering, too. If the black hadn't given up soon, he would have had to.

"Hell," Woody grumbled, "me and Jase softened up that crazy bugger for you." He jumped down into the corral with Ketch and the stud.

The moment Woody Vaught's feet hit corral dust, the stud, in a burst of renewed vigor, lowered its head and charged, tearing the reins from Ketch's hands. It chased Woody until it backed the Slash R foreman against the rails. It reared back on its haunches and struck out with unshod forehooves.

Ketch jumped between the two and slapped the stud's face with his hat, giving Woody the space he needed to scramble under the bottom rail and out of the pen. By the time Woody got to his feet, Ketch again held the reins, murmuring to the seemingly docile horse.

Short on gratitude and long on spleen, Woody yelled at Ketch, "You spooked that damn devil a'purpose. Snaky bastard, you and that bronc. Two of a kind. C'mon, Jase, let's get us a drink. We owe ourselves one for softening the stud up for Ketch."

Woody Vaught's attempt to save face failed. Jase shook his head. He knew as well as everyone else there, that the few moments he and Woody had hung on wouldn't have tired a new colt, much less the stud. If anything, they had made Ketch's ride a helluva lot harder. They'd not only spooked the horse, but worse, taught the animal it could dump its rider.

When Ketch removed the bosal, the stallion stood without restraints while Ketch rubbed it down. He murmured to the horse, "*Diablo*, huh? You're no devil. Not in any language."

Peady and the remaining loungers could only shake their heads in a mixture of disbelief and admiration.

Chapter One

"C'mon, honey. Don't be so unfriendly."

"Let me go." Cindianne Jackson, trembling like a colt with a catch rope around its neck, tried to free her wrist from Woody Vaught's grip. "*What* are you talking about!"

The Slash R foreman pulled her closer. "You know damn well what I'm talking about. You're that little queenie been shacking up with Ketch over to the other side of the ridge."

"I told you. I don't even know any 'Ketch.' I'm Cindianne Jackson...Mrs. Tom Jackson, to you."

"Hey, Jase, listen to the little hussy putting on airs. 'Mrs. Tom Jackson,'" he mocked in a falsetto. "Who the hell's *Mister* Tom Jackson?"

"I am, you son of a bitch!"

The voice came from behind Vaught at the same time he felt himself being spun around. All he saw was the flash of a hard-knuckled fist that met his face head-on. Woody's head snapped with the blow as he tumbled a full five feet back into the dusty street and on into oblivion.

Jase sprang to his foreman's aid. "Damn you, Ketch, you didn't give Woody a chance!"

He didn't give Jase one, either. Ketch pivoted, drove two rapid lefts into Jase's gut and another, higher, into the solar plexus. As Jase doubled over in pain, Ketch straightened him out with a solid uppercut that kited the hired hand ass over elbows into the dirt next to his boss.

Ketch towered over the two sprawling figures, hoping that at least one of the bastards would get up so he could knock him down again. Jase shoved up onto one elbow, no farther. Woody Vaught stayed out.

Ketch said, "You tell that damn foreman of yours if I ever catch him manhandling my wife again, I'll kill him. That goes for you, too, Jase..."

Behind him, Ketch heard a woman cluck her disapproval. "Look at that. Brawling over that strumpet right out in the middle of the street and in broad daylight, too."

Ketch turned to face the woman, adding, "...or anyone else who hurts my wife."

Cindianne grabbed Ketch's arm. "Please, Tom, let's go home. No more trouble, please." Tears streaked her plain face.

Some of the tension washed out of Ketch as he looked down at her. He brushed the hair away from her face. "Sure, Annie, whatever you say."

He walked her to the buckboard where he'd been loading their supplies. "Is there anything else you need? Anything you'd like for yourself?"

Cindianne shook her head and allowed Ketch to hand her up onto the buckboard. She was close on to four months along and already showing. Ketch treated her as if she were a porcelain figurine rather than the sturdy little Kansas farm girl he had married.

He flicked the team into motion, slowly down the main street. As they rode along, he ignored the snubs tended him and the girl at his side. He hoped she didn't notice. *Damn those bitches, anyway.* Whatever they thought of him, they oughtn't be petty enough to take out on her just for being his wife.

As they neared the edge of town, Nora Peters stepped out of the office of *The Reef Weekly Record*, the local newspaper. Nora had been damn decent so far, but her boss, owner/publisher/editor Charlie Wykle, proved a different breed of cat—one whose aroma rose to the high heavens.

Thought of Wykle further darkened Ketch's mood. Glumly he reflected on the odd set of circumstances that had brought about their first encounter. Ketch had just returned to White Reef, Utah, from a horse-selling trip to an army fort in Kansas, the biggest deal he'd turned so far. And when he came back, he brought Annie with him as his bride.

While he'd been away, old Ed Duerson learned that a prospector he'd grubstaked had struck it rich in Colorado. With his new wealth, Duerson determined to sell out there and head for Denver to see the elephant. He'd heard that, for a price, the gals there would do anything, any time, and any way. A man was never too old to learn, but he had to learn before he was too old to do...though there were many who swore Old Ed had long past reached that stage. In any case, Ed wanted to get on with it.

Duerson owned not just the sandstone ridge west of town that had given White Reef its name, but also the lush green valley beyond it. He wanted to sell; Ketch wanted to buy. Ketch made an offer to Duerson for the land he needed, which translated into as much of the piece as he could afford. Duerson accepted the offer, but Ketch knew Duerson had given him a damn good deal.

A week or so later, Wykle arrived from Pioche, Nevada, and set up shop in town. Only days after that, he had cornered Ketch in town and tried to buy the place from him. But Ketch had no thought of selling. He'd just bought the place, the first solid thing in his life he ever owned. He wanted to make a home there for his "Annie" and for the children they would have together.

But Wykle couldn't—or wouldn't—take "no" for an answer. After Ketch's emphatic refusal to every offer the publisher made, rumors about Ketch and his wife started flying. Hell, he didn't mind for himself. How much could people say about him that *wasn't* true? He owned a salty reputation and was the first to admit he'd done more than his share to earn it.

But that was *before* he had married Annie.

What grated his insides raw as a saddlesore were the unfounded lies the gossips began passing around about her. Nora had passed on to him what she had heard, that Cindianne had been a wheeligo girl who worked the houses over to Pioche. Hell, Annie had never even been out of Kansas until he'd brought her home with him to White Reef.

Ketch rarely came into town and today was the first time in the six months they'd been married that he'd brought his wife in with him. He'd had no idea how bad things had gotten until a few minutes ago, when he ran into Woody and Jase. Talk like that could only have originated with Wykle. Well, you cut a snake off at its head. Same thing with rumors. He'd see Wykle and set that particular snake straight. But it would have to wait till next trip, when Annie wouldn't be with him.

He held his breath now, as they neared Nora Peterson. So far, and despite her boss Wykle, she'd been the only woman from town to come out and visit Annie, even schooling her in reading and writing the couple of times she'd been there. God, he hoped Nora didn't high-hat her today, too.

She didn't. As they drew nearer, Nora waved a hand and stepped out to greet them. "Good morning, Cindianne."

Ketch sighed a breath of relief and slowed the team to pull them to a halt. But catching the faint shake of Annie's head, he kept the team moving, returning Nora's greeting only in passing.

Cindianne gave Ketch an apologetic look. "I just don't feel much like talking with anyone right now, Tom."

Ketch nodded, understanding. Just as well. Once she did feel up to talking, he'd have to come up with some pretty damned hard answers.

Not until they'd returned to their place and Ketch had unloaded the supplies did Cindianne break her self-imposed silence.

"Tom, why would those men talk to me that way, like I was a saloon girl or something?"

His face darkened. "They won't do it again. Woody Vaught gets about half crazy with a few drinks under his belt. He didn't mean anything."

"But that woman, what she said, too. And why did they keep calling you 'Ketch'?"

"Ketch is just a nickname. Remember, I told you I was pretty good with a ketch rope."

"You also told me you lived here all your life, but they acted like they never heard of Tom Jackson."

Ketch looked off and away from her. Hell, even he didn't know his *real* name.

She looked at him steadily, waiting for an answer. She may have been a naïve, uneducated little farm girl, but she was not stupid.

"Tom?"

He gently stroked her arm. Such a sweet, innocent thing, so much better than someone like him deserved. He hated like hell to chance losing her, but she had to know sometime what a nothing she'd married.

"Annie, honey, look..." he came to an immediate dead end. Giving himself time to line up his thoughts, he led her to a chair, seated her, then sat on the floor at her feet. He lifted her hand, toying with the plain silver band on her finger.

"When I met you and your dad, I told you my name was Tom. And when the preacher was going to marry us, I had to pull a whole name out of the hat to give him. I'd been reading through a history of the late war and the name of Thomas Jonathon 'Stonewall' Jackson was fresh in my mind. *Tom Jackson.*"

He looked up at her, saw her confusion. "Annie, I don't have a name. I'm just a bastard some whore dropped out behind a cathouse." The old wound, raw again. The shame didn't quit. "I've had my nose rubbed in that dirt since the day I was old enough to understand. As I got older, I got pretty mean, cut a shine or two, kicked up considerable dust. If I was going to have a bad rep, I might as well have the pleasure of earning it. Never anything too deep, though. Stealing, as a kid to keep alive, but not more than a couple of times and I never got caught. But I did lift a chunk of hell with my fighting and drinking and..." he was about to add *whoring around*, but sensed there were limits to how honest he should be with her "...and enough other stuff to send ten good men straight to hell."

In his defense, he could have added that no one had ever bothered to tell him right from wrong until after the fact. He always had to figure things out for himself, inevitably the hard way. He forced a grin and spoke lightly, trying to hide the real depths of his feelings. "You hear folks warning their daughters about keeping bad company. I was the bad company they mostly warned about."

"I don't think that's funny."

He gave a short, humorless laugh. "Neither do I. That's the hell of it. And when I met you out there in Kansas and you didn't know anything about me and you seemed to like me — I know I should have told you all this, but it's been such a damned hell of a lonely life." Something he'd never before admitted to anyone.

They both sat a long while, not speaking, before Ketch broke the silence again. "Honey, if you think...if it's what you want, I can take you back to your folks. Just, the only thing I ask is that you think some about it before you decide. The hell-raising, that was just something to do before...my way of thumbing my nose at all those 'good' people to let 'em know I didn't give a damn what they thought.

"But I do give a damn about what you think. You've been with me half a year. You know I haven't had a drop of liquor or gone near one hellhole, nor been into a fight since we've been married. Well, not until that little mix with Woody and Jase today. I've toed the line, worked steady, and building this cabin for you from the ground up, just the way you want it, two fireplaces and all."

When she didn't answer, he added quietly, "...and there's the baby coming. I never had a family. I just...I want you and him...or her..." He again fiddled with the ring on her hand, staring at it. "If you'll stay, if you think you can put up with the other, I swear to God I'll be anything, do anything to try to make it so you won't ever be sorry."

He waited through another interminably long silence. She didn't appear to have anything to say. He'd tossed all his chips into the pot and lost. Without looking at her, he started to rise.

Wordlessly Cindianne reached out, laid her hand on his shoulder, pulled his head gently against her breast and held him there.

She said, "You told me I'd always be your 'Annie.' Well, you'll always be Tom—*Tom Jackson*—to me."

Ketch tightened his grip on her hand as if he might lose her just by letting go. He didn't know if what he felt for Cindianne was love. That was something he'd only read about in books and had never seen enough of it to recognize. But what he did know was that she filled what had been a deep and lonely void in his life.

He'd lived with that emptiness before. He didn't think he could ever live with it again. A cold, black feeling shuddered through him.

Dear Jesus, I hope to hell I'll never have to find out.

Chapter Two

Woody Vaught brooded over his drink in a darkened back corner of the saloon. If he hadn't seen that fist coming with his own eyes, he'd have sworn one of Ketch's wild broncs had kicked him in the face. Who the hell ever thought the bronc buster would be so damn touchy over him funning a whore? And that's what she was. Charlie Wykle himself had told him he'd seen her working the cribs over to Pioche. And an important man like Charlie Wykle wouldn't have no damn reason to lie.

In Vaught's mind, the line between decent women and "the other kind" was clearly defined. Hog ranch trulls were dirt, a sub-human breed like niggers, greasers, and injuns, trash like Ketch himself. Why hell, that kind of woman wanted to be used and abused. That's what they got paid for.

He guessed the fact that Ketch laid claim to this whore was what made the difference to the bronc buster. But hell, being taken down that way over a woman like that, especially for the whole town to see, rankled. That had been a week ago, but his resentment, fueled by liquor, became an acid eating at his gut and at his mind. The more he drank and thought about it this afternoon, the more rankled and madder he got.

Well, by god, time to do something about it.

He rose unsteadily, carrying his bottle with him. Yep. That's what he'd do. Pay old Ketch a visit and do something about it.

By the time Woody reached Ketch's place, his brain was as empty as his bottle. He threw the bottle in the dirt yard, slid down off his horse and yelled, "Ketch, you bastard, get on out here!"

He waited for an answer and got none. "Quit hiding, you sonofabitch! Ain't gonna do you no good. You afraid to fight a man that's facing you?"

Silence.

"Come on out or by hell, I'll come in there and drag you out with your woman watching!"

Woody wove his way across the open yard, past the smashed bottle to the house and kicked the door open.

"Where you hiding, Ketch?" He looked groggily around the combination kitchen-sitting room. Empty. He moved on to the curtain-divided bedroom off to the right. Empty, too. But he caught a muffled sound, a faint blur of movement in a smaller room off this one. He blinked a few times, his eyes adjusting to the dimmer light. A half-finished cradle stood in one corner. Cindianne crunched down in the opposite corner, trying to hide.

"What the hell?" Woody blinked a few more times. He stepped closer, leaned over and grabbed her by the arm.

Sudden heat lightninged through him at sight of Cindianne in her thin chemise.

"Where's your man?"

So frightened, the words barely crept out of Cindianne's mouth. "He's...he's not here. He's out on contract, working a bunch of horses for the Diamond."

"You here by yourself?"

She didn't answer so much as whimper. Even befuddled by drink, the significance of their situation didn't escape him.

"Well, if I can't get my hands on Ketch this time, you'll have to do."

Cindianne's eyes widened in terror. "No! Please. Please don't hit me. My baby...you'll hurt my baby."

He intended only to rough-house her a little, a few kisses, whisker burn those soft cheeks of hers, just scare her enough to make Ketch mad as hell, quit his hiding and come to him. Even as he said, "Never took me a pregnant whore before," he never meant more than to frighten her. But the moment he hauled her lush body against his, fire shot through him.

Woody Vaught lost control.

Woody stood, buttoning his pants back up.

"For a gal who's had so much practice, you sure didn't give me such a good roll."

Cindianne lay on the floor sobbing. "I never. Tom's the only one I ever…oh, God!"

Vaught stared at her, some degree of sobriety returning. She didn't look like a whore. More like a hurt kitten. But dammit, she was a whore. God knows he'd never lay a rough hand on a decent woman. He had to hang onto the thought that she was a whore. He pulled a silver dollar out of his pocket and flung it at her.

"Cut rate. For making me work so damned hard for it."

Cindianne pressed her bunched fists to her mouth, tears streaming down her face.

"Tom will kill you for this."

"If you're what you claim you are, you'd be too ashamed to tell him. But go ahead, tell him. If the bastard comes after me, I'll kill him. Then I'll come back here and have you any damn time I want—free. Remember that.

Ketch finished off work early to spend some time with Cindianne. She'd been off her feed for the last month or two. He feared that since she'd had time to think about what he'd told her, she might be changing her mind about staying with him. Or maybe he'd spent too much time away from her. The Diamond's horses had been a big job. Between that and breaking and hauling stone to complete the fireplace in their bedroom, and trying to finish the baby's room and furniture before the little fella came…Ketch shook his head. Then again, maybe Cindianne just wasn't feeling good. Even horses had problems throwing off colts sometimes. God, he hoped nothing like that was in the offing. He ran his hand across his face. Whatever the cause, something sure as hell was troubling her. He felt the gap between them. It would just keep widening unless he did something about it. She hadn't even let him touch her this past month.

Ketch arrived at their cabin as Nora Peters was stepping out the door.

"Nora." He touched his hat brim. Alarm darted through him as he caught the troubled look on her face. "Nora, what is it? What's wrong?" He lengthened his stride.

Nora put her hand on his arm as he started past her.

"Ketch, wait. It's Cindianne, but nothing—well, nothing to get too excited about. May I talk to you a few minutes first, before you go in?"

Ketch cast an anxious glance toward the house. "Sure, Nora, go ahead."

"Another one of those letters came today."

"*Letters*? What letters?"

"You know. Those poison pen things she's been getting. They've had her so upset, but the one she got today…"

"Nora, I'm not following you."

She studied Ketch's face, slowly lifted one hand to her mouth. "Cindianne didn't tell you? Oh, Ketch, I'm sorry. I didn't mean to…oh, damn. I just naturally thought you knew."

"No. This is the first I've heard about it. *Poison pen letters*. So that's what's been bothering her. I thought it was me, something I did."

"Only in the most backhanded, roundabout way. Nothing you should blame yourself for. Anyone dirty enough to send letters like that in the first place, has to be…just has a rotten mind to begin with."

"What did they say?"

Nora flushed, looked away from him. "They're pretty vile. If Cindianne didn't tell you, I don't think I—"

"Nora."

"She's been getting these unsigned notes telling her she doesn't belong around here…that she's a wanton woman…no other kind of woman would have tangled up with…" She hesitated, but Ketch had no problem mentally filling in the blank. "Ketch, I shouldn't be the one to tell you all this."

"Go on, Nora."

Reluctance plain on her face, she shrugged, "Oh, it's just more trash in the same vein—that neither of you is fit for decent people's company; that you aren't really married since you didn't have a name to give to her in the first place; that since you aren't legally wed, your baby will be a...a bastard like, like—"

"Like me," he finished for her.

She nodded.

"What else?"

"That not knowing what you are, your baby might be born red or brown or black or yellow. Anything but white." She looked up at Ketch. "Just enough of a shade of truth hidden in all that garbage to make Cindianne worry about it."

"Yeah. Just enough of the truth." His voice came in such a soft whisper, that it barely carried to Nora. "And the one she got today?"

Nora closed her eyes. "Ketch, that's not for me to say. Cindianne will have to tell you, if she wants to. But I will tell you this. I think it's the last straw. I think it's just about broken her. She's talking foolishly, as if she might do something foolish, to herself I mean. Please, just see if you can't talk sense to her. I feel so bad telling you all this, but nothing I could say comforted her."

Ketch gently gripped Nora's shoulder. "Not your fault. You've been a friend to her. I appreciate that and I won't forget it."

Nora forced a smile. "I—I'd better go."

Ketch entered the house, swearing softly to himself, burning deep inside because of the pain his Annie had been suffering on his account.

She was in their room, lying on their bed, like to crying her heart out. He walked over to her, talking softly, as if calming a skittish colt.

"Annie? It's all right, Honey. Whatever it is, we can make it right." He put his arm around her, wanting to comfort her. But she pushed him away and ran out of the house. A crumpled piece of paper fluttered to the floor. The note Nora had told him about.

He picked up the paper, read its flawless script:

Does your husband know that while

he's been out working the horses

you've been home working the cowboys?

"Oh, shit." He ran outside after Cindianne, caught up with her.

"Honey, I read that note. That's nothing to tear yourself all up over. You know I wouldn't believe a damn lie like that!"

She tried to pull away from him, refusing to look at him.

"Annie. Honey, don't—"

She jerked free of his hold, turned her tear-splotched face to him. "It's not a lie!"

Her response stunned him. "Annie, I know you. I know you wouldn't do anything like that. You could tell me something like that with your own lips from now till doomsday and I still wouldn't believe it."

"Oh, Tom." She ran into his arms.

He held her tightly, smoothing her long hair with one hand. "Tom," she said, "it is true, but not like that note Nora read to me."

Ketch held her out from him, to study her face. "*What* are you telling me, Annie?"

Her face turned white. Slowly, brokenly, the story came out. She swore it happened just that once and the man never came back. The only thing she wouldn't do was identify the man who had attacked her.

Ketch begged her, argued with her. She insisted she didn't know who it was, that she'd never seen the man before. Ketch knew, on this one point, she *was* lying. But she'd put up with so much already, had borne it all these weeks by herself that he didn't want to compound her distress. He was a patient man and a lot stronger-willed than she was. She would tell him eventually and when she did, there would be one dead son of a bitch.

Ketch urged his horse into a jog, anxious to get home to Cindianne. After a night of constant reassurances by him, she seemed to be in better spirits before he left that morning. He'd hated like hell leaving her after breakfast, but he'd promised Clint Brinker he'd meet him in White Reef today to talk about contracting to bust out a herd for him. This promised to be an even bigger job than his last one. Even so, he wouldn't have left her, but he had no way to get in touch with Brinker to call the meeting off. The old fellow lived a good distance north of town and would have made a half-day's ride for nothing. He explained this to Cindianne, then left and met with the man. He and Brinker had come to terms quickly, but ironing out all the details took a little longer than he'd hoped.

He glanced at the sky. Still plenty early enough to take Cindianne up onto the sandstone ridge behind the house, where he'd gotten the rock to build their fireplaces. The last time they were up there was about the last time they'd had any real fun together. She had pointed out which rocks to haul down to build the hearths; hell, all rocks looked alike to him.

Then, coming home that day, a rain had come up sudden and caught them out in the blue clay hills that fanned out below the ridge. When blue clay got wet, it was slicker than a school-marm's thigh and twice as clingy. They hadn't sloshed more than five yards before they looked as if they were walking with buckets on their feet. Cindianne had slipped; he'd grabbed her, then they both went down. Laughing, they decided the hell with it and, like a couple of kids, slid the rest of the way down. By the time they'd gotten home, they resembled rocks themselves and weighed out a good twenty pounds heavier.

They marched straight down to the creek, stripped, and scrubbed the damn stuff off before they concreted into statues. Then afterward, on the bank, they'd made love. A quiet, gentle love. And he was sure that was when their baby had been conceived. Annie said no it was sooner, a whole lot sooner, but he didn't care. That's still what he liked to believe.

A boyish grin brightened Ketch's face as he relived the moment. Maybe they'd do more of the same today! He started whooping for her while still a hundred feet shy of the house. When he reached the dirt yard, he jumped from his horse, dropped the reins leaving the horse ground-hitched, and covered the rest of the distance to the house at a high lope.

He whistled shrilly to let her know that he was coming, then yelled, "Annie! Where are you, Honey? Come on! Me and you're gonna fix us a picnic lunch and ride up onto the White Reef."

He slipped through the doorway into the shadowed interior. "Hey, come on, Girl, where you hiding?" In full high spirits, he whipped into the bedroom.

"Annie—"

His voice sliced off to a harsh whisper, "Jesus God!"

Cindianne lay face up across their bed, the patchwork cover a crimson mess where the lifeblood had pulsed out of her slashed wrists. His straight razor lay on the floor inches away from her dangling right arm.

"Jesus God," he said again, then "...the baby!" Numb, dazed, Ketch worked feverishly, by instinct, trying to take the small, barely formed baby out of her. Twice he'd pulled foals out of dead mares and been able to save them. His Annie was dead, but maybe he could save their baby. *Please God. Please Jesus!*

But their son was already dead when he took him out of her. Dead before he had a chance to be alive.

Ketch sat by their bodies until nightfall, as if his own lifeblood had been drained out of him. At last he forced himself to move, to take care of his wife and baby.

He washed the blood off their bodies, dressed Cindianne in her best dress and the baby in a little gown she had made and embroidered in anticipation of its coming. He upended the cedar wardrobe he'd built for his Annie, lined it with quilts and laid her body inside. He folded the baby in her arms and covered them both.

Dry-eyed, face expressionless, Ketch buried them without saying any words over them. He was burying the only good and decent thing ever to come into his life and be a part of it. He figured God knew that, too, without his being brash enough to tell Him.

Ketch returned to the house and for the first time saw the note on the table. On brown paper, crudely printed in the hand you'd expect of a poor little farm girl who'd never had any schooling:

Ketch
I cant take it no more
Cindianne

He folded the note carefully and placed it inside his leather money flap.

Much later that night, Ketch went into town to get drunk. Knockdown, black-out drunk!

Chapter Three

Heat and smoke forced Ketch to retreat. He stood back, watching helplessly as flames broke through the roof and cracked out the three real glass windows of the house he'd built.

A small crowd gathered, drawn by the red glow over the ridge that could only mean fire. Those on horseback arrived first, taking the shortcut over the sandstone reef that separated his place from the town. Those coming by wagon had to drive the long way around, through the canyon, and were just arriving.

The wooden expression on Ketch's face gave nothing away of what he felt inside. The house was too far gone for anyone to offer help, even if they'd been of a mind to. But Ketch didn't suppose that was why they had come. Curiosity may have brought some, but likely most had come for fear of the fire spreading over the ridge and taking their damn town with it.

No pretenses ever existed between him and the townspeople. And tonight, with frustration pushing him, he recoiled at having to put up with the mealy-mouthed sonsofbitches.

"You've seen your show. Now get the hell out of here. All of you."

Nora Peters stepped down from Charlie Wykle's buggy and laid her hand gently on Ketch's arm.

"We only came to see if there were anything we could do to help, Ketch."

Ketch looked over Nora's head, his piercing look including the few women sprinkled throughout. "Where the hell were all these culls and their 'help' when Annie was alive?"

He felt Nora's hand pull away. He looked down at her, regretting only for her sake what he'd just said. She was, after all, the one exception, the one truly decent person in this whole damn bunch.

Nora had been the only one besides Talbert, the town marshal, that he'd even bothered to tell about Cindianne's death. He'd given the marshal the full details, but withheld the grisly parts from Nora. Even after word of Cindianne's death sifted out, shadowed by rumors, Nora continued to buck public opinion by offering her friendship to Ketch.

But Ketch had too much respect for Nora to let the same thing happen to her that had happened to his wife, so he'd backed off — way off. In his book, the only mark against Nora was the fact that she worked for Charlie Wykle. Yet he couldn't really fault her for that. Single women had few choices when it came to getting decent jobs.

Even as Ketch began to apologize to Nora for the slight, Wykle moved behind her and laid a possessive hand on her shoulder.

The two men glared at each other across her head. Wykle was a big man, not quite as tall as Ketch's six-feet-three inches, but at least thirty pounds heavier and, in his early forties, a dozen years older.

Before Annie was even cold in her grave, Wykle had come, badgering him to sell out. After Ketch's latest flat refusal, Wykle resorted to open threat, then followed up with an article about Cindianne's death in his rag of a paper — a curt obituary, not flattering to her and raising a spate of questions about Ketch, questions that initiated a new flurry of rumors and speculation.

All too aware of the animus between Ketch and Wykle, Nora ignored Wykle and spoke to Ketch. "I'm sorry about this fire, after all the work you put into this house. What happened?"

Wykle loudly cut off Ketch's response. "It wasn't an accident, that's for certain. Coal oil, smells like."

Nods and murmurs of assent rippled through the small crowd.

Wykle moved Nora from between him and Ketch. Although facing Ketch, Wykle was patently addressing the onlookers. "Can't for the life of me understand why anyone would want to burn down a perfectly good house like this one."

Ketch said evenly, "My thoughts exactly."

"Unless..." Charlie continued as if Ketch hadn't spoken, "...unless somebody had something to hide. Something to cover up, maybe even some evidence to destroy."

"Evidence of what?" Ketch asked.

"Why evidence of Cindianne *Jackson*'s death."

"Meaning what?"

"That should be pretty obvious."

"It isn't. You have something to say, spit it out…right here and now, to my face, instead of slurring around behind my back, hiding behind that ass-wipe you call a *newspaper*."

"All right, then. Suppose you tell the people how your 'wife' died."

"That's none of your damn business or theirs, either."

"You say. But there was quite a bit of speculation that the baby she was carrying wasn't yours. And it was common knowledge she'd been entertaining the cowboys while you were out breaking the horses."

"That's a lie," Ketch said, his voice ominously soft. But somewhere in the back of his mind, the thought registered that Wykle's statement ran almost word-for-word with that last poison-pen note Annie received the day before she killed herself.

"Maybe it is a lie," Wykle piously conceded. "I'm not one to judge the dead. That's for a Higher Power than mine to decide. But I am interested in *how* she died. I suspect a crime, maybe a violent crime, has been committed. As editor of *The Reef Weekly Record*, I represent the people, their voices, their conscience. It's my responsibility to search out the truth and lay it before them."

Ketch snorted. "You sound like you're running for election, Wykle. Hell, you wouldn't know the truth if it r'ared up on its hind legs and spit in your face."

"I'd know murder…and everything I've seen here points in that direction. The killing of a woman, any kind of woman, is bad enough. But the taking of an innocent baby's life as well—that deserves punishment. I believe you killed your woman and the baby she was carrying!"

The image of their baby as he'd taken it out of Annie's lifeless body knifed through Ketch. All reason left him. He shoved Nora out of the way and drove his fist into Wykle's damned lying mouth. Wykle dropped in a heap, stupefied, but not totally out. Furious beyond reason, Ketch jumped him while he was still down. Straddling Wykle, Ketch grabbed him by the throat with his right hand while hammering Wykle's face with a lightning barrage of lefts.

The two nearest men grabbed Ketch by the arms. Ketch jammed his elbow into the stomach of the man to his left, jerked that arm free and swung a wild roundhouse into the groin of the man still holding his right arm. A third man came up behind Ketch, gun drawn. *Woody Vaught*. He slashed Ketch behind the ear with the barrel of his gun. Ketch folded soundlessly to the ground as Vaught pistol-whipped him once again, for good measure.

"There, you bastard. See how you like getting taken down from behind." Then he turned to Wykle. "You all right, Mr. Wykle?"

Even if Wykle understood the question, his mouth was too battered to answer. Several of the men helped lift him into the buggy. Nora climbed up beside him.

Vaught took off his hat. "You going to be able to manage all right, Miss Nora?"

She hesitated, looking at Ketch's limp form on the ground. "I'll manage," she said stiffly. Taking up the reins, she flicked the team into motion.

"I'll ride behind you," Vaught offered, "just in case."

Ketch heard the voices and the sounds as if from a great distance. Overlaying the diminishing creak of the buggy came voices closer up.

"You think Wykle's onto something? You think Ketch might've killed his woman?"

"Truth to tell, wouldn't surprise me none. Why just now he damn near Killed Wykle. Would've too, I'll wager, if Woody Vaught hadn't buffaloed him."

With a loud whoosh and crash, the rafters collapsed into the middle of the house.

"Well, there she goes. Can't say as how I'm sorry."

"I am...sorry that bastard Ketch wasn't in there when she fell. He never was no damn account no how."

"Got a point there," the other man laughed.

Ketch shoved up onto his knees and looked up at them, the firelight playing off his blood-streaked, smoke-blackened face. He stared at them without saying a word. Somehow, the total lack of expression on his face made him seem all the more dangerous.

One of the men mumbled something under his breath. Then, as if on signal, the two caught and mounted their horses and followed the rest of the departing gawkers.

Ketch knelt there a long while, physically and emotionally drained, staring into the night's velvet darkness, not seeing the burning logs or the occasional fountain of sparks bursting upward. He was not even seeing half a year's solid work and a lifetime's meager savings going up in smoke. His internal eye saw only one thing — the destruction of the only tangible part of Cindianne that had been left in his life.

No, he thought bleakly. There existed one other tangible reminder of her existence, kept in an otherwise empty money poke — his Annie's suicide note.

By daylight, only the rock foundation and the stone chimneys remained. The chimneys rose above the ashes like the desert monoliths common to Utah's canyon country. Off to the side lay the few charred odds and ends he'd managed to salvage last night before the flames had beaten him back — the cradle, a cupboard, a chair.

Ketch moved wearily among the smoldering embers and stopped in front of the gaping rock fireplaces. While he'd been building them, he used to imagine quiet moments with Annie before the fire, her shy smile, her hair shining red in its warm glow, the two of them sharing the silence. Now the blackened maws of the fireplaces seemed to mock him, reminding him of the times he and Annie had never had together, the times they never could have now.

Ketch turned abruptly and with cold singleness of purpose strode to the slab-wood lean-to where he kept his tools and meager gear. He grabbed up his sledge, the same hammer he'd used to break into pieces the rocks Annie had chosen for the hearths and chimneys.

Someone watching him would have seen him pause in an attitude of prayer or reverence before he hefted the sledge and began swinging in savage fury. The fireplaces and chimneys had taken months to build. He leveled them in a matter of hours.

Exhausted, in an emotional vacuum, he slumped down onto one of the toppled sandstone rocks. He sat minutes, hours, not thinking, not wanting to think. But some subconscious impression kept intruding, teasing at the edge of his mind as he stared at the rock he sat perched on. Where he'd been running his hand back and forth, the texture didn't feel rough and granular like the rest of the rock. It was smooth and cold and metallic.

Taking a short grip on the sledge, he chipped off a fist-sized chunk and picked it up for a closer look. Some kind of metal, melted by the intense heat, had oozed out of the sandstone. He wet his finger and rubbed it some more. Damn stuff shone like silver, but anyone who knew the least little bit about mining knew silver just wasn't found in sandstone. In quartz, yes, but in sandstone? Never. Sure was pretty though. He grinned to himself. Wouldn't Annie have gotten a kick out of his having a thought like that, especially after all the hell he'd raised about "you see one rock, you've seen 'em all."

Thought of Cindianne brought the brief reverie to a painful end. He tossed the chunk of rock onto the pile of rubble created by his anger and frustration. The anger and frustration were gone. So was the dream.

Only the guilt remained. For, like those damned notes, Wykle's accusations carried more than a shade of truth. Just by virtue of who and what he was, no matter how heart-wrenching and unintentional, he was the one most responsible for the deaths of his own wife and baby.

Chapter Four

Revel Bentsen entered the small false-fronted building that housed *The Reef Weekly Record*. She nearly tripped over a drawer of type lying on the floor.

Nora Peters, smiling at the inelegant entrance asked, "May I help you?"

Revel looked over her right shoulder. Tucked in the corner, behind a desk hidden under other stacks of trays, sat a woman about her age, maybe a few years older.

"Thank you, yes. That is, I hope so. I need some information and I thought the town's newspaper office might be the place to get it."

"What kind of information, Miss—?"

"*Mrs*...Bentsen. Revel Bentsen."

Nora rose and extended her hand. "I'm Nora Peters."

Revel took Nora's hand and returned her smile. "I'm looking for a small ranch to buy."

"For yourself?"

Revel hesitated. "Not exactly. My husband will be joining me later on, after I get things organized."

She realized Nora waited for her to go on, but she decided not to elaborate. Her husband, Drew, was languishing in a sanatorium in the mountains of Pennsylvania, a consumptive fighting for each breath. From past experience, she'd discovered the fear with which most people regarded "lung-ers." She herself had shared that fear of tuberculosis.

Drew's physician had informed her in their last consultation that her husband's only hope, a slim one at that, would be to move him to a high dry climate. An auction sale, a few hurried inquiries, and she found herself in this high desert country of southwestern Utah, seeking to establish some means of support for themselves so she could bring him out here. She'd been told that the quickest financial turnover she could make with her limited funds would be to buy, break, and sell horses to the U. S. Cavalry.

She already had a line on a herd that could be bought cheaply, had, in fact, paid a deposit on it. Now she needed a base from which to operate.

"What kind of place did you have in mind, Mrs. Bentsen? How large, what price range?"

"Somebody buying something?" Charlie Wykle came out from the back of the building. The publisher wiped his ink-stained hands on an equally ink-stained apron. Shadows circled his mouth. At first glance, they appeared to be more ink smudges. But, as he drew nearer, Revel realized they were bruises, fading and discolored.

"Charlie," Nora said, "this is Mrs. Bentsen. Mrs. Bentsen, Charlie Wykle, Editor-in-chief of this illustrious newspaper—as well as publisher, writer, sales manager and typesetter. He is also a calligrapher who can provide you with hand-written notices, invitations, and announcements, from handbills to—"

Charlie held up a hand in feigned modesty. "Whoa. I don't go quite that far in trying to earn a living in this fair community. Besides, I'm certain Mrs. Bentsen can tell just by looking that this is a one-horse operation." Offering his most engaging smile, he added "...and one woman. Nora tries to keep me organized. A lost hope, but one that keeps her busy as well as gainfully employed. Pleased to meet you, Mrs. Bentsen. Now what can I do for you?"

Revel repeated her query for Wykle, adding a few details regarding her specific needs.

He nodded. "I see. Have you hired any men, yet? A foreman? Hands? Bronc busters?"

She shook her head. "I haven't gotten nearly that far. I'll be very frank with you, Mr. Wykle. I don't have unlimited funds. Money has to be a factor."

Wykle thought a long moment before removing his dirty apron. "I know of a couple of places that might suit you. I'll hitch up my buggy and take you around, if you'd like."

"Yes, I'd like that very much. But I certainly don't want to inconvenience you or interfere with your work."

"Not a problem. I work mostly at night. Just had a few odds and ends to attend to, but I'm through here for today. Nora can hold down the fort for the few hours we'll be gone, can't you, Nora?"

Nora readily agreed, but Revel thought her smile a trifle strained.

"Do you need to stop anywhere or do anything else first, Mrs. Bentsen, or are you ready to go right now?"

"Now would be fine with me, Mr. Wykle."

"Make that 'Charlie'."

Charlie Wykle and Revel Bentsen returned just before dark, Revel tired and disheartened.

Charlie said, "C'mon, let's have supper at the hotel."

"Thank you, Mr. Wykle, but I don't think—"

"I won't take 'no' for an answer. And the name's Charlie, remember?"

She forced a small smile. "Charlie."

After Wykle put up the team, they walked to the dining room at the hotel. He ordered generously for them both.

Wykle ate heartily, but a troubled Revel pushed the food around on her plate. All the "outfits," as Charlie had called them, cost more than she could afford and still allow enough of her available funds to be left over to hire the help she would need. The ranches she could afford either lacked water or adequate graze for the size herd she was buying.

As Wykle watched her from across the table, an idea began to form at the back of his mind. He leaned forward and laid his hand across hers.

"You look worried. Don't be. Things have a way of working out."

Revel set down her fork and, trying not to be too obvious about it, withdrew her hand from under his.

"I wish I could be as confident about that as you are, Mr. Wykle. I'm afraid I've started something that I can't finish." Revel's voice caught in her throat. For a brief moment, she toyed with the idea of confiding in Charlie Wykle. However, without really understanding why, she held back.

"I'd better leave now. I've already taken too much of your time," she said.

"Nonsense. It's been my pleasure."

As they left the dining room, Wykle pulled out a cigar and lit it. Through the haze of blue smoke, he glanced around the small hotel lobby and the few loungers seated in the wicker chairs. He took a few puffs before speaking again.

Drawing Revel to one side, he spoke confidentially. "While we were in the dining room eating, Mrs. Bentsen, a thought came to me — a way around your problem that I might be able to help you with. Why don't we walk back down to my office for a few minutes where we can talk without anybody overhearing." He tilted his head, indicating the loungers.

Revel hesitated, again without understanding why. Charlie Wykle had been nothing but helpful and courteous all day. Yet now, for no apparent reason, she felt an internal alarm sounding. She shook off the sensation, feeling foolish. Besides, it cost nothing to listen and the Lord knew that at this point she needed all the help she could get. Even as she admonished herself, another thought flashed through her mind — *But what was in it for Charlie Wykle?*

"Well," she decided, "I — I suppose that would be all right."

The office appeared dark and empty when they arrived. Wykle lit a lamp, moved a composing tray off a chair to clear a place for Revel to sit.

"Have a seat, Mrs. Bentsen." He paused a long, theatrical moment. "Stop me if I'm off the track or out of line. When we first met today, you mentioned that money had to be a factor in determining your selection of a property. Now the Slash R we looked at was really a pretty good buy. And Hugh Reid did tell you his foreman Woody Vaught could stay on and run the place for you. Woody's a good man. And you won't find a more perfect set-up for your needs than that place. Yet as good a deal as Reid proposed, you didn't make an offer.

"Forgive me for being blunt, but I sensed...something right close to desperation in you a few minutes ago at the hotel. I'm assuming the reason is that your funds are even more limited than I had supposed?"

Revel looked down at her hands. Her funds were even more limited than *she* had supposed. But since she didn't know what Wykle was leading up to, she just gave a noncommittal shrug.

Wykle held back a smile. He'd opened the door plenty wide for her to confide in him, but she kept shutting it. She obviously had a mind of her own, but he felt confident he could still work on her pressing need, whatever it may be.

"Mrs. Bentsen, what if I were to offer you however much more money you need—at minimal interest, of course—to buy the Slash R?"

She looked directly at him and replied without hesitation, "Then I would have to ask you *why*."

This time, Wykle did permit himself a small smile, appreciating her prudence or shrewdness, whichever it was. "You're absolutely right," he admitted. "I do have an axe of my own to grind. Other than the small interest I'd collect, I would ask a small favor in return."

Revel stiffened. "And just what would the nature of that favor be, Mr. Wykle?"

"There's a fellow lives out here in the Canyon. He's a sometime wild-horse hunter and a contract bronc buster, that is, a horse-breaker. Calls himself *Ketch*. He's just what you need to make this operation of yours work. If you let me be your *silent partner*, so to speak, the deal is this—that you hire this man. This Ketch."

Revel felt a little surge of relief. She'd been afraid the favor Wykle was going to ask might be of a more personal nature. She chided herself. *Vanity, thy name is woman*!

"That's it? All I have to do is hire this friend of yours to work for me?"

"That's it, plus the small amount of interest I said I would charge. Say, three percent? Full amount due on the sale of your horses. No one, but you and me would have to know about our agreement. Not even Ketch."

Revel nodded. That seemed a small and reasonable enough favor, yet...

"This man, *Ketch*, you called him? You said he's one of the best 'bronc busters' in the business?"

"Tops, from all I've been told."

"Then I don't understand. If he's so good with horses, why do you need to go out of your way to line up a job for him?"

"Let's just say it's a personal debt I feel obligated to pay. With your help, I think I see a way of doing just that. As to *why* he needs help getting a job, I'll be perfectly honest with you. Ketch isn't too popular in these parts. He's got a drinking problem and he's a general all-around troublemaker and hell-raiser, to boot." Wykle fingered the healing marks around his mouth and added, without realizing he was saying it aloud, "Yep, a real hell-raising bastard."

At Revel's raised eyebrows, Wykle caught himself. "I didn't mean that figurative so much as literal, Mrs. Bentsen. The circumstance of his birth, to put it delicately, is somewhat clouded. That fact has left him with a curdled outlook on life and a disposition to match. But what I said about his ability as a buster still stands. Besides, with Woody Vaught to stay on and rod for you, Ketch won't get a chance to act out of line, least of all with you."

The way Wykle had put this whole proposition, he was doing her a favor and wanted nothing more in return than to pay a favor he owed to this Ketch fellow. Reasonable on the surface, yet she sensed something deeper involved. But even if there were, that was no real concern of hers. Drew's welfare was—*had to be*—her first and only concern. She must face up to Drew's and her situation. Both time and funds were running out.

As if keyed into her mind, Wykle said, "It's a small favor and when you come right down to it, do you have any other choices?"

An edge in his tone of voice caused her earlier flash of wariness to return. She had the sudden conviction that she'd been maneuvered into something beyond her control or understanding. Wykle had asked and answered his own question. He was waiting only for her to confirm it.

She dropped her eyes and said in a soft voice, "No. No, I guess I don't have any other choices."

Charlie stood and took her hand. "It's a deal, then, Revel?"

"Yes, *Mister* Wykle. It's a deal."

Revel left immediately, anxious to get back to the solitude of her room. Somehow, her hand felt dirty, contaminated, and she wanted to wash it.

As soon as Revel left the newspaper office, Nora stepped in from the rear of the building.

"How long have you been here?" Charlie asked.

"Just a while. I saw the light and came in through the back door. What is going on between you and her anyway?"

Charlie chuckled. "You sound like a jealous wife."

"How can I sound like something I'm not?"

Charlie interpreted that to mean that Nora was referring to the "wife" part, not the "jealousy." What he didn't understand was that her thoughts were of Ketch and not him.

Charlie pulled Nora close to his chest and gave her a long penetrating kiss. She let him have his way. When they separated, she said, "You still didn't answer my question, Charlie."

"I've just engaged Mrs. Bentsen's help in getting Ketch out of our hair."

Nora laughed and leaned into Charlie. "If *I* couldn't get past first base with Ketch, what makes you think little Miss Priss can?"

"I don't."

"Then what—"

"Why Nora, my dear, have you never heard of *the sacrificial lamb?*"

Chapter Five

"For hell's sake, Ketch, move your ass! Mrs. Bentsen wants to talk to you."

Ketch's full length stretched out between the barrel chair he slouched in and the scarred tabletop his booted feet rested on. Deliberately, he tossed off the rest of his drink and refilled the glass before answering Woody Vaught.

"So?"

A half grin worked across Ketch's lips. Being sent down here on an errand-boy chore must be graveling the hell out of the Big Slash R foreman. His grin soured. *Serves the fool right, working for a petticoat.*

"She's waiting down to the ho-tel lobby." When Ketch remained seated and uninterested, Vaught added, "Come on, dammit. She don't have all day and neither do I."

Ketch shrugged. "Well, I do. If she wants me, I expect she knows where to find me. She knew where to send her flunkey."

"Listen, you drunken sonofabitch, it's hard for trash like you to understand about such things, but Mrs. Bentsen's a *lady*. Women like her don't set foot in joints like this."

"If she plans to see me, she'll have to. Tell her I'll be helling around down here for the next few days."

"Yeah. And drying out down to the jail the rest of the week."

"Probably."

Ketch knocked off his drink, poured another, then leaned back until his chair balanced on its two hind legs. He tugged the brim of his broad hat down over his eyes, his half of the conversation ended.

Vaught leaned over him, knuckles bunched, tempted to kick the chair out from under Ketch. He would have, too, if he were sure Revel Bentsen wouldn't fire him off the job. He pulled down a good salary from her, more than Reid ever paid him. But that didn't concern him as much as the extra wages he was pulling down on the q.t. from Charlie Wykle to work for Revel Bentsen. The editor had confided that he was bankrolling Mrs. Bentsen in her crazy venture, as a personal favor to her. Vaught guessed Wykle had something else up his sleeve, but hell, what difference to him? This deal gave him a chance to put a stake together for himself. No way was he going to spend the rest of his life looking at the wrong end of other men's cows.

Woody forced his hands open. As the Slash R foreman stalked out of the deadfall, he called over his shoulder, "Be seeing you soon...bastard."

Ketch had been watching the foreman through slitted eyes. His lips tilted into a thin humorless grin as he murmured at Vaught's retreating back, "I'll just bet you will."

From snatches of talk he'd caught around town, Ketch knew all about *Mrs.* Bentsen that he cared to. Apparently she'd arrived a week or so after his place burned down. From some place back East, he'd heard. Richmond or Boston or Philadelphia, one of those places. Hell, didn't every lady from east of the Mississip' come from Richmond or Boston or Philadelphia? Married, too. No doubt to some old geezer with more money than brains. Her husband probably bought the Slash R as a whim-wham for her to play with.

Jesus, just what this town needed—another "good" woman. Only pleasure her type seemed to get out of life was making life miserable for poor bastards like him or pecking away at kids like Cindianne until they finally...

Swearing bitterly under his breath, Ketch gulped down his drink, reached for the bottle, and refilled his glass.

Minutes later Vaught's bullhead and beefy shoulders reappeared above the saloon's batwing doors. So did a bobbing green hat with a ridiculous feather sticking up out of it. Vaught was looking down at the top of that hat and, from all appearances, arguing with its owner.

Ketch shook his head. "Unless he's caught himself an ostrich, I'll bet myself a drink that's Woody's new boss-lady."

The batwings swung open and a slim erect young woman entered.

She headed for Ketch's table. Her eyes, as green as the silly little hat on her head, arrowed in on him. She stopped at his table.

"Owe myself a drink," Ketch muttered and drained his glass.

"Mr. Ketch?"

"I'm Ketch," he acknowledged, but made no effort to rise.

She looked around self-consciously. "May I sit down?"

Ketch waved his hand at a chair. "Help yourself. Last time I looked, this was still a free country."

Revel Bentsen perched stiffly on the edge of the chair across from him. He thumbed his hat back from his forehead and eyed her boldly. A damned good looker; he'd give her that. Certainly a lot better than what he'd pictured in his mind's eye. Stiff-necked, though. She needed some of that starch shaken out of her.

Filling his glass to the brim, he asked innocently, "You one of the new girls working upstairs for Katie?"

Her cheeks rosied up, but she maintained some composure.

"No," she answered, "I'm Mrs. Bentsen, the new owner of the Slash R ranch."

"Too bad," he said, letting her interpret that any way she wanted to. "Better watch your step coming in here, then. Another fella who's not as much a gentleman as I am might not be willing to take just your word for it."

Recovered from her initial fluster, Revel said flatly, "Perhaps. But that's of little concern to me. I know the kind of person I am and if someone is stupid enough to mistake me for something I'm not, that is his misfortune, not mine."

Ketch pursed his lips. *Feisty little heifer.* "I'll drink to that," he said. "How about one for you, *Lady*?"

Revel ignored his sarcastic inflection. "No, thank you, Mr. Ketch. Shall we quit sparring and get right to the point? I have nearly seventy head of five- and six-year-olds that need to be broken. I'm working on a very tight schedule and I...it is imperative that I have them ready for the army buyer who expects to be coming through here the first of next month. I've been told that you're one of the best horse-breakers in the business and probably the only one in a hundred miles who could come near to meeting such a deadline."

"Well, Lady, whoever told you that is absolutely right."

"Then you'll do it?"

"No."

"But why not? You just said—"

"In the first place, Mrs. Bentsen, I have some very serious drinking planned for the next couple of days. And in the second place, I'm not interested in pulling down wages off a female in the first place."

"Money is money, no matter who is paying it out."

When Ketch didn't respond, she asked, "Mr. Ketch, are you drunk?"

"Not yet, Honey, but I'm sure as hell working on it."

Revel's face stiffened as she fought against her building anger and frustration. Ketch wondered which would surface first.

Taking a deep breath to calm herself down, Revel said, "I wouldn't interfere with your work, Mr. Ketch. Actually, you'd be working under Mr. Vaught's supervision."

Ketch laughed. "Like hell, I would."

"What—?"

Ketch settled whisky-sullen eyes on her. "Lady, I don't work for anybody but myself and least of all *under* that sonofabitch. But all that aside, you're missing the point. I'm flat out not interested in working your damn horses. I got something more important of my own to work out.

"As for your deal, you backed yourself into some kind of hole, dig yourself out. And one more thing—for future reference—any time there's an exchange of cash between me and a woman, you can be damn sure it goes the other way."

His meaning wasn't lost on her. The flush that crept across her face purely gratified Ketch.

Determined, Revel tried one more time. "Look, Mr. Ketch—"

Ketch wagged his head, a grin escaping in spite of himself. "Why in hell do you keep calling me *that*?"

"Calling you what?"

"*Mister* Ketch."

"That is your name, isn't it?" she asked uncertainly, exposing the first real crack in her composure.

"Sure enough. But lady, you can't tag 'mister' onto a front name and, if you're up on local gossip, you know I don't have any other."

"I don't think—"

"C'mon, now. Cards on the table. No one's told you that I'm a bastard and a hard-drinking one at that?" He held up the half-emptied glass. "I can't believe that whoever steered you onto me would have missed an opportunity to pass along that prime piece of gossip."

She regarded him steadily.

"As a matter of fact, yes, I do recall hearing something of that nature about you. But I've also heard that in this part of the country people are..." she groped for a delicate way of putting it "...are *democratic* about such things."

He laughed. "Sure. All kinds of bastards inhabit the *Wild West*. Trouble is, not all bastards are created equal. And when you're a hometown product like me, all kinds of speculation bobs up. Folks like to think I'm the unexpected product of some passing drover, but that don't stop them from trying to match up my face with the local banker, or preacher, or even the town marshal, since I seem to like to spend so much time in his establishment—though not necessarily by choice."

"Very interesting. What has all that got to do with *me*, Mr. Ketch?"

"Mrs. Bentsen..." he hesitated, and then a sly humor glinted at the corners of his eyes. "...Mrs. Bentsen, you seem like a damned decent sort, so I'm going to tell you something I've never told another soul. I do have a last name—it's *Colt*. The full moniker's *Ketch Colt*. Now if you're of a mind to call me mister, to keep things right and proper, you can feel free to call me *Mister Colt*."

This unexpected concession threw her off stride. "Why, thank you...Mr. Colt."

Ketch's lips twisted in a sardonic grin. "Mister Colt," he repeated, letting the words roll over his tongue. "Even I have to admit, Lady, that that does sound a hell of a lot more respectable than plain old Ketch."

Revel took a deep breath and started again. "Mr. Colt, even if you are not a man of breeding, you obviously have some education..."

He interrupted her again even as he took in the left-handed compliment and chalked one up for her side. Still, he found himself enjoying himself for the first time in months by virtue of the simple fact that he must be at least as aggravating to her as she was to him.

"That would all have to depend on your definition of education," he said. "As far as formal schooling goes, I have to plead innocent.

Never had the chance to be corrupted by any. But as for *education*, you'd be surprised at how much a person can learn hanging around hellholes like this one. If you're interested, I'll be glad to teach you some of the more interesting aspects...and without charge."

"Let's stick to business, Mr. Colt. I'm offering you a business proposition."

"Well, Honey, what the hell do you think I'm offering you?" He flicked his eyes over her. "I dunno, though, you look like a filly that'd run more to show than performance. Now that one over there" — he lifted his chin in the direction of one of Katie's Palace's "queenies."

Catching his look, the painted woman sashayed over to the table and joined them.

Rising, Ketch clamped one hand around the neck of his nearly empty bottle. His other slid around the woman's waist and, cupping his hand under one of her breasts, squeezed. The slattern giggled.

Ketch pulled the woman close against his side and led her up the stairs where the cribs were located. As they climbed, he shot a glance over his shoulder at Revel. She still sat stiffly by the table, color high on her cheeks. But she returned his look with a level and unwavering one of her own.

Some perverse devil had set him out to humiliate Revel Bentsen the way he and his Annie had been humiliated so many times by "good women" like her. From the look on Mrs. Bentsen's face, he'd done a fine job of it, too. But now that he had, he felt neither elation nor satisfaction. When he reached the top landing, he stood there, staring at her until she finally left. But her disgust and a fleeting image of Cindianne's disapproval reached out and wrapped themselves around him.

Dammit! He was thinking too much. What he needed was to get a good healthy drunk on. That's what he'd come to Katie's Palace for in the first place.

"Ketch?" The floozy tugged at his arm.

He let go of her and slipped two cartwheels into her hand. Patting her ample behind, he said, "Another time, Honey, huh?"

"Sure, Ketch, you bet." The woman dropped the silver dollars in the gap between her sagging breasts and slewed away.

Ketch, watching her swaying rear, wasn't even tempted. That was part of his trouble. Whores disgusted him. For all he knew, one of these bats could be his mother—some were sure old enough. And decent women were beyond him. He'd learned his lesson about that. Hell of it was, it had been Annie, not him, who'd suffered most for the accident of his birth. He'd never subject another woman to that again.

He shook his head as if he could throw off the tortured memory.

Lord, he didn't need to get a good healthy drunk on—what he needed was the long sought-after, but as yet unattained goal of getting "knock-down, black-out drunk."

Chapter Six

Revel Bentsen left the deadfall the way she had entered—body erect, chin elevated. But now bright red spots colored her cheeks and tears stung at the backs of her eyes. After meeting the man, she decided Wykle's appraisal of the horse-breaker hadn't gone far enough. What was the word Wykle had used? *Curdled*. Mr. Ketch Colt was all that and a lot worse. If ever a soul were beyond redemption, his had to be it. No wonder he had no friends. Who wouldn't balk at hiring a man like him?

Woody Vaught gaped at Revel. "Damn, I knew I shouldn't have let you go into that dive alone. What'd that boozehead say to you anyhow?"

She sighed and shook her head. "It doesn't matter. You were right. I shouldn't have gone in there. I just thought that if I could talk to him in person, but Mr. Colt—"

"Who'd you say?"

"Mr. Colt."

"Mrs. Bentsen, you was supposed to talk to a man called *Ketch*."

"Right." She nodded her assent. "Ketch is his first name. Give the devil his due, he at least gave me the courtesy of telling me his full name. *Ketch Colt*."

"Son...of...a...bitch!"

"Mr. Vaught!"

"Excuse the pepper, Mrs. Bentsen. That wasn't meant for your ears. You mind walking back to the ho-tel your ownself?"

"Where are you going?"

"Back in that joint to have a word with that damn — that drunk. Should have busted open his skull when I had the chance."

The Slash R foreman wheeled around and headed back toward the deadfall. Revel caught up with him just short of the bat-wing doors.

"Mr. Vaught, wait! Please. What's got you so angry? What did Mr. Colt do?"

"Dammit, Mrs. Bentsen, don't call him *that*."

Her face reflected her befuddlement. "I don't understand."

"I know you don't, ma'am. That's just the point. But Ketch does, the dirty son—" Woody Vaught bit off the rest of the expletive.

"Mr. Vaught, I do not want you to go in this place and start a fight. I *do* want you to explain what has you so riled."

When he clamped his lips together, she said firmly, "That's an order."

"It—it ain't decent Mrs. Bentsen."

"Then all the more reason for me to know."

Woody stared at the toes of his boots. Hell, a man just didn't talk about such things in front of someone like Mrs. Bentsen. But she did have a point and, more importantly, she was his boss. An idea struck him and he offered a compromise. "All right. But I can show you easier than I can explain it."

He turned and walked away, fists clenched, thick shoulders bunched as if against a storm.

Revel followed, running to keep up with him—across the dusty thoroughfare, down the street, to the edge of town, to the livery stable opposite the newspaper office.

Woody stopped by an enclosure that held a magnificent black stallion. As Woody lifted a foot to the pen's lower rail, the beast reared back almost onto its haunches and pawed the air. Whistling a shrill challenge, the horse thundered right up to the railing and slammed against it. Vaught jumped back, snatched off his hat and slapped at the horse's head.

The hostler ran out of the stable. "Hey! Get the hell away from that hoss!"

Vaught turned to the man. "Just me, Peady."

"Well, dammit, Woody, you ought to know better. That there stud's a sure as hell mean one."

"Mean? He's a damn killer. You ought to shoot him."

Peady scrubbed his bearded jaw. "If he wasn't such a damn good breeder, I'd sure enough be tempted." Only then did Peady see Revel standing behind Woody Vaught.

He jerked off his battered hat. "Ma'am."

"Peady," Vaught said, "this is my new boss, Mrs. Bentsen."

Peady bobbed his head. "Hod do, ma'am. Hope you'll pardon the corral talk. Didn't see that you was here with Woody."

Revel acknowledged the introduction with a nod, her attention focused on the horse. "Does he let you get close to him, Mr. Peady?"

"No, ma'am. Ain't never been but one man I seen handle that crazy hoss—he even got up on him oncet and rid him to a standstill. Bronc buster by name of Ketch."

Vaught grunted. "Yeah. But you got to remember, Ketch and that devil horse are two of a kind."

"That's a fact," Peady agreed, rubbing his bristly chin. "But let me tell you…in the right hands, either one of them critters, this hoss or Ketch, could turn out to be right fine specimens."

"I'm not sure I agree with the latter part of your assessment," Revel said. "I met your Mr. Colt this morning."

"Mr. Col—" Peady's eyebrows bunched up. He gave Revel an odd look before a small grin broke across his face. "Yeah, *Mr. Colt*. That's pretty good," he snickered.

As for Woody Vaught, his face churned like a man with a mouthful of chaw tobacco and no place to spit.

"Well," Peady said, still grinning, "I'd best be getting back to my chores. Just watch out, Woody. Don't let the lady get too close to this here devil…or the other one, neither."

As soon as Peady moved out of earshot, Woody said to Revel, "Mrs. Bentsen, Ketch isn't mister nobody. I told you, don't you go calling Ketch by that other name."

"But—"

"That's what we come here for, remember? Let's move over here." He stopped by the bigger corral and again propped a foot on the lowest rail.

"You see that colt over there, Mrs. Bentsen?"

He pointed to a scruffy sunken-chested piebald that barely topped fourteen hands.

Revel nodded.

"Now supposing," he said, "I wanted to sell you that sorry-looking little fella and told you that it was of that black devil's get?"

"You mean sired by the black stallion?" She gave Woody a dubious look. "Even *I'm* not *that* gullible. That poor animal could not possibly have the black's blood in him."

"Right. That's just purely right." Woody nodded in satisfaction, waiting for her reaction.

Revel just looked at him.

"Don't you catch on, Mrs. Bentsen?"

"No. I can't say that I do."

Woody took his hat off and ran his fingers through his bushy hair.

"Mrs. Bentsen..." he whooshed out a breath of air, studied the hat in his calloused hands, his scuffed boots, his eyes wandering everywhere, refusing to meet her steady gaze. "...Mrs. Bentsen, you'll have to excuse me, but there's no way for you to know unless I tell you plain out."

"That's what I've been trying to get you to do."

"Well, ma'am, *Ketch Colt* ain't a name. It's corral talk...for *bastard*."

With a slight groan, Revel folded her arms over the corral rail and dropped her head onto them.

Woody towered helplessly over her, watching the slim, shaking shoulders. Although he'd been in her employ only two short weeks, his protective feelings already spread far beyond the ordinary "loyalty to the brand."

In an awkward but gentle gesture, he patted her shoulder.

"Here now, Mrs. Bentsen. Don't go at it so. That damn Ketch ain't worth it."

When Revel tilted her head to look up at Woody, his mouth dropped open in surprise, making him look almost stupid. Revel Bentsen was not crying. The crazy woman was *laughing*.

Brushing at her eyes with the back of her hand, Revel reassured Woody. "It's all right, Mr. Vaught. We just learned something about our *Mr. Colt*. He has a sense of humor. A little warped, perhaps, but maybe there is some hope for the man after all."

The best response Woody could muster was a puzzled look.

Revel bit her bottom lip, thinking. After a bit she murmured as much to herself as to Woody, "I wonder if he can take as well as he can give? Mr. Vaught, is there a pharmacy or a physician here in town?"

"Doc Booth, back in the middle of the town at the barber shop. If he's not out doctoring, he should be down there, cutting hair."

"Ah. I want you to run down and ask Dr. Booth for a vial of chloral hydrate."

"What the hell is *that*?"

"Here. I'll write it out for you." At that moment, the faint grin on her face bore an uncanny resemblance to Ketch's own usual sardonic one.

Chapter Seven

The heavy pine-oil smell stung Ketch's nostrils, sickened him. Splinters from the rough plank floor dug into the palms of his hand and scraped his face as he tried to raise himself out of the puddle of disinfectant water. The effort set a green bronc to bucking blind inside his skull. Slumping back down, Ketch ultimately settled for propping just one eyelid open. Even that hurt...and a damned sight more when some of the pine solution dribbled down into his eye.

Someone had doused him with the pine oil solution. *Why, for God's sake?* The sour taste in his mouth answered the question for him.

Oh hell, he thought, I never been sick before...not even coming off my worst drunk.

Obviously he'd finally achieved his elusive goal of getting "knock-down, black-out drunk." But how in hell had he done it? One thing sure, it was a once in a lifetime deal and not all it was cracked up to be.

He squeezed his eyes shut, trying to recall just what the hell had happened.

He'd been bending his elbow with renewed vigor down to Katie's hellhole, working on that long-promised high-lonesome when someone had joined him at his table. After that Bentsen woman had left? Yeah. Who the hell was it?

Ah, yeah—that hollow-horn, Woody Vaught.

Remembrance returned to him in snatches. He'd figured the foreman came into Katie's looking for trouble and he was primed for a temper-cooling fight himself. But Woody—no, they didn't fight.

Woody had offered to buy him a drink. A few drinks. Then he had reciprocated. Pretty soon the damn thing turned into a boozing contest, which should have been no contest at all. Hell, hadn't he been in serious training the past month or two? So, why was he the one in jail with a buffalo herd stampeding inside his head? And where was Woody Vaught?

Lord, his head hurt. Thinking hurt. His eyelashes and fingernails hurt.

A booming clamor jolted Ketch's eyes open. Who the hell was beating on the bars of his cell with a crowbar? His whole body vibrated with the ungodly clanging until he felt like the clapper in the meeting-hall bell.

He moaned. "Stop that damn racket!"

"Well, gee, Ketch, you got a visitor." The "racket" emanated from Orlie, the jailor, his keys rattling against metal as he unlocked the cell door.

"I don't need any visitors. I need a drink." But the very thought of liquor churned his stomach. That never had happened before, either. And his mouth felt dry enough to spit cotton clear to Alabama.

"Mr. Colt."

Ketch groaned out loud when he heard that voice.

Aw, not her! His eyes rolled heavenward and he mumbled aloud, "God, You sure enough have it in Your mind to punish me today."

Despite the pain ratcheting through his brain, Ketch shoved up into a half crouch. His clothes reeked of the pine oil puddled around him...and a hell of a lot worse. Cursing under his breath in self-disgust, he ran the back of a shaking hand across his whisker-stubbled chin. He leveled a flat, albeit bloodshot, glower on Revel Bentsen.

"What do you want?" he growled, even though he had a pretty good notion of what was coming up. He'd humiliated the hell out of her yesterday and it was pay-back time. *Take your lumps, Ketch,* he told himself. *You sure as hell earned them.*

"I came to collect on that wager you lost last night."

"The *what?*" His forehead wrinkled.

"The wager you made—and lost—with my foreman."

He stared at her, confused. Was she talking about the drinking bout between him and Woody? He didn't remember any bet on the line. Anyway, what in the name of all that's holy did that have to do with her? Damned if he could remember him and Woody putting up any kind of stakes. He shook his head.

"You're reneging then?" she asked.

"Lady, I never welched out on a bet in my life." But neither did he intend to concede he had no recollection of any damn "wager." "Vaught has nothing to worry about. I'll pay off whatever I owe. Just give me a week or two to get myself straightened out."

"That wasn't the agreement. You know I don't have that much time to spare!"

Ketch squinted at her, a faint glimmer of what the bet might have been teasing around the edge of his soggy brain.

"The details...I don't recollect all of them exactly."

"Mr. Vaught wagered the going rate for breaking my bunch of horses against your taking the job for me at the same rate."

Again, Ketch swore under his breath. Sounded like some damfool kind of bet he might make, especially given his certainty that he could drink Woody under the table any day of the week and twice on Sunday.

"All right," he said. "I'll meet you at your place as soon as Talbert springs me."

"I've already spoken with the marshal. You're free to go with me now — if you can make it."

He shot her a black look. "I can make it."

The saying proved easier than the doing. Hanging onto the bars, he jacked himself the rest of the way up onto his feet. He swallowed hard and repeatedly to hold back the surge of nausea the motion stirred in his gut.

To Orlie he said, "You got my hat and pocket stuffings?"

"You bet, Ketch." Orlie creaked across the room to the marshal's desk to retrieve Ketch's few belongings. "Ain't no hat here, Ketch. Come to think of it, you didn't have none on when the marshal drug you in. He handed Ketch the "pocket stuffings."

"Oh, I durn near forgot. Some kid brought this here for you this morning." Orlie held out a sealed note.

Ketch's stomach sank. Same stationery. Another one of those vicious notes. For a moment, his face turned savage. *Didn't the bitch, whoever she was, know that Annie was dead?* He jammed the folded paper into his back pocket, unopened and unread.

Revel Bentsen's rig sat hitched and waiting outside the one-room jailhouse. When Ketch did not offer to hand her up, Revel mounted the buckboard by herself and began unwinding the reins from the brake.

"Where's my horse?" Ketch asked.

"Marshal Talbert's keeping it until you pay off your fine. Your saddle is in the back of the buckboard."

Ketch glared at her. Between Revel Bentsen and Marshal Talbert, they had him pretty well whip-sawed. He had to work for Revel Bentsen to earn enough money to get his horse out of hock. Without his horse, he'd be a virtual prisoner out at the Slash R. Wouldn't surprise him if Talbert hadn't cooked up this deal with the Bentsen woman just to keep him dried out and out of the marshal's hair…at least for a little while.

Ketch grunted his irritation and sprang up onto the seat beside Revel.

"Move over," he said, taking the reins away from her. "Be damned if I'll ride with a woman driver."

Revel gave him a wicked look, but bit back a retort, knowing that she still held the reins figuratively, if not literally. She swallowed a smile — no reason to fight a battle when you've already won the war.

Clucking to the horses, Ketch set the team in motion down the road to the west of town. At the first split in the trail, he veered north.

"You're going the wrong way," Revel said.

Those were the first words spoken by either of them since they had left town. The *only* words. Ketch didn't respond. When it became apparent he wasn't going to, Revel said, "Mr. Colt, the south fork of the trail goes to my place."

Ketch continued to drive in silence and Revel wavered. She hadn't been in the country long enough to know all the shortcuts. But at the next fork in the road, Ketch made another right. Even she could tell they were heading back in the general direction of the town.

Revel glanced anxiously at him. The secluded road had gradually petered out into little more than an overgrown animal track.

"Mr. Colt, I don't know what you have in mind, but this is not the way to the Slash R. I must insist that you turn back to the main road. Right now!"

If her voice didn't betray her building fear, her next words surely did.

"My foreman and the marshal both know that you and I left White Reef together." Her hands, tightly clasped together, trembled.

Ketch drew the team to a halt and stared at her. *By god, she was afraid.* A smile formed in his mind. Good, he thought, let her worry a little. He wished he could look inside her head and see what she was imagining. What was it with these so-called good women anyway? Seemed they thought all a man was interested in was how to get inside their bloomers. With the size of his aching head, Revel Bentsen or any other living female was down at the bottom of his present want list. Hell, he didn't even want a drink!

His lip curled, half in disgust, half in amusement. Maybe he ought to give the little gal something to worry about. He continued to stare at her, then slowly tracked his eyes up and down her body, letting them stop and linger on the swell of her breasts. He ran his tongue over his lips, gave the best horny leer in his repertoire. He stopped short of panting out loud. After all, he didn't want to overdo it.

Apparently what he'd done pulled the right trigger. Revel drew herself rigidly upright, edged toward the outer side of the seat, one hand braced on the outer rim. Ketch bet that if he so much as twitched an eyelid, she'd bail out over the side of the rig. Not that there was any place to jump—they were stopped in the middle of a narrow-walled canyon.

His lips quirked into his usual aggravating grin as he clicked the team back into motion.

After another mile or two, the narrows opened abruptly into a lush green park half a mile wide and three or four deep, that formed a natural corral if the opening they'd come through were closed off. A darker green line on the diagonal marked the meandering path of a small spring-fed stream. Not too much beyond lay the west wall of the sandstone ridge that separated the meadow on this side from the town of White Reef on the other.

Ketch didn't think Revel could get any stiffer, but when he halted the team in front of a slab-wood shack she looked as if somebody tightened the strings on her corset a few more notches.

Ketch toyed with the idea of grabbing her and carrying her inside, past the cowhide-covered doorframe, just to hear her squawk. But the million and a half jags of pain that lightninged through his head when he jumped down from the rig quickly disabused him of that notion.

He steadied himself against the side of the buckboard until certain his head wouldn't spin right off his neck. He stood a few minutes longer, head hung. In his worst nightmares, he never imagined this granddaddy of all drunks. He ran the back of his hand across his face. His stomach was empty, his hands shaking…and he needed a slug of whiskey.

Ignoring Revel, he approached the shack, kicking aside the tin cans and bottles that littered the way. He brushed the cowhide "door" to one side and tied it back with the rawhide thong nailed to the frame for that purpose, allowing light into the windowless shed. The neat interior of the one-room shack contrasted sharply with the squalid exterior.

To the right of the door stood a one-lid potbellied stove with a well-seasoned but clean cast iron skillet on it. In the corner beyond the stove, piled quilts served as a sleeping pallet; a pile of rumpled but neatly folded clothing lay on the floor next to a slightly charred cradle; a fire-blackened cupboard leaned against the left wall; a makeshift table, an inverted nail keg, and a scorched straight-back chair filled the center of the room.

Ketch headed for the cupboard, reached in, and pulled out a bottle. He uncorked the quart and lifted it to his mouth. The raw smell belted him in the gut. He fought down the nausea, could do little about the shakes. Good Lord! Even if he could hold his hands still long enough to get a good slug down, his stomach wouldn't keep it down. He slammed home the cork and set the bottle on the small table without lowering the liquor line.

Pivoting abruptly, he reached over to the pile of clothes and dug out a few items, grabbed his chaps and then some "necessaries" off a rough board nailed to the wall. He hesitated as he picked up his straight razor…probably slit his throat if he tried to shave. What the hell. That might be preferable to working for Revel Bentsen. He placed the razor in the middle of the clothing and rolled the things together in a ball and tucked the bundle under his arm.

As he turned to leave the cramped room, he nearly collided with Revel who had followed him as far as the doorway and had been standing there, watching.

Ketch grimaced, then brushed past her without a word. Revel followed at a safe distance. When Ketch walked right on past the buckboard, she called after him.

"Where are you going?"

Angrily he spun around to face her. "Down to the crick to wash some of this stink off me. You want to come down and watch that, too?"

He strode away without waiting for an answer. He didn't care if she watched or not.

Like hell misery loves company.

What he wished was that she'd climb up onto that buckboard and gallop the hell out of there and leave him alone.

Ketch had no idea how close Revel had come to doing just that. But she needed Ketch badly and she had more than herself to think about. The back of her mind always held Drew as a priority. She sighed and began ambling around the clearing, taking the opportunity to stretch her legs.

A large blackened area beyond the parked rig drew her attention. Curious, she walked past the buckboard for a closer look. Unlike the littered yard around the shack, the ground here had been neatly raked, the rubble piled to one side. As she neared the burnt-over land, she stumbled on some sort of projection just below the soil's loose surface. She brushed her foot back and forth and discovered a rock and mortar edging.

The rocks were charred like the cupboard she'd caught a glimpse of inside Ketch's shack. She supposed there had been a house here at one time that had burned to the ground and that Ketch probably salvaged the piece of furniture from this wreckage when he first squatted here.

Revel picked up one of the loose rocks. As she turned the heavy rock around in her hand, the sun reflected brightly off the metal extrusion that ran through it. Pretty. She'd never seen one like it and she pocketed it. It would make a nice paperweight.

On the far side of what she figured to have been the house's foundation, Revel discovered a grave-like mound. No cross or marker though. Maybe just an old dumping ground.

She was still idly poking through the burnt litter and debris when Ketch returned.

Revel looked at him in surprise. Ketch looked entirely different—almost human—even with the nicks his shaky hand had carved in his face. Anything she might have said froze in her throat at Ketch's look of barely controlled rage.

"What the hell gives you the right to go nosing around *here!*"

Too startled to answer, Revel drew back, bewildered and admittedly frightened. "Why—what—I wasn't..." her voice trailed off.

Her anger overcame her fear. "Look, you dragged me out here. I thought looking at burnt ground would be a lot more interesting than watching you trying to make yourself over into something half-way human."

Ketch ran his fingers through still-wet hair, the anger ebbing out of him. She probably was only passing the time. Maybe the good people of White Reef hadn't told her *every* damn thing about him after all.

Chapter Eight

By the time they reached the Slash R, Ketch's hands shook so badly he could scarcely hang onto the reins.

Revel glanced at him, a little conscience-stricken. She suggested, "Why don't you go down to the bunkhouse and get settled in. Mr. Vaught or I will let you know when supper's ready."

Ketch barely nodded. His hat disappeared from his other gear at the jailhouse and he didn't own a spare. All day he felt as if the brassy sun were boiling his brains inside his skull. And he was sick. *Oh, God, he was sick.*

He stepped down gingerly from the buckboard, trying not to stir up another cattle stampede in his head. He stumbled across the yard toward the bunkhouse, each step shooting blinding jags of black lightning across his eyes.

Range etiquette demanded that a new hand occupy only an unclaimed bunk. Ketch didn't give a damn about range etiquette. He collapsed on the first bunk he came to. Hell of a thing to do, but he had a hell of a head on him.

In a matter of seconds, Ketch fell dead asleep.

An hour and a half later, Revel rang the supper bell. When Ketch didn't come up to the big house, Revel sent Woody down to rouse him.

Woody bit back his refusal, seething inwardly. As soon as he cleared her range of hearing, he began swearing a double stream of cusswords, some that hadn't even been invented yet. Hellfire, he didn't hire on to wet-nurse no lousy damn drunk. If he wasn't drawing down those extra wages from Wykle, by damn, he'd quit on the spot.

Woody barreled into the bunkhouse, still grumbling. What he saw cut short his tirade...in fact, left him speechless. In a room with eleven empty bunks, Ketch had to squat on *his*.

"Well I'll be damned! If that don't tear the rag off the bush!"

Woody grabbed the edge of the cotton mattress, bent his knees, and straightened, raising his arms like a weightlifter, heaving the pad up to shoulder level.

Ketch jettisoned through the air, landed hard. He bit his tongue as the back of his head bounced on the dirty wooden floor. The ocean roared in his ears; the salt tang of blood filled his mouth. In a red haze, he tried to figure out what in hell happened. Forcing his eyes into some kind of focus, he saw two Woody Vaughts standing at the end of the room, their knuckles on their hips. The room tilted, his eyes lost their focus, and as the images began to fade, they merged into one.

Before he blacked out entirely, Ketch managed an earnest "You son-of-a-bitch."

Along about midnight, a persistent banging on the front door shook Revel Bentsen out of her sleep. She tied her wrap around her as she ran to the door.

"What is it? What's the matter?"

"It's me, Mrs. Bentsen," Woody answered. "Sorry as he—heck to trouble you this time of night, but I'm gonna need help. It's that bum, Ketch. He's real sick. We're gonna have to get a couple a shots of whiskey down his gullet."

She pictured Ketch. *Whiskey was the last thing that man needed.*

"Why whiskey, Mr. Vaught?"

"He come off the booze too quick."

"I don't have any whiskey. What will happen to him if he doesn't get it?"

Woody just shrugged. He'd heard of people pulled off the booze too fast to suddenly keel over and die. Not that he gave a particular damn about Ketch one way or the other. But the barkeep down to Katie's had seen him doctoring the bronc buster's bottle last night.

"I got a bottle down to the bunkhouse, Mrs. Bentsen, uh, for medicine. Offered Ketch a snort, but he wouldn't have none of it off me. I thought maybe if I drug him up here to the house and you was to give it to him…"

Before Woody finished the sentence, Revel pulled her wrap tighter around her and started at a half-run for the bunkhouse.

Woody hesitated, then followed, complaining. Hell, bunkhouses were off-limits to women. Wasn't no way right for a lady like Revel Bentsen to go hell-bent for election into the bullpen to spoon-feed no damn worthless drunk of a hired hand.

When they arrived, Ketch was sitting on the edge of a bunk, hunched over, his arms clasped around his middle, his whole body shaking violently, unaware anyone had even entered the bunkhouse.

His head jerked up as Revel draped a blanket over his shoulders. Face chalk white, eyes dull as two burnt-out coals, he stared, uncomprehending.

The moment Revel's presence registered on him, Ketch's eyes flamed to life.

"Get her out of here, Vaught. What the hell did you go and bring her down here for? Dammit, man, where's your sense…to let her see…" The words choked off in his throat as he turned his head away. "For God's sake, get her the hell out of here!"

"Hey, now, watch that language, Ketch."

But Revel put her hand on Woody's arm and shook her head. She motioned for him to follow her back outside.

"Mr. Vaught, you don't think the chloral hydrate…"

Woody shrugged. "Ketch's got the shakes worse'n any I ever seen."

"But a few drops of the drug in that concentration shouldn't have affected him that badly."

Woody stirred, uncomfortable.

Revel gave him a sharp look. "How much *did* you put in his bottle?"

"Enough to make sure he got knocked out, like you wanted."

"How much, Woody?"

"All of it."

"The whole vial? Dear Lord!" She'd seen Drew's physician administer just a gram or two and put Drew out for hours. And what Ketch had, mixed with the alcohol—no telling what might happen to the man!

"I told you to add just a few drops, the absolute most. You'd better ride to town for that Doctor Booth you told me about."

"Hell no, I don't," Woody stated emphatically. He didn't want any more people to know what he had done. "Doc Booth couldn't help a hen lay an egg. And listen, the treatment's the same for the shakes whether you're coming off a small drunk or a big one. Only thing that'll help him is a hair of the dog that bit him. Course, if we do give him a couple of shots, there's a good chance he'll take off on another toot again."

"Thanks to you, that's a chance we'll have to take."

Woody grunted. "But how the he—heck am I supposed to get him to swallow it? Hold his nose and pour the damn stuff in? I told you, he wouldn't have none when I tried to get him to take a slug. That's why I went and got you. Thought maybe you might could talk him into it."

"No. You saw. Do you think you can get him to drink some tea or coffee?"

His voice betraying exasperation, Woody answered, "Mrs. Bentsen, ain't no tea or coffee that's going to help what's wrong with him.

"If it's laced with canned milk and some of your whiskey, it might."

Woody thought about that, then nodded. "I'll give her a try."

"You'll do more than give it a try, Mr. Vaught. You will get it down him, even if you do have to hold his nose and pour it in."

By daylight, Woody looked in worse shape than Ketch did, his eyes red-rimmed and sandy from staying up all night nursing Ketch—not to mention the liberal doses of the "hair of the dog" he'd helped himself to between times.

An unusually subdued Ketch looked across the empty bunks at the Slash R foreman. Ketch couldn't forgive Woody for laying a rough hand on Cindianne that day in town a few months ago, but the man had stayed up and helped him through a damn bad night. Ketch figured he owed it to Vaught to make the first move.

"Woody. Thanks," Ketch offered tentatively.

Woody glowered, spat a brown stream across the rough wooden floor, missing the sandbox by a foot. Running a tobacco-stained sleeve across his mouth, he said, "Don't fret yourself none about it. Was it up to me, I would've dumped your sorry ass on the dung heap back of the barn and have done with it."

Ketch's face tightened, but he said mildly, "Fair enough." Then, after a short pause, he said, "Woody, if we're going to be working and bunking together, there's a little story you'd best keep in mind."

"Yeah?" Woody gave him a sidelong glance, not sure what to expect.

Ketch began, "The way the story goes is that this old farmer ordered himself a catalogue wife. He hitched up his best mule to the wagon and went down to the train to pick the gal up. As they were driving back to his place the mule acted up balky. Farmer didn't much care for that, what with his new wife looking on and all, so he says to the mule, 'That's one.' And he took up his whip and cracked the mule a good one on its noggin. The mule started up, but after a bit, it stopped to pull at a bunch of grass. The farmer said real quiet like, 'That's two,' and really laid the whip on him this time. The mule trotted along right respectful after that for a while. But, being a jackass, and not too smart a one at that, the mule decided to try out the farmer one more time. The farmer said, even more quietly than the other two times, 'That's three.' And without another word, he hauled out his hog rifle and plugged that mule right between the ears. Now that last bit of meanness was just too much for the farmer's new wife and she lit into him, read him the Scriptures up one side and down the other. When she finally run out of words, the farmer looked at her and said quietly, 'That's one.'"

Woody eyed Ketch uncertainly. "So?"

"So," Ketch said, "two nights ago, you doped up my booze and suckered me into a bet I couldn't win. *That's one.* Then last night when I was sicker than a sheep with a mouth full of dip, you dumped me off your lousy bunk. *That's two.*

Ketch pushed to his feet, a hard grin on his face. "...think about it."

Chapter Nine

Ketch felt some better this morning, if a little unsteady. He fumbled with tobacco and papers as he sauntered across the yard toward the corrals. He squinted against the glare of the early morning sun and swore bitterly at himself—for losing his hat, for getting suckered into this deal like some dumb greenhorn and, most of all, for dropping his defenses in front of Woody Vaught down to the bunkhouse earlier. Not as if this were the first time in his life he'd had a peace offering thrown back in his face. But godsakes, you'd think after having it drummed into his thick skull all these years, he'd have learned better. Wasn't anyone going to do anything for him without there was something in it for themselves. Why he thought any different, even for a moment, he could only chalk up to the whiskey-head he was toting around this morning.

The half-rolled cigarette crumbled between his fingers.

Ah, to hell with it. He dropped the makings to the ground and jammed his hands into his back pockets.

As he crossed the yard, he gave the layout the once-over. Yesterday he'd been too booze-blind to notice much, but this morning the Slash R showed every evidence of being a hardship outfit. No hands around. Of the twelve bunks in the cabin, only the one had been staked out—Woody's. A place this size without a crew could mean only one thing. *No money.* Hard to believe, but Revel Bentsen looked to be strapped for ready cash.

Well, dammit, that was her problem. Just like the infernal buzzing in his head was his problem. But if she expected him to keep his end of this deal, she damn well better be prepared to keep hers.

Ketch's eyes narrowed as they settled on a tightly cinched horse standing hipshot, its head tied close against the hitch rail. He moved over to the animal, loosened the *cincha* and the tie rope and nodded to himself. If that horse's being here meant what he thought it did…He spat in disgust.

Revel stood by the corrals, watching her herd of green broncs mill about. As Ketch approached her, he fixed his lips in the most irritating, most arrogant grin he could manage, given the condition he was in.

With mock deference, he said, "Good morning, Mrs. Bentsen…ma'am."

"Good morning…*Mister Colt.*" Then in a qualm of conscience, Revel added, "Are you feeling better today?"

"Enough to start working off my debt, if that's what's worrying you." His words punched out cold and flat.

"That isn't what I—." She shook her head in frustration. After a thoughtful pause, she straightened her shoulders and faced him directly.

"Mr. Colt, I've thought about this. I need your help desperately. But I can't force you to work for me under false pretenses. That bet between you and my foreman wasn't above-board. I don't want you to blame Mr. Vaught. He was just following my orders. But the truth is, the other night I had him slip…"

"…knock-out drops in my bottle," he finished for her.

"You know? How?"

"Lady, the minute I tried to open my eyes down to Marshal Talbert's steel-barred hotel, I knew I'd been snookered. I just didn't know why and it took a little sobering up to figure the how."

"You aren't mad?"

Ketch gave one of his short humorless laughs.

"What for? I aimed to drink myself into oblivion. All you and Vaught did was get the job done quicker and a hell of a lot cheaper than if I'd done it myself."

Revel flushed. "Of course, considering the circumstances, you're under no obligation to honor the bet."

"*Of course*. That's damn white of you, Lady. You know that I've been dealt off the bottom of the deck. Woody knows it. And I know it. But I'll bet Marshal Talbert doesn't nor the good people of White Reef, do they?"

"I was under the impression that you didn't particularly care what 'the good people of White Reef' thought of you."

Ketch focused out in the distance. "That's mostly so. Folks have a pretty damn rotten opinion of me and I don't see me doing much to change that. But even my worst enemy will admit two things about me—" He turned to face her, " —I'm a damn good bronc buster and my word is my bond. Not a helluva lot to walk proud around, but it's what I've got and I'll hang on to it. I'll break your horses for you because I said I would. But I'll get paid the going rate for it, too. Make no mistake about that."

Ketch set a foot on the bottom rail of the corral and folded his arms over the top bar.

"Getting these broncs wrung out will cost you close to nine hundred dollars. Eight eighty-five, if my count's right. And that's cash on the barrelhead. When I turn out that last horse after its last ride, I expect you to be standing by the gate with the money in your hand. I'll grab it as I trot on through. You'll be rid of me, and before the dust has a chance to settle, I'll be long gone from this petticoat outfit."

As Ketch talked, Woody ambled over and joined them. "Come again with those figures you was throwing around, Ketch? A little slower this time," he said.

Revel answered, raw discouragement in her voice. "Mr. Colt says I'll have to pay him eight hundred eighty-five dollars for him to break these horses."

"Oh, like hell!"

Ketch tilted his head to look at Woody, then pointed his thumb toward the penned animals. "She's got sixty-seven head of horses in here. But look, that bay over there has got too much white marking on it. The buckskin over there by the snubbing post has got to be fourteen years old, if it's a day. Whoever sold her these horses slipped in a couple of mares. There's a geld that stands close to seventeen hands and at least three more that don't make the fifteen-hand requirement. Now, unless the Army's changed its general orders on cavalry stock in the last couple of weeks, we got at most here fifty-nine head the

Army will accept. Once I get to handle each horse, I can give you an exact count. But figuring her as she stands, eight eighty-five it is."

Revel looked at Ketch in amazement. "You're right about there being sixty-seven horses here. When did you have a chance to take a count?"

"While we were standing here, talking."

Amazement turned to grudging respect. "And you believe the Army will buy only fifty-nine of them?"

"At most."

She did some quick mental calculation, finally got down and used a stick in the dust as she'd seen cowboys do. The figure she came up with both stunned and appalled her.

"You're going to charge me fifteen dollars a head just to break the horses!"

"Or my neck. Whichever comes first."

"But Mr. Wyk—but it was my understanding that the usual charge for breaking horses is only five dollars a head and that was our agreement—the going rate."

"It is, dammit," said Vaught. "And you know it, Ketch."

Ketch jerked a look at the foreman. "Whose going rate, Woody? Sure as hell not *mine*."

"That's all old man Neidlinger charges over to Quail Crick."

"Then drive the bunch over to Quail Crick and let old man Neidlinger do the damn job." Ketch turned to Revel. "Neidlinger's a good man and he can do a good job. But he can break only about four horses a week for you, depending on how many saddles you want."

"You mean I have to buy saddles for all these horses, too!" she asked, truly despairing.

Ketch gave her a pitying look. The woman didn't know crap about the horse business.

Forestalling the biting comment on Ketch's tongue, Woody explained, "A 'saddle' means a ride, Mrs. Bentsen. You usually turn a horse over to a buyer after five to seven 'saddles'."

"Sometimes you can get by with three," Ketch added, "depending on who's doing the buying and who's doing the breaking. When did you say that Army buyer is due?"

"The first of the month." At the question in Ketch's eyes, she appended, "Today is the seventeenth. We have exactly two weeks from today."

Ketch whistled through his teeth, wagging his head. "Hell, Lady, even working ten horses a day at three saddles a horse, that's impossible! Look here, first day sacking and rigging, maybe a few saddles. Figure then, we can handle seven the first day. Second day, I can get to ride ten, maybe even stretch that to twelve. Third day I'll give seven of them their third saddles…"

Quickly, he continued figuring in his head. "Not even allowing for hammerheads and older stuff like you've got in this bunch—which are a damn sight harder to break than the younger stuff—you got to figure the most I could have for you by the end of two weeks would be forty-eight head."

"That won't do. That won't be enough." She couldn't hide the desperation in her voice. In her mind Revel tallied the expenses facing her, the loan, the interest, Woody Vaught's wages, Drew's hospital and medical bills, his transportation out here, food, medicine. "Either you've got to break more than that or you can't charge me that much!"

Ketch gave her a probing look. He'd picked up on the genuine anguish in her voice. She wasn't trying to be difficult. She was in some kind of trouble.

"Mrs. Bentsen, you got some other kind of sucker bet going here?"

"You'd probably call it that. But it's none of your concern…or business. I'm telling you the way it must be. I have no choice."

"Sure you have a choice. Send your errand boy up to Quail Crick to jigger old man Neidlinger's drinks on him, too."

Revel shrugged off Ketch's goading, but Woody squared around, fists bunched. Revel stepped between them, facing Ketch.

"All right," she said, "I had that coming. "Mr. Vaught, I left your breakfast warming on the stove in my kitchen. You go on up there. I have some more things to discuss with Mr. Colt."

When he didn't move, she said, "Now. Please."

Grumbling, Woody spun on his heel and headed for the big house.

Revel picked up the raveled threads of her exchange with Ketch. "If I had the money, I would hire Mr. Neidlinger to help, too. But I don't. I was lucky to talk another horse-breaker into working with you, but I'm only paying him a dollar a day."

Ketch's glance drifted over to the tightly cinched horse that had been left to stand out in the sun. "That's about two-and-a-half dollars a day too much, if it's who I think it is."

"Nueces Pecado."

"Huh-uh, Lady. No way short of hell I'll let that lousy crossbreed bastard work on a herd I'm responsible for."

"What did you call Mr. Pecado?"

"Just what he is—a lousy breed bastard."

"I can't believe what I'm hearing! What a classic case of the 'pot calling the kettle black'." Revel was outraged. "You of all people...to call someone a...what you called him! By your own admission you're nothing more than a...a *ketch colt* yourself."

Ah, so she knew or someone had told her what 'ketch colt' meant. Her words stung and he couldn't pretend otherwise, but he wouldn't back down on what he said, either.

The fixed smile returned to his face, his voice holding a weary acceptance of a fact not of his doing and beyond his control. "Well, Lady, you got that right. I'm a lousy breed bastard myself. For all I know, I might be Chinee-Nigro-Jew with just enough Cherokee, Scots-Irish, and Russian tossed in for spice."

Staring at Ketch, Revel recognized at least some truth in his statement—straight black hair, bronzed skin, and high cheekbones more than hinted at early American ancestry. Yet his startling blue eyes bespoke a northern European heritage somewhere in there, too.

Ketch continued passionately, "Regardless of what I am, there's no way I'll ever work with that *other* breed bastard. Just look at this." He grabbed her by the arm, half-dragged her over to Nueces' horse, then jerked up the leather *mochila* to expose a brutally spur-scarred side.

"Look at those bear tracks on this poor horse. I may not have much to walk proud around, but I do take pride in my work. There are a lot of names for the work that I do: bronc buster, peeler, stomper, twister, snapper. Take your choice. But that goddam Pecado is a bronc-*fighter*. And if you can't figure out the difference between what he does and what I do, you have no damn business messing with horses."

He let go her arm, suddenly drained of anger. "And look at this, Mrs. Bentsen." He reached for the bridle and the animal threw its head wildly. "Head shy," he muttered. He caught the animal's head and opened its mouth.

"See that?" He pointed to the animal's cut mouth and the cruel spade bit that damaged it. "That breed's got this poor horse so cold-jawed he has to use a damn pitchfork in its mouth to get it to rein. You want these horses broke, not ruined, don't you?"

There was an unconscious plea in his voice before it hardened. "Of course, they're your animals. You can do whatever you damn well please with them. But I'll tell you flat out—you can't have both me and Pecado working for you. That's the way of it, plain and simple."

Ketch turned his attention back to the abused horse. When he looked back over his shoulder, Revel Bentsen was gone.

He shrugged and headed back to the holding pen. As he passed the barn, Nueces Pecado came charging out, dark eyes glittering like polished knives. The *mestizo* threw his steeple-peaked hat at Ketch's feet.

"Sonofabitch!" Pecado hissed, the sibilance of his accent sounding like a snake about to strike. "You son-of-a-bitch," he repeated, "you cost me this job."

Ketch spit on the ground near Nueces' hat. "I sure as hell hope so."

"*¡Hijo de puta!*"

Ketch grinned. Pecado had called him a "son of a whore." Too bad Revel Bentsen didn't catch *that* pot calling *this* kettle black. He turned his back on the smaller man and began to walk away.

Nueces flicked his arm and the leather quirt hanging from his wrist jumped into his hand. Another ophidian move and the lead-weighted poppers at the end of the short whip slashed Ketch across his bare neck.

As Ketch turned toward his attacker, Nueces lashed him across the eyes, momentarily blinding him. Ketch backed away from the quirt, which now seemed a darting, biting extension of Pecado's arm, flicking, striking like the tongue of a snake. Bloody welts rose on Ketch's arms as he lifted them to protect his eyes and face from further damage. Ketch stumbled backward into the vee formed by Nueces' ill-used horse and the hitch-rail. Nueces' indiscriminate slashing bit into the animal's hide and sent it into a bucking frenzy.

With nowhere to go but toward his attacker, Ketch lunged forward. As he collided with the smaller man, they both crashed to the ground at the horse's feet. The frightened beast tried to rear up onto its haunches, jerked down heavily. A flailing hoof struck Ketch on the thigh. He rolled away just as the horse broke its headstall and buck-jumped to the other side of the yard.

Nueces scrambled to his feet and tried to run away, but Ketch reached out and caught him by the ankle, jerked him back to the ground and clamped his arms around him. Ketch shrugged his shoulder to wipe the blood from his face. He shoved to his feet, yanking Nueces up with him.

"Now, you damned snake, we'll see."

He tore the quirt out of Nueces' hand, held him with one hand and grabbed hold of the smaller man's britches with his other. Hauling down hard, Ketch ripped Nueces' pants right off him along with the filthy underwear beneath.

In a swift, unexpected move, Ketch dropped to one knee and, with a single fluid motion, flung Nueces across his other knee. Holding the squirming kicking man in place, Ketch whipped the mestizo's bare buttocks until tears ran down the man's face.

When he begged Ketch to stop, Ketch dumped him into the dirt. Favoring his injured leg, Ketch limped across the yard and caught up the man's jittery horse, re-adjusted its cinch, then lifted and tossed Nueces face down across the animal's back.

"There," Ketch said, "now maybe your ass will be too sore to ruin any more horses for a while."

Ketch lightly flicked the quirt across the horse's rump, sending it into an uncontrolled gallop out of the yard, with Nueces doing his miserable best to hang on.

Ketch again wiped his face with his sleeve. Revel and Woody were standing there, watching him.

Woody said, "You're a sure-win fighter, aren't you? If you can't take a man down from behind, you find one half your size."

Ketch looked the burly foreman up and down. "You're facing me, Woody. You're my size, and then some. Step up any time you've a mind to."

"When I settle up with you, bronc buster, you can just bet it will be permanent."

"Yeah." Ketch dismissed Woody and turned to Revel. "You want these broncs twisted out, let's get going. We're short on help; you've got a deadline. What I'd like to know is, are you going to sit on your front porch giving out orders or is this important enough for you to pitch in and carry your share of the load?"

"I'll do anything I can to help."

"Good. You can help plenty—if you can ride."

"I can ride."

"We'll see. Go get some riding clothes on and we'll get started. He watched as she turned to leave, a thin grin forming on his face. He couldn't think of any single thing that would give him more pleasure than working her starchy little bustle off.

Fifty-nine horses in two weeks. *She'd learn.*

Chapter Ten

Ketch reached down and picked up Nueces' abandoned headgear in hopes of using it for himself. As he straightened, pain jagged through his head.

Good God, when would he get over this drunk? At least he wasn't seeing snakes—yet. Probably the next step in his headlong gallop to hell. And, after that? What the hell did it matter?

Deliberately, Ketch thrust aside that morbid line of thinking and turned his attention to Nueces' hat. He thumbed back the sweatband and found the lining alive with "graybacks." *Just my luck.* He scudded the hat across the yard onto the dung heap.

Should have dumped Pecado there, too, instead of on the back of that poor horse. He realized with self-repulsion that was just about the same as what Vaught had threatened to do to him back at the bunkhouse a little while ago. Made sense. When you got right down to it, he didn't differ all that much from Nueces, especially these past few months.

His eyes flicked up toward the house. What the hell was keeping Woody and Mrs. Bentsen anyway? He began fidgeting, anxious to get started. He didn't much relish taking on a bunch of green broncs, but that would be a sight better than standing around, thinking. Truth to tell, even though he'd been coerced into this deal, he was looking forward to it. He hadn't worked since the deaths of his wife and baby. No one had offered him a job and he hadn't sought one.

He went down to the corral where he found a limited choice of working horses. He selected a gentle-looking geld for Revel, a more spirited one for himself—a blood bay that looked to have a lot of bottom. He led the two horses toward the holding pen.

Halfway there, Vaught challenged him.

"What the hell now?" Ketch asked wearily.

Woody said, "You ain't going nowhere with that bay horse."

"*Somebody* around here has to get this damn job started."

"Well you ain't using that horse. He's out of my personal string."

"That so?"

Ketch circled the animal, running his hand over withers, flanks, hips. "Funny as a broken tooth, Woody—only brand I see on him is a Slash R."

"That don't make no never mind. I've used that bay ever since I started working for Hugh Reid, back when he owned this outfit. Ain't no one but me ever rode him then, and ain't no one but me going to ride him now."

"Hugh Reid doesn't own the Slash R anymore. He used to have eighty head you could pick a seven-horse string out of. Mrs. Bentsen has exactly five working horses on the whole spread. I've picked one for her and one for me. You can pick any of the other three."

As Ketch started to lead the horses away, Woody grabbed him by the shoulder.

"Goddammit, Ketch, it's about time someone shortened your stake rope. I'm foreman here and *I* give the orders."

Comprehension clicked in Ketch's head. Virtually overnight, a man used to giving orders found himself having to take them…and from a woman, no less.

He'll raise all kinds of hell when he finds out I'm bossing this job. Might as well spell it out for him now.

"Woody, I don't know if Mrs. Bentsen didn't make it clear enough to you or if I didn't make it clear enough to her. When I work broncs, there's only one boss—*me*. It's my bones that'll get broke or my head that'll get stove in. Each ride I make, I lay my neck on the block and the simple truth is that I'm the only one who gives a damn whether or not it gets chopped off. Now, if you want to argue the point, take it up with the lady who's footing the bill. Here she comes now."

Ketch had Revel Bentsen and, by extension, Woody Vaught over the proverbial barrel. She had no choice but to back him over her foreman. Hell, even Woody wasn't too stupid to realize that in her present circumstances, Revel Bentsen needed Ketch to bust her broncs a lot more than she needed Woody to ramrod a non-existent crew.

Ketch and Woody exchanged scowls, but when Revel got within three yards of them, Woody's look wavered, then fell. As he stomped off to choose himself a horse, he passed Ketch and muttered loud enough for the buster to hear, "Bastard."

Ketch grinned at the retreating foreman's back. Sure was stacking up to be one hell of a fine day.

Revel had changed into an emerald green riding habit with fitted waistcoat and long flowing skirts. The silly green hat with the feather was pinned to her piled gold hair. A riding crop dangled from her wrist and she carried a light sidesaddle. *A striking, lovely, altogether feminine picture.* Not what Ketch had in mind for the rough and grubby work ahead.

"Have you changed your mind about helping out?"

"Not at all. You told me to get into my riding clothes. I did and here I am."

A grin worked across his face. Not his usual go-to-hell grin, but one of genuine amusement. For godsakes, she really thought she was going to work in *that* outfit.

"You can't work in those fluffy duds."

Revel shot him a frosty look. "There are some civilized people who recognize a riding habit when they see one and who, contrary to that silly gloat on your face, do not find this kind of attire so ridiculous as to be laughable."

"Well, Lady, you can count me among that last bunch. I think you and your outfit both look beautiful. But horses aren't as easily impressed as I am, especially once all that stuff starts flapping around and spooking them. Mrs. Bentsen, as pretty as your *riding habit* is, it's just not safe for you...or for me. Look, we've already lost way too much time this morning standing around squabbling. For now, you can just watch Woody and me and try to get the hang of things. But tomorrow at daybreak, you be down here, wearing a pair of britches. And forget that lopsided pancake you're holding. You'll be using a stock saddle and riding squaw style."

"Squaw style?"

"Astride. You know, one leg on each side of the horse."

"You can't be serious!" Revel's face reddened. Ladies just didn't wear men's clothes and ride *that* way. "Mr. Colt, isn't there any end to your impudence?"

Ketch cut her off with a sharp gesture. "Look, Lady, I'm not trying to hoo-raw you. But neither am I going to waste time spelling out every damn order I give."

"Every order *you* give!"

"Do you have to repeat everything I say? Yes. Every order I give. If this job's going to get done at all, it's got to be my way. We can save a hell of a lot of time and wrangling the sooner you and your foreman hot-iron that fact into your brains."

Revel glowered at him. "Believe me, Mr. Ketch Colt, I'll do anything I can to hurry this job along...even take orders from you. Because the quicker I'm through with it, the quicker I can be through with you, too."

Ketch shrugged his shoulders. Way to go cowboy—Pecado, Vaught, and now Revel Bentsen. That makes it unanimous. If they were holding elections for a lynching today, he sure wouldn't have to buy any votes.

Ketch and Woody hazed fifteen head from the big pen and drove them into a smaller corral. Dismounting, Ketch took his coiled rope off his saddle.

He said to Vaught, "Cut out that chestnut for me."

Woody scoffed. "Hell, even Mrs. Bentsen could ride that rocking chair."

"This isn't a fourth of July rodeo with me looking to pick up beer money, Woody. The longer I keep all in one piece, the more broncs I can snap for your boss. Now move."

The look of venom Vaught shot at Ketch was lost. Ketch had already turned and shaken out his loop, ready to make his toss.

Riding a heavy-chested dun, Vaught cut the chestnut from the bunch of milling broncs and drove it toward Ketch. As the chestnut whirled by, Ketch made a "slip pitch," the loop vertical, its top against the chestnut's chest, the bottom just a fraction off the ground. As the bronc's forehooves stepped into the loop, Ketch hauled back, digging his heels into the dirt, ready to bust the horse. But just as Ketch threw his weight against the rope, Woody spurred on through, instead of veering off. Ketch saw Woody's spiteful grin just before the big dun shouldered into him, knocking him end-over-end into the corral dirt.

Ketch's foot got fouled in one of his rope's coils as he fell. The chestnut he'd forefooted spooked and crow-hopped around the corral, dragging Ketch behind him. All the other horses in the corral broke into a round of bucking and kicking. The chestnut, with Ketch dragging helplessly behind, ran up against another horse. The sudden stop slackened the rope for an instant. Ketch rolled onto his side and curled his body enough to get a hold on the catch-rope above his ankle. When the other horse jumped away, the chestnut bolted forward again. Ketch hung on to the rope and pulled himself forward, hand over hand, until he had enough slack to hang on with one hand and work his foot free with the other.

Just as Ketch cleared himself, Woody rode up to him on the dun. He leaned over and Ketch grabbed the foreman's arm and sprang up onto the dun's rump behind Vaught. Revel ran to open the gate and Vaught rode them out of the pen.

Ketch slid off the back of the dun. Woody smirked down at him, but threw a bit of mock solicitude into his voice for Revel's benefit.

"Sure got yourself into a helluva mess that time, Ketch. Good thing I was around to drag your irons out of the fire."

Ketch nodded to him, returning the smile.

"Woody—"

"Yeah?"

"That's *three*."

Ketch grabbed Woody by the shirtfront and hauled him out of the saddle. Before Woody could gain his balance, Ketch drove a knotted fist into the bigger man's middle. Woody doubled over, clutching his stomach. As he bent forward, Ketch brought his knee up, catching the foreman flush under the jaw. The audible crack of Vaught's teeth made Revel Bentsen shudder. The foreman collapsed, a sodden heap at Ketch's feet.

Revel ran to Vaught's limp form and knelt beside him, as if to protect him from further harm. She glared at Ketch.

"Are you crazy? What kind of man are you! How could you beat Woody like that, after he just saved your worthless neck!"

Ketch didn't try to explain. That and a nickel would get him a cup of coffee...maybe.

Chapter Eleven

Now that he'd taken care of the preliminaries, Ketch hoped to get down to some serious bronc stomping. He brushed past Revel and Vaught. If her horses were ever going to get broke, she'd better learn to keep that cur dog of hers on a leash.

Ketch gathered up his rope, giving Woody a couple of extra moments to collect himself. Once the foreman's eyes stopped rolling around in his head, Ketch leaned down and offered him a hand up. Vaught shoved Ketch's hand aside and levered himself up under his own power.

Ketch smiled. "Let's try 'er again, Woody. Cut that chestnut out and drive it by me one more time."

Ketch could have done the job himself by neck-roping the horse and choking it down. But he didn't for two reasons. First, it takes more time to calm down and handle a horse that's been roped by the neck, rather than forefooted. Secondly, the chance of injury to the horse was greater that way. Revel Bentsen had neither the time nor the horses to spare.

Woody separated the chestnut from the rest of the bunch. As he hazed it toward Ketch, Ketch approached it from its near side. He gave the rope an inward twist as he tossed it over the animal's right shoulder and a little ahead. The rope flipped backward against the chestnut's knees and the horse stepped right into the waiting loop. Ketch threw his weight back against the rope, jerking the animal's front legs out from under and busting it to its side.

Quickly he worked hand over hand up the rope, keeping the horse's legs stretched out. *Damn, but he could sure use another hand on the rope with him.* The chestnut scrambled its back legs under and started pushing to its feet.

"Head down the sonofabitch, Woody! Head 'im down!"

Woody hesitated for only an instant. He was a top hand and instinct won out over resentment. He jumped from the dun, ran to the chestnut and straddled its neck. Grabbing its nose, Woody twisted the head back with both hands until he and the horse were staring into each other's eyes.

While Woody pressed his considerable weight down on the horse's neck, Ketch threw a half-hitch around its forelegs, doubled the rope to make a loop, ran it back between the forelegs, and drew the horse's lower hind foot forward into the loop he made, and tied it off. He made a bowline over its shoulder and "crow-hobbled" the top hind leg, just in case he needed the extra control.

Like a rodeo competitor working against the clock, Ketch grabbed the bay's tail in one hand and pulled out his pocketknife with the other. Using his teeth to open the blade, he cut the tail. He moved closer to Vaught and trimmed the short mane over the animal's withers.

"You have the hackalea?" Ketch asked.

"Got it right here."

"Put 'er on and we'll get this fella on his feet."

The moment Vaught slipped the hackamore in place over the bronc's head, Ketch slipped the loop from the chestnut's bottom hind hoof, took up the "McCarty"—the hackamore rope—from Woody. Holding the rope to the forefeet secure in one hand and the McCarty in the other, he yelled to Woody Vaught.

"All right, throw off!"

Vaught jumped off the bronc's neck and the animal lunged to its feet.

While memory of being busted was still fresh in the bronc's mind, Ketch worked the head rope from side to side, holding the foot rope taut, trying to convince the horse it was still tied and that if it moved, it was apt to be busted down again.

Once Ketch felt comfortably sure that the horse understood that much, he urged the animal toward the snubbing post in the middle of the corral. Ketch fastened the ropes to the seven-foot-high, twelve-by-twelve puncheon. He spoke softly, reassuring the animal, handling him, touching him all the while he worked the horse.

"Let's go ahead and sack him out."

Woody handed Ketch an empty grain sack. As he talked to the animal, Ketch raised the sack in front of its head, letting the animal smell it. Then, gently, he moved the sack forward and began massaging the bronc's eyes with it. The calmed horse accepted Ketch's ministrations without a twitch or tremor. Ketch dragged the burlap slowly back over the bronc's head, let it lie there a few moments, swung it across the neck, slowly, patiently working over the horse's entire body, getting a little rougher as he went along, sometimes flicking it, but all the while keeping up his soothing chatter.

Ketch, Woody, or Revel Bentsen would repeat this time-consuming process each day, as often as time afforded. Ketch wanted to be sure that any horse he turned out would be a reliable one. Toward the end of this first "sacking-out," Ketch started draping his weight against and across the chestnut's back.

When the bronc seemed as reconciled to the sack as it would ever be on its first workout, Ketch untied his stiff yellow rain slicker from behind the cantle of his saddle. The oilskin "fish" crackled as he worked it over the chestnut's body, as he had the sack. After a first startled reaction, the chestnut also accepted the slicker.

"Let's try a saddle. Get the rig off my horse, Woody."

Woody frowned at the order, resentment simmering just below the surface. Ketch understood what Woody must be feeling. It was a hell of a thing for a ranch foreman to serve as flunky to a contract buster.

When Woody brought the saddle, he dumped it into the dirt at Ketch's feet.

Ketch let the insult pass with nothing more than a slight tightening of his lips.

"You want to blind him?" Woody asked

Ketch shook his head. As Woody had already sarcastically pointed out, the chestnut didn't seem to be a particularly ill-natured brute. A blindfold seemed superfluous.

"Let him see what's coming. He's crow-hobbled."

The horse took the rig on its back and let Ketch lace it up without much of a fuss. Once the animal got used to the idea of the saddle,

Ketch began putting his weight first in one stirrup, then in the other. He did this several times before removing the saddle. Then he put it back on.

After a half hour of that repetition, Ketch put his full weight in the stirrup, then astride the saddle, mounting and dismounting, both from the near and off sides of the horse.

"Tie a sack of grain on his back, Woody. As soon as he seems settled with it, take the crow-hobble off, but leave him hobbled and turn him into the breaking pen."

Woody's lip curled, contempt rich in his expression. "You want a sack of grain tied onto its back?"

Ketch flushed. Using weights galled him, as it would any good bronc rider. But dammit, he wasn't in this for show. With the time constraints imposed on him by the boss lady, he'd use whatever he had to, to soften the mounts up for riding.

"Dammit, just follow orders."

Shortly afterward, Ketch and Woody prepared to repeat the same process with the next bronc. After they completed the whole routine with the second horse, they returned to the breaking pen where the chestnut still stood with saddle and filled grain bag on its back.

The chestnut was ready for its first saddle.

Ketch buckled up his chaps while Woody went for the dun horse. By the time the foreman rejoined him at the breaking pen, Ketch had already removed the sack of grain and tightened the cinches on the chestnut.

He looked at Woody and asked, "Ready?"

Woody gave a curt nod, then added sarcastically, "Need me to ear this juggernaut down for you?"

The thin go-to-hell smile curved Ketch's lips. "This one's a rocking chair, remember?"

Taking a firm grip on the hackamore, Ketch crouched by the chestnut's near side and loosened the hobble from its forefeet. Slowly, without flourish, he brought the McCarty over onto the bronc's shoulder and tied it to each side of the hackamore to fashion reins. He took up the slack, the reins, and a handful of the cropped mane in his left hand and braced his left shoulder against the chestnut's. With his free hand he twisted the near stirrup, and then slipped the pointed toe of his boot in only as far as the ball of his foot. At the shift of Ketch's weight, the chestnut surged forward. The motion propelled Ketch up and into the saddle.

The chestnut bucked straight-away, pumping up and down like a well-oiled pump handle with no tricks or show of imagination. Ketch smiled to himself. *Damned if he hadn't picked himself a rocking chair after all.*

On the whole, the next five broncs Ketch picked proved relatively easy rides, too. He'd gotten grassed a few times, but there was no shame to a bronc snapper being piled by an honest bucker.

The sixth bronc proved a whole different story.

"You sonofabitch of a hammerhead!" Ketch swore heartily at the horse. "Hold the bugger's head, Woody!"

Even Vaught forgot that Revel was standing at the corral rail watching and let loose his own flood of choice profanity.

"Let the sonofabitch go, Ketch. That coon-footed hay burner is shit crazy as that black devil of Peady's."

"I've got his hind leg caught up. Have to leave the hind hobble on." Ketch shook his head. "Maybe you're right, Woody. Maybe we ought to let the bustard go. But the boss needs him and he's going to have to be busted sooner or later. If we let him go now, after he kicked up all this hell, he'll be twice as hard to work on later."

They worked sack and slicker close to an hour-and-a-half before putting the saddle on. Ketch checked the western sky. Getting along toward dark, and he had hoped to handle a dozen horses today, roughing out at least seven of them. With Revel helping with the sacking-out, they'd accomplished the first goal. But he'd given only five horses their first saddles. If he waited any longer, it would be too dark to give this one his. Ketch made his decision.

"We're losing too much time on this widow-maker. We just don't have the time to let him buck the saddle. I'm going to twist him out."

Woody handed the reins of his dun over to Revel so he could help Ketch.

The bronc fought them all the way, trying to kick their heads off along with the hobbles, biting and snapping at any part of their bodies that got within striking range.

Woody asked, "Want me to ear him down?" No sarcasm this time.

"Blind him *and* ear him down for me."

Ketch held the ropes against the struggling beast while Woody yanked off his kerchief and tied it over the bronc's eyes. He grabbed up the halter in one hand, one of the horse's ears in his other and sank his teeth into the tip of the nearer ear. The horse held motionless against the pain, giving Ketch the moment he needed to throw off the hobbles and scramble aboard.

"All right," he yelled, "let 'er rip!"

Woody threw off and the bronc sprang straight up in the air, hitting the ground ramrod stiff. Leather popped, dust clouds plumed. As its hindquarters exploded, the breath whooshed out of Ketch's lungs. His spine felt as if it had been driven clear up through his hat—if he had had a hat. *Couple more like that, and he wouldn't even have a head!*

Before Ketch set himself in the saddle, the bronc humped its back and made a series of violent, spine-jolting, pile-driving turns, jumps, and landings. The horse was a sure enough "close-to-the-ground bucker." It changed direction so quickly while hurtling through the air, kicking sideways with such fast and violent action, it was nigh impossible to keep either sense of direction or timing.

As determined as the bronc was to unload Ketch, Ketch was even more determined to stay on. Ketch didn't know how many more of those grinding shocks he could take. But just as he felt himself weakening, Ketch caught the bronc's rhythm. He raked blunted spurs back and forth along the lunging brute's sides, shoulder to hip.

Mentally and physically, this was the one thing Ketch was born to do. For a few minutes, his lithe body became one with the horse's. So perfectly timed was his wiry frame to the bronc's movements, that man and animal seemed to merge into a single jack-knifing centaur.

And then the bronc began twisting in an erratic weaving motion, none of its feet hitting the dirt at the same time. Ketch gripped the horse's barrel tighter with his legs, using his whole repertoire of quirt, spurs, rope-end and, more than once, a fist between the ears.

The punishment was not all one-sided. Blood began to dribble from Ketch's nose and one ear. He felt his strength ebbing. He hadn't eaten today; he wouldn't have been able to keep it down, had it been offered. But with skipping meals, coming off one mean drunk, and twisting out five broncs before this one, Ketch had few reserves to draw on. The bronc, however, seemed to be revving up to its second wind.

Unless he could get the bronc as tired as he was, Ketch didn't have a chance in a hundred to ride the brute out.

"Open the gate!" he yelled to Vaught. Woody leaned over the dun's neck and swung open the corral gate. Ketch spurred the bronc on through.

Frustrated at being unable to separate itself from the human burr attached to its back, the bronc exploded into a new frenzy of blind bucking, running into and over anything that got in its path. When it headed toward a pile of old corral posts, Woody spurred his horse hard to intercept the chestnut and haze it away. But the crazy animal plowed right on through Vaught and the dun.

Ketch hammered his fist down on its nose and stopped the chestnut just short of the woodpile. Whipping and spurring, Ketch guided it into a wide running arc three miles long that eventually brought them back to the breaking pen.

"Get the gate!" Ketch yelled to Vaught.

Revel reached the breaking pen first and flung open the gate just as Ketch and the bronc reached it. Woody hurried to help her. They swung the gate back and held it shut as the hammerhead turned to run back out.

As the bronc made its last defiant gesture, Ketch clubbed the horse between the ears with his fist. The bronc took another pitching fit, but the run had burned the steam out of the animal. Ketch began drawing up the hackamore rein, pulling the bronc's head higher and higher until it was hard put to do any decent kind of bucking.

All at once, the horse stopped dead.

Ketch had ridden the bronc to a standstill.

Gently, Ketch urged the quivering animal into a slow walk around the breaking pen until the chestnut fully cooled down.

Ketch's legs trembled in exhaustion when he finally dismounted. His spine ached; his back throbbed like hell; his head was exploding in three different directions. Nevertheless he waved off Woody and off-saddled and rubbed down the bronc himself.

As Revel walked across the pen to join him, Ketch sleeved the paste of blood, dirt, and sweat from his face. Before walking away, he said to Revel, "That, Lady, is the difference between bronc-busting and bronc *fighting*."

He wasn't bragging. The horse had done more damage to him than he had done to it.

Ignoring Ketch's arrogant grin, white in the closing darkness, Revel moved closer to the chestnut. She'd seen the way Ketch spurred that animal...the hypocrite, after all his disparaging talk about Nueces.

She touched the animal's flanks and shoulders. Not a drop of blood. Not a scratch on its hide. To her absolute incredulity, not one spur mark showed on the bronc Ketch had just broken.

She had no choice but to re-assess her perceptions of Ketch Colt, if not as a man, certainly as a bronc buster. What she had taken as arrogance proved less insolence than self-assurance, the ingrained confidence of a man who loves his work, knows his work, does that work exceptionally well, and is justifiably proud of it. Even the way he moved suddenly translated into something different. What she originally perceived to be lazy indifference, she now recognized as a singular economy of movement.

If nothing else, Revel Bentsen now understood one thing with clarity — today, she had seen bronc-busting at its roughest — and at its best.

Chapter Twelve

Working by lantern light, Ketch and Woody completed cold-shoeing the six broncs Ketch had ridden. At about the same time, Revel called them up to the big house for a very late supper.

A basin of warm water, a cake of lye soap, and some flour sacking had been laid out on the side-porch of the ranch house. Woody washed his hands and went inside. Ketch did a more thorough job of sloughing off the day's accumulated grime, but stood uncertainly outside the kitchen door when he finished. She had called Woody up here to eat this morning, but not him.

Revel cracked the door open and stuck her head out. "We're waiting for you, Ketch."

"I wasn't sure…"

Revel gave him a perplexed look, then clapped her hand to her mouth. "Oh, Ketch, have you eaten at all today?"

He shook his head. "It's all right. I didn't have much of an appetite on me today." Mentally, he qualified, *not for food*. The liquor was working out of his system and he was jittery and distracted. He never needed a drink more or wanted it less.

"I'm sorry, Ketch," Revel said. "I just wasn't thinking. I'm really sorry."

"No big thing." He brushed aside the apology.

"Well, please come in now. Any time I call or ring the bell for breakfast or supper, that certainly includes you."

Ketch unbuckled his chaps, folded them, and laid them on the porch outside the door.

At the table he ate sparingly and finished long before either Revel or Vaught did. He started to pull out the makings, glanced over at Revel who was just beginning her pie, and returned the Bull Durham and papers to his pocket.

Eating hadn't helped him. He was still edgy, nervous. Revel misunderstood his restlessness.

"You don't have to wait for us to finish," she said. "You can leave any time you want to."

Ketch gave her a strange look. If he'd wanted to leave, he'd have left without waiting for anyone's permission. He started to rise. "Fine meal. Thanks."

Revel returned Ketch's long steady glance and a silent exchange passed between them. Quickly she asked, "Are you sure you wouldn't like another piece of pie or cup of coffee first?"

Something flipped over inside Ketch. Revel Bentsen understood. She was giving him a legitimate excuse to prolong his stay at the supper table if he wanted to. And he did. Tonight he needed company a lot more than he needed food.

"I could go another cup of coffee," Ketch said, easing back down into his seat.

Revel lifted the pot off the stove and refilled their cups all the way around.

When she settled back down at the table, Revel asked, "You appeared to be spurring that last horse very hard."

Ketch took a moment to weigh her statement, wondering if it were born of criticism or curiosity.

"You bet I was spurring hard — damned hard."

"Then why weren't its sides all marked up like Nueces' horse?"

"Spurs aren't decorations, but they aren't supposed to be instruments of torture, either. They're used to control, not punish. Did you get a close look at my spurs?"

"Not really."

He reached down and slid one off his boot and held it up for her to see. "If you look here, you can see I've filed down the points of the rowels. Rounded off like that, they won't scour the hide off a horse. Now Pecado, he does just the opposite. He sharpens those damn Mexican spikes he wears and he's not at all shy about screwing down when he's got an honest bucker under him."

"Screwing down means...?"

"Well, he'll sink those meat hooks under the cinch to hold himself in the saddle. You see, Mrs. Bentsen, Mexican spurs aren't bad in themselves. Hell, they're just like that spade bit I showed you that Pecado uses. Spurs and bits are as good—or as bad—as the hombre using them. I've seen some fine Mex *vaqueros* use a spade bit and never more than tickle the roof of their horses' mouths. Yet they could put their horses through paces you wouldn't believe possible."

"Do you mind answering another question?"

"Shoot." He liked the interest she was taking in her new business enterprise.

"Why did you cut the horses' manes and tails?"

"Just the ones we worked on. Tomorrow when you go down to the corral and look at all sixty-seven head, you'll see why easy enough. Makes it a lot simpler to pick out the ones you've already worked on from the ones you still have to do. There's another reason, too. With all the things that can go wrong when you've giving a bronc its first saddle, you try to eliminate beforehand anything that's a potential source of trouble, like getting a spur hung up in a mane or tail.

"That's why tomorrow I want you to wear britches instead of an outfit like you had on this morning." He couldn't help but grin at remembrance of her seriousness as she came down to work in that fancy outfit.

Revel flushed and replied stiffly, "Mr. Colt, I do not own a pair of *britches*. The fact may have escaped you, but I *am* a woman."

"Yes, ma'am. I noticed that about you right away." Ketch's face broke out in a smile that lightened the dark shadows of his face.

This was the first time Revel had seen Ketch without a guarded expression on his face. The transformation stunned Revel.

Why, he's handsome!

She quickly stomped on the errant thought. It had been too long since she'd been with Drew and even longer since they had...

"Look, Mrs. Bentsen, if you really want to help in the morning, you'll need to rustle that pretty little bustle of yours and don some real pants."

Ketch clamped his teeth shut. Dammit, he hadn't meant to put it in quite those terms. But before he had a chance to backtrack on his words, Woody threw in his two bits.

"Curb that saloon talk around here, Ketch. That ain't no way to talk to a lady."

"You're right," Ketch admitted humbly enough.

But Woody, who up to this point had been busy stuffing his mouth, pushed the issue. "Just 'cause you never been around a decent woman before don't give you no leave to—"

"All right, Vaught. That's as far as you go, unless you want to land through that wall across the way."

Revel tried to intervene. "Ketch, Woody didn't mean anything, certainly nothing worth getting all upset about."

"How the hell do you know? There isn't a woman living, born, or died any more decent than…" Ketch stopped short, unable, unwilling, to dredge up Annie's name in front of them. "Just go to hell. The both of you."

He pushed to his feet and stormed outside.

As soon as the door closed behind Ketch, Revel said, "Well doggone that man anyway!"

Woody Vaught smiled unpleasantly. "That's the mildest damnation I ever heard wished on Ketch."

She shook her head. "Why is he like that? What is wrong with the man?"

"If you figure that out, Mrs. Bentsen, you'll for sure be the first."

"But he's such a different person when he's working horses or even talking about them. I guess if there's one good thing to be said about him, he is what he claims…a fine bronc buster."

"Hell. Don't take no more than a heavy seat and a light brain to be a bronc buster."

Revel shrugged off Woody's comment. "What I can't understand is what brought on that sudden show of temper? Do you know what it was he started to say, about there not being another woman as decent as—*who*?"

"Ah, he brought him a woman back after one of his horse-selling trips somewheres. Just trash like him. But he tried to pass her off as a decent woman—claimed she was his wife. Now you tell me, what good girl would take up with the likes of Ketch, right?"

"Then Ketch is married?" She was remembering the bronc buster's crude pawing of the painted woman at Katie's Palace the day she first encountered him.

"He was, if you want to call it that, till a couple months back. But even she couldn't take no more of Ketch."

"His wife left him?"

"Yeah, but there's some question about *how* she left him."

"What do you mean, Mr. Vaught?"

"The woman's dead. Nora Peters—now there's a fine lady—believes the gal killed herself. Said she heard there'd been a suicide note. But Wykle says that's bullshit...pardon my language. Wykle don't believe the girl had enough schooling to even read or write. Ketch won't talk about it. Marshal Talbert won't do nothing about it. But Wykle figures Ketch killed his woman. The gal was carrying a baby at the time. And from the looks of her, pretty far along. Town gossip had it that the kid probably wasn't even Ketch's. Wouldn't surprise me none. She was pretty free with her favors. Why even I—"

At the look of revulsion on Revel's face, Woody dropped that line of talk. "Begging your pardon for talking so loose, Mrs. Bentsen, but you wanted to know what Ketch was so thin-skinned about."

She nodded, but still a little perplexed. "Woody, you said *Wykle* thinks Ketch killed his wife?"

"...and her baby, too, don't forget."

"Would that be *Charlie* Wykle you're referring to?"

"The same."

"But I was under the impression that Charlie Wykle and Ketch were rather good friends."

"Where in hel—heck would you get an idea like that? Ketch and Wykle *friends*?" Woody laughed at the thought. "Why, not more'n three or four weeks back, Ketch like to of beat the living crap out of Mr. Wykle. Happened the night Ketch burned his place down...I think it was just before you come to White Reef."

"Ketch burned down Mr. Wykle's place?"

"Nah. His own. Just a damn shack with a room and a half with just a curtain—" Woody bit off his words, realizing he might be saying too much.

"I'm having trouble following this, Woody. Why would Ketch do anything so foolish as to burn his own house down?"

"Mr. Wykle figures Ketch done it to destroy the evidence of what Ketch done to his woman."

"Does anyone else besides Mr. Wykle believe Ketch killed his wife? I mean, if the man is suspected of committing a crime that serious, wouldn't Marshal Talbert do something about it?"

"Aw, Talbert's about the closest thing to a friend Ketch can claim. The way Talbert tells it, Ketch come in when his gal died and reported her death legitimate and all the rest is confidential. Talbert's damn quick to point out, too, that his jurisdiction ends at the town line. That never stopped him from crossing over that line a time or two to catch hisself a rustler. He just don't want to go after Ketch. You ask me, Talbert's too flat out scared to cross Ketch. Why hell! Nobody even knows where Ketch planted his gal."

Revel shuddered, remembering the cleanly raked mound of earth and the savage look that twisted Ketch's face when he found her poking around there.

Just what kind of deal had Charlie Wykle pulled her into?

Chapter Thirteen

Ketch rolled and lit a cigarette, dragged deeply on it as he paced the bunkhouse floor. God, his nerves were raw. He hadn't meant to jump both feet down Revel Bentsen's throat up there at the big house. She had no idea what Vaught was talking about. And he'd welcomed her interest, appreciated the opportunity to talk with a woman without having to pay for her time, jumped at the excuse to delay this moment when he'd be by himself and have to fight off the loneliness...the need for a drink...the guilt.

Always the guilt.

He finished one cigarette and lit the next from it. He really didn't *want* a drink. The thought made his stomach churn. But even if it didn't, one drink would lead to another and that wouldn't be smart, not in the middle of a busting contract. But Lord, he *needed* one.

Ketch was in the process of lighting his fourth "Dur'm" in a row when Woody returned to the bunkhouse. Ketch watched the foreman over cupped hands.

Vaught stared belligerently at him. Then, with purposeful malice, the foreman reached into his warsack under the bunk and pulled out a quart of whiskey and set it on the inverted half-barrel next to his bunk. He poured some of the amber liquid into an enamel cup, stretched out on his bunk, his back against the wall, and took a long satisfying pull from the mug.

A fierce flash of joy creased his face as he saw Ketch's eyes caressing the bottle.

Ketch didn't miss the expression on Vaught's face.

The sonofabitch would give his saddle to have me beg for a drink.

Even knowing this, Ketch stepped closer to the makeshift table with the bottle on it, as if forced beyond his control. His hands balled into fists and he stood there a moment longer before wheeling out of the room, Vaught's mocking laughter echoing after him.

Spurred by his restlessness, Ketch strode over to the barn and saddled up the bay he'd used that day. A good horse and it hadn't had that much of a workout.

It would get one now.

Revel heard the pound of hooves outside and rushed to the front window. Shading her eyes against the lamplight, she peered out into the darkness.

Was that Ketch on the bay, stampeding out of the yard as if all the demons of Hades were nipping at his heels?

She tossed a wrap around her shoulders and ran down to the bunkhouse.

Vaught was there alone, slouched on his bunk, sipping from the cup. He jumped to his feet when he saw who it was.

"Where did Ketch go?" Revel demanded.

"How the he—heck should I know? He got a burr under his blanket again and just took off."

Then she spied the half-empty bottle on the inverted barrel alongside Vaught's bunk. She fought down a sudden rage.

"Hitch up the buckboard," she ordered.

"This time of night? What for? Hey, you aren't—you *can't* go running after *him*."

"I can do anything I please, Mister Vaught, including firing you, if it comes to that. Now get me that buckboard. You know how much I need him to break those horses."

And, as much as she hated to admit it, even to herself, an urgent inexplicable concern for Ketch himself nagged at the back of her mind.

From sheer force of habit, Ketch headed for his place. The moment he arrived, he was sorry he'd come. Too many bad memories here for him. Worse, there on the table sat his bottle where he'd left it the other day when he'd stalked out with Revel Bentsen at his heels.

He took a chipped cup out of the cupboard and set it down next to the bottle.

The temptation was damned strong.

As he did the other day, he turned abruptly away from it and went to the small pile of tousled clothes in the corner. Revel Bentsen said she didn't own a pair of britches. He'd give her a pair of his.

He swore softly. His troubled thoughts kept jumping between her and the whiskey. Neither one would do him one damn bit of good.

As he rummaged through the pile trying to find the smallest, cleanest pair, he saw the soiled jeans he'd worn during his stint in Marshal Talbert's hotel. Most of the stench had left them, but they still badly needed laundering. He emptied the pockets and found the note Orlie had given him. He balled the note in his fist and threw it on the floor, unread.

"Whoever you are, you lousy bitch, you can't hurt Annie anymore ...not where she is," he said aloud.

He returned to the table—and the bottle. He'd been a heavy drinker before he met Cindianne, but he had no trouble giving the stuff up altogether when he married her. Never before had he had this deep, bone-aching need for a drink nor, paradoxically, had he wanted it less. Part of his problem, he realized, was the woman urge burning inside him. Liquor was a hell of a poor substitute for what a woman could provide, but the best he'd been able to come up with since Cindianne's death.

He stared at the bottle. *This is stupid. If I had a lick of guts or brains, I'd heave the damn bottle out the door.*

But that wouldn't solve anything. If he wanted a drink badly enough, he'd just go into town and buy himself another quart. Either he'd face this thing down or he'd be swallowed up whole by it.

He pulled the room's single chair closer to the table and sat unthinking, staring past the feeble candle glow to the night's blackness beyond the open doorway. Finally he rose, picked up the note he'd thrown on the floor. Like the booze, this was one more thing he had to face up to.

He slipped his finger under the seal and opened it.

The note wasn't, as he'd thought, for Cindianne, but for him. It made as little sense as any of those Annie had ever received:

This should be interesting, watching you and Woody Vaught sharing the same woman again.

The "again" had been underlined so hard, a hole had been torn through the paper.

Ketch studied the note, wondering what the hell it was supposed to mean. He recalled the rape of his Annie, then that last note she'd received accusing her of "entertaining the cowboys." Could Vaught have been the man? He shook his head. Woody was a low-down sonofabitch, but it would take more than a note from some anonymous and vicious woman to convince him that even Vaught could be *that* low down.

And who was the woman he and Vaught were supposed to be currently "sharing?" Revel Bentsen? That thought was outright laughable. Besides, the note was waiting for him before he was "recruited" to work for Revel Bentsen. Who, besides Revel Bentsen, would even have had an idea that he'd agree, albeit under duress, to bust out her horses?

The only thing he knew with any degree of certainty was that whoever was writing these poison-pen letters, as Nora had called them, must be a woman. The writing looked too fine, too fancy to be a man's, although he'd heard that accountants, engravers, sign-painters and such could write pretty fussy. *What about newspaper editors?*

Ketch reached into his hip pocket and pulled out his worn-thin leather money pouch and opened it carefully. For the first time since her death, he looked at Cindianne's note and smiled grimly. The only thing she had ever written him...and the last.

He turned the back of his chair toward the table and straddled the seat, folding his arms across the chair's back.

What a contrast between the elaborate script of those other notes and this one of Annie's, with its crude print.

Anger and guilt put a bitter taste in his mouth as he read and re-read the *suicide* note until the words blurred.

God, but he missed her. He missed her gentle acceptance of him in spite of what he was. He missed the clean smell of her hair, the warmth of her body next to his at night, her cold feet on his legs. He missed her...he needed her...and dear Christ, he was lonely.

He stared at the bottle before him, the ache for his Annie as real and throbbing as his need for a drink.

When Revel came to the open doorway of the little shack, she found him still sitting at the table, trying to steel himself against the urgent needs clamoring inside him. Ketch sensed her presence before he actually saw her. When he tilted his head up and saw Revel, a quick warm stir of excitement pulsed through him.

"What are you doing here?" he asked softly.

Revel's glance swept over the nearly empty bottle, the empty cup, Ketch's disheveled appearance. Her expression flickered, became a cool mask. She gestured toward the bottle. "That should be obvious, Mr. Colt, even to you."

The warmth, along with its unwarranted hope, died a quick cold death. His face stiffened. Who the hell appointed the oh-so-good Mrs. Bentsen as president of the Watch and Ward Society to guard his morals? Just another self-righteous bitch, no different from those in town, he thought bitterly. *Quick to judge, ready to believe the worst.*

Didn't she realize how her following him, being here alone with him in this isolated place at this time of night, could lay her own behavior open to question? What if he jumped to wrong conclusions about her, the way she always seemed to be doing to him? He ought to give her a dose of her own medicine, scare the hell out of her, jolt that holier-than-thou attitude out of her.

He pushed to his feet, quirking his lips into their usual cynical grin. Quietly as a puma stalking its prey, Ketch walked around the table until he was close enough to feel the warmth of Revel's breath. Before she could grasp his intent, Ketch caught her wrist and folded her arm behind her waist. His other hand molded to the soft rounded undercurve of her hips as he pulled her body snug against his. When she opened her mouth to protest, Ketch closed his lips over hers, his kiss deep and probing.

What Ketch had intended as an object lesson backfired—big time! The moment his taut body pressed against her soft yielding curves, he caught fire with a driving need that he believed had died with

Cindianne. He backed Revel against the wall and moved in hard against her.

Revel worked her free arm between them and drove the heel of her hand upward. The solid jolt to his Adam's apple made Ketch aware of Revel's desperation, of how far he'd gone.

He stepped back abruptly, breathing heavily, but under control. The habitual grin returned to hide his confusion, the depth of his feelings.

He laughed harshly. "Hell, Lady, you aren't getting anything you weren't begging for. That should be obvious, Mrs. Bentsen—even to you." He threw her earlier words back at her. "Why else would you follow me here...alone...at night. You asked for it and you know it. Who the hell are you trying to kid? Yourself?"

Revel retreated a step. "I came because I was concerned about you. But Ketch Colt, you aren't worth worrying about. If I didn't know what *Ketch Colt* meant before, I certainly do now. You are a bastard—in every sense of the word."

"Well, Honey, you aren't the first person to figure that out. And if you don't ease off a little on the bridle, I might show you just how much of a bastard I can be."

"You already have. Just keep away from me. You're disgusting. No wonder your wife killed herself!"

An explosive moment of silence followed Revel's assertion. Ketch seemed to stop breathing, and Revel shrank as if she expected him to strike her. But the blood had drained from his face and he caved in the middle, as if he'd been kicked gut-high by a locoed bronc. Pain showed raw and naked in his face.

"Damn you, Revel Bentsen," he said in a hoarse whisper, then shoved past her into the night.

Long minutes later, Ketch knelt by the unadorned mound alongside the fire-blackened foundation, his fingers sifting through the dirt and ash, only vaguely aware of the rumble of Revel's rig as she drove off.

Images flooded his mind: picnicking in the pasture, Annie asking him if he had ever noticed the way the prairie sunflowers turned their heads to the sun. And after a rain, her wondering, "Will God let us smell the sagebrush when we die and go to heaven?" And he'd told her, "Darlin', you have a long time before you need to start thinking on things like that."

Annie, honey, do you smell the sagebrush now?

The thought brought darker images: vivid pictures of Annie lying in a bed of her own blood; the small limp form of their son, nearly lost in the bigness of his own two hands as he'd taken the tiny fellow from her lifeless body.

Remembrance brought gut-wrenching agony. His fist tightened convulsively around a clump of the charred earth.

Oh, Jesus. God. Annie.

Then, alone in the darkness with no one to see and no one to hear, Ketch Colt cried.

Chapter Fourteen

Revel stood motionless as Ketch stalked out of the little shack. She had to. Her knees kept trying to collapse under her. She barely made it to the table before her legs gave out altogether.

She'd caught Ketch's look of ragged hurt, but she wasn't sorry she'd thrown his wife's death in his face. If she hadn't, there was no telling how far he might have gone...or how far she might have let him. It had been eight long months since she and Drew had had any physical contact, even to kiss or touch. And never had she felt so alone.

Ketch's hunger wasn't any deeper than her own. She still felt the hard persistent thrust of Ketch's body against hers. She resisted his violence, but for a moment, when his kiss softened, the sense of underlying gentleness and corresponding need in him nearly undid her. To her shame, for the briefest moment, she had yielded.

Revel gripped the edge of the table to steady her trembling hands, closed her eyes, trying to calm herself. She waited until some of the tension left her, took a deep breath, and opened her eyes.

On the table directly in front of her was a rough hand-printed note. Something she had accidentally intruded upon and had no right to read. But that single glance was all she needed to identify it—Ketch's wife's suicide note.

So that was what he'd been mulling over when she had barged in. He hadn't been drinking. She discovered that when he'd kissed her. There'd been no alcohol on his breath.

Partially covered by the suicide note lay another one. At first glimpse, the second note appeared to be written by the same person, even though one was calligraphic in style and the other in block print. On second glance, the difference appeared more marked, with the calligraphy of one so precise and the other ink-smeared and comparatively crude.

Then what was it, she wondered, that had given her that fleeting impression of sameness?

She let her eyes float across both papers as she had at first. After several passes, the more obvious struck her. Not only was the height of the letters uniform in each case, but both writings, however different their styles, had the same unusual slant. Actually, a *non-slant*. Like a left-hander, she thought, trying not to write with a backhand tilt.

Ketch was left-handed. Quick alarm jolted through her. If Ketch had written this "suicide" note, then it wasn't a suicide note at all. Could Charlie Wykle be right about Ketch?

She studied the second note, this time reading for content. *Ketch and Woody sharing the same woman*? That little revelation could explain the explosive animosity between the two men. She remembered Woody's critical comments about Ketch's wife and he had been describing the inside of Ketch's "shack" just tonight when he cut himself off.

Her forehead puckered. Certainly whoever had written this note could not have been referring to her? Absurd. She recognized the same expensive stationery that had been handed to Ketch at the jail. The note would have to have been written before she hired Ketch. So the note couldn't be referring to her at all since she was the only one who knew she was going to hire both Ketch and Woody.

No. Charlie Wykle knew, too.

The furrow between her eyebrows deepened. She let out a long breath. Too many things were going on around here that she either didn't understand or that Charlie Wykle had deliberately neglected to tell her.

The small room seemed to close in on her. She didn't know where Ketch had gone. He might return at any moment. She must get out of here, but she wasn't returning to the Slash R. Not yet.

First, she was going to town to see Charlie Wykle.

Revel arrived in White Reef near midnight, though you couldn't have guessed the time by looking at the town. The saloon vibrated with voices and the rhythmic thrum of an out-of-tune piano; people walked both sides of the main street, lights shone from the marshal's office, the mercantile, and even THE REEF WEEKLY RECORD office.

She went to the newspaper office first. Initially, she had considered going to Talbert's office to report Ketch's misbehavior, but, as Ketch had pointed out, her own conduct might have precipitated the incident and could very well bring her own reputation into question. Besides, Charlie Wykle knew things she needed to know. She must talk to him first.

Both Charlie and Nora were at the newspaper office. Unlike Ketch, Revel could not put on a poker face at will. Wykle's solicitousness confirmed that her face revealed her distress.

Wykle said, "Revel! My dear, here, come here, sit down." He cleared one of the perpetually cluttered chairs for her and she dropped onto the wooden seat with a heavy sigh.

"Are you all right, dear?"

"Yes, Mr. Wykle, but I have to talk to you—alone." She cast a meaningful glance in Nora's direction.

Before Wykle could respond, Nora said, "That's all right, *dear*. Anything you have to say to Charlie you can say in front of me. As Charlie's partner, I know about your business arrangement with him."

Wykle shot Nora a murderous look. "I regret to admit it, but Miss Peters overheard us the night we struck our deal, Revel."

The smug look on Nora's face raised serious doubts as to which of them was telling the truth. Nevertheless, the woman had gotten her point across—*she did know*.

"I'll certainly be glad to talk with you Revel," Wykle said. "How may I be of service to you?"

"Mr. Wykle, you've not been honest with me. I learned some things tonight...things that should have been told to me right from the beginning. Had I known then what I know now, I don't believe I'd have ever entered into our agreement."

"How have I not been honest? I've never lied to you."

For starters, Revel might have pointed out that he had already broken his promise not to reveal their "partnership" to anyone. Instead, she said, "You led me to believe that this horse-breaker Ketch was your friend."

Wykle gave her an injured look. "Now wait, Revel, I never told you any such thing. That was an assumption you made on your own. Frankly I didn't see any reason to correct that assumption. The nature of my business with him is of a personal nature and of no real concern to you."

"Of no concern to *me*! You believe this man killed his wife and child, yet you practically coerce me into hiring him and having him stay at my place? Mr. Wykle, I'll not beat around the bush. I want you to release me from our agreement."

"Say, come on, Revel. You're taking all this much too seriously. I may have suspicions about the man, but that's all they are. Besides, with Woody Vaught out there with you, too, you don't have to worry. He wouldn't let anything happen to you."

"So far, Woody Vaught has done nothing but cause trouble. And he certainly wasn't with me tonight when I could have used his help."

A brief, wicked satisfaction flared in Wykle's eyes. "Did Ketch do something tonight? Threaten you? Harm you in any way?"

"No, not really," she hedged. The editor's eagerness to hang blame for something on Ketch put Revel on her guard. After thinking about it, she realized that if Ketch really had wanted to, he could have done anything with her he pleased, what with just the two of them out in the middle of nowhere. Maybe the man honestly misunderstood her motive in following him. Plus, she hadn't entirely convinced herself that her sole motive was to make sure he wasn't drinking and might be unable to work the next day. Too many uncertainties muddled her mind.

"No, he didn't threaten or harm me, but I did see something that I thought someone besides me should know about. Perhaps I should have gone to Marshal Talbert's office instead of coming here."

"Not at all. If it's important, Talbert wouldn't do a blessed thing about it anyway. What did you see?"

"A note. It was supposed to be Ketch's wife's suicide note. But I don't think she wrote it."

"You actually *saw* a suicide note?"

"Yes. Tonight. At Ketch's place. I saw that note and another lying with it."

Revel told Wykle and Nora about the notes, the gist of their contents, along with a rather detailed description of the two distinctive styles of writing. "I'm convinced both were written by the same person, probably someone left-handed."

"Why, Ketch is a left-hander," Nora said. "And if Cindianne didn't write that note, it's possible that Ketch did. That's what you've been saying, Charlie. This could be the evidence you've been looking for — that Ketch did kill his wife."

Revel's eyebrows lifted. If Nora were Ketch's special friend, as Woody Vaught had implied, she had a peculiar way of showing it.

Revel was so intently studying Nora's face, that she didn't catch the look of pure fury on Wykle's.

"Yes, Nora," Charlie said thickly, "that could be the proof I've been looking for."

"No," Revel said flatly. She surprised herself by defending Ketch. "If Ketch had forged his wife's suicide note, why would he send that second vile letter to himself?"

Nora answered, "To throw suspicion off himself. What else? It's obviously worked on you. Besides, how can you be certain that was the *second* note? He could have written it before Cindianne's death."

Revel shook her head. "No. I was at the jail when a boy — maybe ten or twelve years old — gave that note to Orlie for Ketch. There's no mistaking that stationery. Quality vellum — not a paper you see much around here. Furthermore, her note would be just what Ketch would need to establish proof of his wife's death as a suicide. There'd be absolutely no sense in writing another one, particularly with that reference to another woman. That would really muddy up the waters, raise a lot of unwanted questions. I'm finding out Ketch is a lot of things. But one thing he's *not* is stupid."

"True," Wykle said thinly, "but it would appear that some other people are." He riveted his burning gaze on Nora's face as he continued to speak to Revel. "Just too bad you didn't have the forethought to bring those notes along, Revel. I'd have liked to study them myself."

"I had no right to read them, much less take them. Look, Mr. Wykle, I do not want to be involved with whatever problems you and Ketch may have. I do not want to be in the middle of them. The Lord knows I have enough problems of my own. So, I'm asking you again—will you release me from our agreement?"

Charlie turned his attention from Nora to Revel, his expression considerably cooled down. "Of course, my dear, any time you wish..." then he added bluntly, "...all you have to do is return the money I loaned you plus, of course, the agreed-upon interest."

"I see. You know I can't do that until I sell the horses and I can't have the horses ready to market until Ketch breaks them. The spider has very neatly woven the web. But for what purpose, Mr. Wykle?"

When Wykle didn't answer, Revel looked to Nora, hoping for some support from that corner, but none was forthcoming.

Revel spoke quietly, evenly, "I don't like being used, Mr. Wykle, and you are using me. To what end, I can't even begin to imagine. But if I ever find out that it is something that—"

"As you pointed out, Ketch is my problem," Wykle interrupted. Then stepping to the door, opening it, dismissing her, he said, "Just leave Ketch to me. You've done your part and you've got your money. That's all you need to worry your pretty little head about. Now, it's getting late, Revel. I think you ought to get back to your ranch." He added very softly, "It's not always safe for a lady traveling by herself at night...*not safe at all.*"

As soon as Revel closed the door behind her, Charlie Wykle whirled on Nora.

"You bitch! You stupid damn bitch! Just what the hell kind of game are you playing?"

Nora lifted her head and gave Wykle a sidelong glance. "I don't have the faintest idea what you're talking about, Charlie."

"The hell you don't." Wykle stepped closer and pinched her face in his hand, jerking her close to him. "Quit lying, you damn slut. I burned down Ketch's house to make sure those notes I wrote his wife were destroyed. You're the only one who could forge my writing style, even my calligraphy. Why in God's name did you send that last note? What the hell are you setting *me* up for? And what the hell is this suicide note? Don't you think Ketch would know that dumb bumpkin he married wouldn't know how to read or write?"

"I told Ketch I was teaching her to read and write...that she wanted to surprise him."

"But why, for gawdsakes, a *suicide* note? How the hell is that supposed to help me get his place!"

Nora shouted back at him, "I needed something to protect my —" She cut herself short."

"To protect your what? Yourself?" Wykle asked, a hard suspicion coming into his eyes. The significance of what Nora let slip came to him in a rush. "Why damn your eyes! You killed her, didn't you? *You* killed Ketch's wife."

The fear in Nora's face became a living thing. Wykle had read her and he knew the truth. He slapped her hard enough to knock her into the side of the press.

"All we needed to do was drive them off that damned piece of property. I want a clean title to that place. There's a fortune sitting there waiting for me."

"For *us*." Nora wiped tears from her stinging cheek. "Don't you see? Without Cindianne we're that much closer to getting Ketch's place. Cindianne's just one obstacle out of the way."

Wykle considered what she said. "Cindianne's death in one way *was* a godsend...it gave me a chance to work the town up against Ketch. But the suicide note you wrote to cover your tracks also protects him. That must be the reason Talbert stood up against public opinion and refused to take any action against Ketch. And if Revel Bentsen takes what she knows or suspects to the marshal, we could be in for a hell of a lot of grief. Damn! I ought to beat the living hell out of you just on general principle."

Nora massaged her bruised shoulder where Wykle had slammed her into the printing press. "If you hadn't dragged that Bentsen woman into this, Charlie, we'd be set up right now."

"*We*? Like hell! I'm starting to see a lot of things more clearly all of a sudden. You intended that note to protect Ketch as well as yourself. You figured to step into that little dowd's shoes once she vacated them. You and Ketch and to hell with Charlie Wykle, right? Ketch fooled the hell out of you, old girl, didn't he? You aren't the god's gift to mankind you like to picture yourself. Nora Peters — *femme fatale* of Pioche, Nevada. Let me tell you, Honey, it doesn't take much to be the femme fatale of Pioche, Nevada."

"You think you're so goddam smart, Charlie Wykle, that no one else has half a brain in their heads. Just don't forget who steered you onto this deal in the first place. It was *me* Murphy spilled the beans to. I cut you in, not the other way around. Don't think for one minute I'm going to sit back and take just whatever crumbs you're willing to throw my way!"

"Without me, Nora, you wouldn't even have crumbs. You can't think past a mirror. Of all the stupid things, to kill a woman..."

"Man or woman, what's the difference? I was with you when you took care of Murphy, out on the desert. Remember?"

"I'm not likely to forget with you around to remind me. I should have left you out there with him."

Murphy had been a local character around Pioche, an assayer with a self-vaunted reputation for finding ore in what other assayers would consider dubious samples at best.

A bunch of loafers, out-of-work miners, decided to play a joke on Murphy. When a sandstone grindstone shipped out of White Reef to Pioche got broken in transit, they hammered off a chunk and took it to him. After Murphy tested out the sample, he told the jokesters the piece was rich in silver chloride.

But as any miner worth his salt knew, silver was not found in sandstone. So Murphy's claim was enough to discredit him in the eyes of the miners and they ran him out of town on a rail.

But those miners were wrong!

Only Wykle gave Murphy's assay any credence. When Nora had told him about the joke the miners played on Murphy, Wykle recalled running a filler in a paper he had worked for back East, about a mine in Germany where silver *was* found in sandstone several hundred years before.

Even lacking Wykle's tidbit of lore, Murphy was convinced he was right — so convinced, in fact, that he planned on going to White Reef to stake himself a claim, just to prove those doubting loafers wrong.

Wykle had intercepted the assayer and tortured what information he needed out of Murphy, with the intent to appropriate Murphy's hoped-for stake for himself.

When he arrived in White Reef with Nora at his side, Wykle did not want to ask questions that might stir up questions. Carefully he gathered information. One thing he had learned put a crimp in his plans. In California and parts of Nevada, the Spanish colonial mining-camp rules were in effect: that is, you could stake a claim anywhere you found it. But here, in Utah, you had to own the land.

While Wykle continued his cautious inquiries, Ketch snapped up the Ed Duerson place, right under Wykle's nose. Ed Duerson's place included the sandstone ridge that gave the town of White Reef its name.

Wykle's insides churned. *That damned horse-breaker is squatting on a fortune in silver and doesn't even know it.*

"I had no choice with Murphy," Wykle said at last. "There are times when you get boxed into a corner and there's just no other way out."

"Well, then—"

"Well then what?"

"Revel Bentsen. Get rid of *her*."

"Because she's in your way like Cindianne was?"

"In your way, too."

"Only because of that last damn stupid note you sent to Ketch."

Nora shrugged. "No matter the reason. You said yourself that she knows too much now. You're boxed into that very corner you were talking about. Besides, you're the one who set her up as the 'sacrificial lamb.'"

"Not that kind, dammit! You're a cold-blooded bitch, Nora." Wykle rubbed his chin, thinking, then let out a ragged sigh. "Go ahead and finish what you started."

She gave him a smug grin of satisfaction, but the grin faded at Wykle's next words.

"Just remember one thing, Honey. When you dig someone else's grave, it's pretty damn easy to tumble into that pit yourself."

Chapter Fifteen

Ketch brooded, his thoughts bleak. Of all the damn sorry things he'd done in his life, tonight's business with Revel Bentsen had to be the sorriest. And he couldn't even blame it on the booze. He'd been stone cold sober when he treated her like one of the faceless two-dollar lays down to the Palace. God, he went after her like a cur dog after a bitch in heat.

What started out as a hard, punishing kiss slipped out of control into something warm—no, dammit, face it—into something hot and passionate. He'd always been indifferent with Katie's girls and infinitely gentle with Cindianne. But with Revel he experienced a new threshold of emotion and desire.

Even worse, by his reckoning, was how close he'd come to raising a hand to her when she'd thrown Annie's death in his face. Hell, it's one thing when you're a kid to strike out blindly, to pay out hurt for hurt, to blame others for troubles mostly of your own making.

For the first time in his life, Ketch grasped how he'd let the burden of his illegitimate birth shape and shade his character. Sure, folks had shoved his nose into the dirt of his birth. But maybe others wouldn't have made such a damn big case of it, if he hadn't himself. He'd raise a chunk of hell, and then excuse himself because he was a "ketch colt." He pretended he didn't know any better because he had no one to show him. All a lie. Early on, he knew right from wrong. He just wanted to give people as much grief as they had given him. Maybe people had done him the same way for the same reason.

How many generous impulses in others had he killed off with his reckless be-damned attitude?

Ketch, you ain't a kid any longer, he told himself. And after the way he'd acted tonight, he could hardly claim to be much of a man, either. The straight fact was that every word Revel Bentsen had thrown at him tonight was the God's own truth.

He ran a shaking hand through his unkempt hair. That's what I get for coming off the bottle — the shakes and the truth. At the moment, neither one brought him any comfort.

When Ketch returned to his shack, he noticed the chair at the table had been reversed from the way he'd left it. On the table lay the notes, lined out side by side.

Looked as if Revel Bentsen had taken the time to do a little reading. His black depression sank deeper. Well, what difference did it make now, anyhow? The woman couldn't think much worse of him than she already did. He stared at the papers a moment before snatching them up and jamming them in his back pocket. What a damn rotten mess he'd made of things.

He did have the power to right one of the messes, though. He'd backtrack to the Slash R, see Revel Bentsen, and do something else he'd never done before — apologize.

Ketch caught up the borrowed bay, put spurs to it, and reined it onto the Slash R trail.

He'd covered a little distance along the south fork, stopped and sniffed the air. No scent of fine dust sifting through the air, stinging his nostrils. A rig with a team trotting at the clip Revel Bentsen had whipped them to would have raised up a pretty good cloud.

The only other direction she could have taken would be toward town. *To report him to Talbert?* Couldn't half blame her for that. Might as well get all the bad news over at once.

Ketch reversed direction and put the horse into an easy, ground-eating lope.

When he reached the town limits, he slowed the horse to a walk and headed directly for the marshal's office. But Talbert, out patrolling, spied him first and angled toward him.

"Ketch."

Ketch nodded. "Marshal."

"How's it going out there to the Slash R?"

"Fair to middling," he said, tensing, waiting for the stinger.

It didn't come. Talbert just said, "Hope you ain't planning to lift no chunk of hell around here this late at night."

"Not planning to."

Satisfied with Ketch's answer, Talbert lifted a finger in salute and walked away.

Ketch frowned in thought, staring after the marshal's retreating back. Talbert was one of the few town people he respected. Over the years, Ketch had gotten to know the man pretty well, albeit from opposite sides of the jail-cell bars. The marshal had always been fair. And though long on patience, Talbert wouldn't sidestep an issue or back off from a confrontation. If Revel had come to town, she evidently hadn't said anything to the marshal about his antics out at the shack.

So where could she be? Could she have come in to rent a room at the hotel or the boarding house? He felt a swift flicker of shame.

Hell of a thing for a woman to be scared of returning to her own home for fear of a drunk of a hired hand pawing her.

Heeling the bay into motion, Ketch scanned the broad main street for sight of Revel's rig. A buckboard and team were parked outside the newspaper office. He reined toward it for a closer look.

Revel's outfit, all right. He recognized the horses. From where he sat on his borrowed horse, he saw the paint-embellished windows of The Reef Weekly Record office. The question slipped across his mind, *Had Wykle done that fancy lettering on the windows himself?* The thought slid away as he saw Revel Bentsen inside with Wykle and Nora.

Nora was probably Revel's friend, too. Good old Nora. *Everybody's* friend.

Dismounting, Ketch led his horse into the alley at the side of the building. No point going in. He'd told Talbert he wasn't in town looking for trouble and any encounter with the editor would be certain to whip up another go-round. He'd just bide his time until Revel came out.

He did not have long to wait. Ketch had no more than dismounted and leaned up against the side of the building before he heard the front door open and Wykle's voice, deep and firm, "…just leave Ketch to me. You've done your part and you've got your money. That's all you need to worry your pretty little head about. Now, it's getting late, Revel. I think…"

Ketch didn't hear the rest of whatever Charlie Wykle was saying to Revel. He'd already heard more than he wanted to. He had no cause to be either surprised or disappointed. But as he retreated into the shadows, he felt both…poignantly.

Butts littered the floor around Woody Vaught as he idled in the bunkhouse doorway, watching, waiting for Revel to return. From time to time, he'd amble over to the inverted half-barrel by his bunk and take another pull from the bottle he'd taunted Ketch with. Forcing a patience he didn't feel, he rolled and lighted another Dur'm before checking his pocket-watch for the tenth time in the last half-hour.

If Mrs. Bentsen didn't show up soon, he'd go looking for her. No telling what a booze head like Ketch might do if he got her off to hisself. It'd be her own damn fault if something bad did happen, her chasing after Ketch that way.

He wondered what the hell her husband must be like. Couldn't be much, he decided. Any man who'd let his wife go traipsing all around the country by herself like that. Of course, she'd made it plenty clear she had a mind of her own and would damn well do whatever she pleased. But this foolishness, her going off alone and at night to run after a drunken bum…it was almost as if she was hunting up trouble.

An ugly thought crossed his mind — *maybe she was.*

Maybe the fine, innocent lady Mrs. Bentsen wasn't so fine, so innocent, or so much a lady after all. Maybe she wasn't even a "missus," just using the title to give herself some respectability like that little whore of Ketch's done.

And here, him pussyfooting around all the time, tripping over his damn words, careful not to cuss or chew or say the wrong kinds of things in front of her. Why, he bet for all her refined talk and snooty ways, that underneath those fancy Eastern duds she wasn't one scratch different from those cats down to the Palace.

This time, when Woody went back into the bunkhouse, he carried the bottle back outside with him. He took a hefty slug. The drink burned going down, spreading a fire inside him that set flame to his building anger and expanding imagination.

He could just picture her and that bastard Ketch wrapped together. To Vaught bastard and Ketch were one word like damnyankee.

Vaught tilted the bottle back and this time drained it. *What the hell kind of woman was Revel Bentsen anyway?*

He ran the back of his hand across his lips. Maybe tonight he'd find out for himself.

The light still burned in the front window of the big house casting faint shadows across the ranch yard.

Not wanting to wake her foreman, Revel slowed the team to a soft walk and halted the rig just outside the ring of mottled light. She stepped down and led the horses one by one through the shadows alongside the barn to the corral.

What a night! She'd been crying ever since she had left Wykle's office. If Woody Vaught saw her red, swollen eyes, he'd surely blame Ketch and go after the horse-breaker. And she didn't want any more trouble. She'd already made her decision. She'd swallow her losses and go back to Pennsylvania, unable to have helped her husband the way she wanted to. At least she'd get to spend Drew's last days with him.

She crossed the yard, stepped lightly up the steps and sent a furtive glance in the direction of the bunkhouse, making sure she hadn't disturbed Vaught.

As she turned and reached for the door, she walked into the solid mass of a man standing there. She pushed at the figure and screamed.

The "shadow" scratched a sulphur match into flame.

"Oh, Woody!" She held her hand to her throat and breathed a sigh of relief, "It's you, thank God. I thought you were in the bunkhouse fast asleep. You frightened me half to death."

"Who'd you think it was," he asked coldly, "your bastard boyfriend?"

His sour whiskey breath stung her nostrils and she backed up a step.

"Woody, I'll excuse that. That's the liquor talking. You're drunk."

"Sure. Isn't that what a man has to be to get some notice around here?"

"I've had a very difficult day and night, Mr. Vaught. The last thing in the world I need or want is to quarrel with you, too. Please just go back to the bunkhouse and if you think there's something we need to discuss, we can talk about it in the morning when you're sober and I'm rested."

"No, by hell," he slurred. "We're going to get every damn thing straightened out now. I seen you first. I'm tired of having to take that bastard Ketch's leavings. Anyone's got dibs on you, it's me, not him."

"You've said quite enough, Mr. Vaught. No one has any *dibs* on me but my husband. You'd do well to remember that. Now step aside!"

Revel started past him. As she reached for the doorknob, Vaught clamped his huge hand down over her slender one.

Revel reacted without thinking. She raised her foot and stomped down with all her might. Her graceful ankle-high lace-up shoe had a study inch-and-a-half square "military" heel that drew a howl from Woody as it crunched down on his instep.

Woody released her in favor of grabbing his injured foot. While he hopped around on the other foot, yelping like a coyote, she rushed past him into the house and slammed the door shut behind her. She reached out and took hold of the straight-backed chair that stood near the door and lodged it firmly under the doorknob.

A breathless moment of dead silence followed. Then she heard a thud, a smothered groan, then several more thuds as if Woody, in his drunken state, had tumbled down the porch steps.

Revel didn't waste time looking outside to investigate. Instead, she ran to the roll top desk where she'd seen a gun, a big rusting thing left there by the previous owner. She was absolutely clueless as to whether the gun was loaded or even if it would shoot. But just the weight of the heavy long-barreled pistol in her hand gave her some feeling of security.

She blew out the lamp and stood crying uncontrollably, the gun poised in both hands, ready to shoot at anything…any one…who dared to step through that door.

Chapter Sixteen

Woody Vaught hunched over, massaging his injured foot and cussing a blue streak.

"Damn feisty bitch," he grumbled. "She like to of broke my damn foot!"

"Vaught," a quiet voice behind him.

"Huh?"

As Woody lifted his head to see who spoke, Ketch grabbed him by the ears and jerked forward and down. In the same movement, Ketch snapped his knee up into the tender triangle formed by Woody's nose and two eyes.

The crunch of a breaking nose…the sough of a cut-short grunt …no other sound.

Ketch lowered the foreman to the porch, then grabbed a fistful of Woody's shirt collar and the back of his vest, thumped the big man down the front porch steps, and dragged him all the way across the yard into the bunkhouse where he dumped him onto the floor.

Ketch sat on the edge of Vaught's bunk, rolled and lit a cigarette, waiting for the foreman to wake up. Ketch finished three cigarettes before Vaught collected himself enough to push to his feet.

Woody stood spraddle-legged, wobbly as a newborn colt. He ripped the dirty neckerchief from around his throat and dabbed gingerly at his nose. Both eyes were already turning black.

"You sonofabitch!" Woody yelled at Ketch through his blocked nose. "What'd you want to go and do that for!"

"Just to break a bad habit of yours—pawing other men's wives. Collect your gear, Woody. You're finished here."

"The hell I am. You just want to clear the corral for yourself so you can keep whoring around with the Bentsen woman."

None of the white fury roiling inside Ketch showed on his face. As if in slow motion, he lazily rose from the bunk, shook his head, then let Vaught have it—a precise sledge-hammer left to Woody's already fractured nose. The ramrod landed sitting flat, pain forcing tears out of the corners of his eyes.

"You sonofabitch!"

Ketch laughed. "You already used that one, Woody. Try another."

Vaught's rage left him speechless. He heaved to his feet and threw what would have been a tremendous roundhouse, had it landed. But Ketch easily blocked with his left arm, countered with a right to the gut, then a left again, to the middle of Vaught's face. Once more the foreman found himself sitting on the floor.

Ketch said, "This can go on all night, Woody, or you can dig out your bedroll and drift."

The foreman sat there quietly. At last he shook his head. "I'll clear out." His face took on a canny look. "Just give me a moment to throw my gear together."

Ketch stepped aside to let the ramrod get at his things from under the bunk. Vaught reached down, pulled out a rumpled pile of clothes, his extra pair of boots, some extraneous gear, and, last of all, his warsack to stuff all the paraphernalia in.

As Woody reached into the warsack, Ketch lifted up his foot and stomped down hard on the bag. Vaught screamed holy hell and jerked his hand back out.

Clicking his tongue in mock reproach, Ketch leaned over, reached inside the canvas bag and pulled out a Schofield-Smith and Wesson. That .45 could blow a hell of a mean chunk out of a man's middle.

Woody made an awkward stab for the gun. Ketch easily brushed his arm aside, then jammed the barrel straight into Woody's pulpy nose. A strangled cry of pain shot out of Vaught's mouth, a cross between a gargle and an explosion. His nose had to have hurt worse than three kinds of sin, but Ketch felt singularly unsympathetic.

"Quit whining." He dug his fingers into Vaught's shoulder, hauled the bigger man to his feet and shoved him out the door. "You don't take a damn thing with you now but what you've got on your back."

Vaught's face twisted with hate. "I'll kill you for this."

"Sure. But for now, haul your miserable ass the hell out of here before I boot it out."

Ketch followed Vaught to the barn and watched, detached, while the ex-foreman painfully saddled a mount.

"Make sure you leave Mrs. Bentsen's horse at the livery when you get to town. And don't even think of trying to claim it for your own or I'll sic Talbert on you. Now go on, clear out of here."

Ketch riveted his eyes on Vaught until the ramrod rode out of sight. He still held Vaught's gun in his hand, looked at it, shrugged, and shoved it in the waist of his jeans.

Like Vaught and most other cowboys, Ketch carried a rifle on his saddle, but he'd never had much use for a handgun. Hell, last thing a bronc-stomper needed was an extra four, five pounds of deadweight iron slapping at his hip.

But he wasn't busting broncs tonight and it wouldn't be a bad idea to keep Woody's gun handy, just in case the big man decided to return during the night. *Should have taken the damn fool's rifle, too.* He hadn't seen the last of Vaught, not by a long shot.

Vaught blacked out or drifted off a number of times, yet somehow managed to keep his saddle. Each time he awoke, though, his thoughts were always the same —

If it's the last thing I ever do, I'll kill that bastard Ketch.

He continued to think it, but was in no shape to do it...not tonight, anyway. Nor could he go crying to Talbert about it. Between the beating and the booze he was too foggy-minded to slick up the right answers fast enough if anything came up about the Bentsen woman.

As Revel had done earlier, Vaught decided to go straight to Charlie Wykle for assurances and direction.

Close to 3:00 a.m., Woody reined in at the front of the Reef Weekly Record office. Wykle quartered at the back of the building. And since it was general knowledge that Wykle preferred working at night and sleeping late into the day, Woody was not surprised to see the office still lit up.

But Vaught *was* surprised to meet Nora Peters just leaving the building at that hour of the night.

He sat his horse dumbly as Nora looked him over twice before recognizing him.

"Woody Vaught? Is that you? What happened!"

"Gotta see Wykle. That bastard Ketch..."

Nora's mind began clicking. "Charlie's not in the office right now," she lied. "I was just taking care of some last minute details before we go to press tomorrow. Let me take you to my place where I can help you and you can tell me all about it. We can get word to Charlie later. It's more important to get you taken care of first."

Nora took the reins of Vaught's horse and led it, with Vaught on its back, to her bungalow at the fringe of town. She ushered Vaught inside and gave him a pan of water, soap and cloths to clean himself up. He cursed steadily as the lye soap bit into his cut and battered face.

Nora watched him without offering to help. When Woody was finished and seated at the kitchen table with a hot cup of richly laced coffee in his shaking hand, she began to ply him for information.

Talking hurt. Nevertheless, Vaught spoke freely, anxious to broadcast his altered story and to place his actions in a more favorable light.

"When I caught Ketch trying to manhandle Mrs. Bentsen, I jumped him. Would have beat that bastard up, too. But I had her, sniffling and crying, to worry about. When I shoved open the door of her house, to get her inside where she'd be safe, that damn Ketch hit me with something from behind."

Nora figured there'd be no percentage in pointing out to Vaught that all the damage she could see had been done to the *front* of his face. Rather, she clucked sympathetically.

"Actually, I'm surprised," she said. "Not about Ketch trying to take advantage of a woman, but that she didn't let him. She is *that* kind, you know. A woman can always tell."

Vaught raised an eyebrow. "I didn't know, but I've sure as hell been suspecting. Truth is, she's been kind of throwing herself at that sonofabitchin' drunk."

"I probably shouldn't be talking about it, Woody, but she — no, I better not say anything."

"Say, now Miss Nora, you can say anything you want to me. Hell, I mean heck, I wouldn't say nothing to nobody else."

"Well, Mrs. Bentsen isn't really *Mrs.* anybody, if you catch my meaning. She's...how shall I say it...a *kept woman.* Charlie Wykle's. That's why he put you out there with her and Ketch. He knew he could trust you to keep her honest. But it looks as if she's playing her old games, in spite of that. Just like Ketch's woman before her."

"Yeah. Tramps, both of them. Had both of them myself," he blustered, getting deeper into his lie before thinking better of it. "Excuse me, Miss Nora. I shouldn't talk that kind of trash in front of you."

"That's all right, Woody." She moved closer to him. "Sometimes women like me wonder what it would be like to, well, you know — especially with a man like you so strong and powerful...and big."

"Yeah?" Vaught blinked his eyes as she moved closer still and laid a hand on him. He may have had too much to drink and his face might be a hell of a mess, but the rest of his machinery was in working order.

"Well, Miss Nora — honey — " he placed his hand on her breast and when she didn't slap him or draw away, he pulled her closer " — you don't have to wonder any longer."

Because of their rarity in this part of the country, women, especially *good* women, had remained something of a mystery to Woody Vaught, something to be idolized and put on a pedestal. But tonight he came to the conclusion that all women were whores at heart.

Woody wasn't as dense as his ponderous ways seemed to suggest. He gathered that Nora was leading him on to some end of her own as she urged more whiskey on him. But he made sure that she matched him drink for drink.

So, while Nora worked her wiles on him, determined to win him to her side as a formidable ally against Ketch or Wykle, as the case may be, Vaught in turn pumped her for information as to why she needed an ally in the first place.

The liquor had loosened Nora's lips more than she'd intended and by morning, Woody knew all about Wykle and Murphy and the silver on Ketch's place. He also knew that the man who "didn't have no damn reason to lie" had lied plenty. The thought crossed his mind that maybe Wykle had lied to him about Ketch's woman, that Cindianne *Jackson* or whatever the hell she called herself, wasn't the kind of woman Wykle had made her out to be. Maybe she really was Ketch's wife. Woody's momentary doubt caused a brief twinge of conscience which he and the liquor immediately quelled.

He had figured at the outset that Nora was just leading him on while hinting at something in it for him. Well, the little lady was due for a big surprise. He damn well would see to it that there'd be something in it...and something BIG...but for *himself.*

At daylight, Nora slipped from the bed they had shared. Vaught pretended to be still dead to the world. Through slitted eyes, he watched her dress. She glanced in his direction before sneaking over to his rifle and pulling it out of the saddle boot that lay on the floor. She tucked the long gun in the folds of her fully gathered skirt.

He didn't know what she was up to and he didn't care. Because from this point on—whether Nora realized it or not—they were in this deal together...all the way.

Woody smiled to himself, then rolled over and went back to sleep.

Chapter Seventeen

After Ketch made certain that Woody Vaught hadn't doubled back, he led the bay into the barn and put it up for the night. He still felt a shade uneasy about not taking the ramrod's saddle gun away from him, too.

As Ketch offsaddled, he removed the rolled-up britches from behind the cantle. He returned to Revel's house with the small bundle in hand and stationed himself outside her front door.

Ketch unbuckled his chaps, laid them on the porch, and put the appropriated gun on top, within easy reach as he settled down beside them. Closing his eyes, he leaned his head back against the wall, one leg hitched up to keep from sliding forward.

God, he was tired, too tired to even roll himself a cigarette. The broncs had done their job on him today, but emotional exhaustion had taken its toll as well. And his mind wouldn't give it a rest.

He kept chewing on the exchange he'd overheard between Revel and Wykle. Learning that she was somehow tied up with that sonofabitch had hit him hard. A helluva lot harder than he'd have thought possible. He flat out did not want to believe the worst of her although he wasn't sure why.

Somehow, time had bunched together and packed down in the past couple of days, making it seem, in his mind, as if they'd known each other longer than they actually did. He kept replaying that kiss, too. Maybe it was just wishful thinking, but for a moment there, he was sure she had yielded to his need. He felt something for Revel Bentsen that he never before had felt for any other woman, not even Annie.

He forced the thought from his head, his brain too cluttered to think straight.

Sleep came at last, a restless one filled with troubled and kaleidoscopic dreams. Notes and letters. Annie and Nora. Wild horses and Nueces Pecado. Woody Vaught and Revel Bentsen. Flaming houses and melted rocks. And over and through it all, Charlie Wykle stood, hiding behind the garishly ornate front window of his office, pulling strings, orchestrating the whole dream-scene, like some traveling-show puppeteer.

When Ketch awoke at first gray light, he felt as if he'd been beaten with a stick. The night's torments had left him more exhausted than if he hadn't slept at all. A slow drizzle had begun during the night, too, accompanied by a new chill in the air.

Shrugging the stiffness and some of the soreness out of his back and shoulders, Ketch rose and peered through the living room window. In the poor light he couldn't make out more than fuzzy shapes and shadows. As the sky lightened, details sharpened.

Apparently Revel had spent the night much as he had. She sat on the floor, back propped against the wall opposite the front door, ankles crossed, legs drawn up under her long skirts, forming a well. Her hands lay in that well, clutching a long-barreled Navy model Colt's that probably hadn't seen action more than a decade ago, since the War Between the States or, as Talbert the Texas transplant had always referred to it, *The War of Northern Aggression*.

His face softened as he watched her. Poor kid must have been scared as hell last night. First him, then Vaught. At least she wasn't lacking for spunk.

A rare smile blurred the hard lines of Ketch's face, then as quickly faded.

What reason in God's heaven would she have for teaming up with someone of Wykle's ilk? And what did it have to do with him? Hell, he was just a poor bronc snapper. He didn't have anything anyone would want, much less a man like Wykle.

It was beyond his understanding why any man, even one as vindictive as Wykle, would hound another just to get his hands on a relatively worthless piece of property. The man was like a spoiled kid who couldn't stand not to have his own way. Damn the man anyway for all the trouble he was causing.

Whatever Wykle's game, Mrs. Revel Bentsen appeared to be up to her pretty green eyes in it. And from what he saw last night, probably Nora, too. He didn't know what the hell was going on. No matter how you cut it, he felt like a blind man playing dealer's choice against a stacked deck.

Nearly two hours passed before Ketch heard Revel stirring around inside and a good half-hour beyond that, before she finally came to the door.

Ketch stepped in front of the opening, his tall frame filling the doorway. Revel leaped back, startled at his unexpected appearance. Her eyes looked frantically beyond him.

"There's no one here but you and me," he said, meaning to reassure her. But as soon as the words leaped out, he realized they had just the opposite effect.

Revel back-stepped again, trying to slam the door shut on him. Ketch stuck out his hand and held the door open.

"Hold it. Easy now." The same calming words he used on the broncs. "I didn't mean to spook you."

He stood at the threshold, palm flat against the door, but made no move to enter. He didn't want to panic her further. "Woody Vaught's gone." Ketch looked down at his barked knuckles, unconsciously rubbing them against his britches. "He won't be bothering you again. Neither will I."

Revel gave him an uncertain look.

"Here. I brought you these." He held out the wrinkled pants to her, hoping she'd accept them as they were intended, as a kind of peace offering. "If we're going to work together today, you'll be needing them."

"You have unbelievable gall, Mr. Colt, to even show your face here after the way you mauled me last night."

Ketch had the decency to flush. "Mrs. Bentsen, you've got broncs that need to be broke. I promised you I'd do the job and I will, come Hell, high-water, or Judgment Day."

He consciously avoided the sarcasm that usually colored his voice. Still, Revel eyed him skeptically.

He felt a wash of frustration. "Look, about last night...I'm sorry." He shook his head. "Jesus, I've been sorry my whole damn life. I just honest-to-God don't know what the hell you and folks like you expect of me."

Revel laid a level glance on him. "And just what do you expect from yourself?"

Ketch laughed softly, bitterly. "Hell, I don't know that either."

"Then let me enlighten you. You got out of me exactly what you expected, because you set me up for it. You can't wear your bastardy like a banner and *not* expect people to notice it. When we first met, why did you tell me your name was 'Ketch Colt'? Why not John Brown or Joe Smith or some other name, a real name—*any* other name?"

At her question, an elusive thought lightninged through his head, too quick for him to catch hold of it. He forced his thoughts back onto the tenuous thread of their conversation.

"We're getting off track here. I'm not offering this as an excuse, but last night when you came to my place with your spurs high and jumped to the conclusion that I'd been drinking myself into a stupor, I got mad. I aimed to curb your bit and scare the hell out of you. Honest to God, that's *all* I intended. Things got a little out of hand. I hadn't reckoned with myself—I'd been a long time without a woman. And once I got started in that direction, it was pretty hard to rein in. But with a little help from you," the irony returned to his voice, "I managed. Look, all I can tell you is it won't...nothing like that will happen again."

"I can guarantee that, Mr. Colt." She reached behind the partly open door and dragged out a heavy suitcase. "Last night I made up my mind to leave here and return to the East. I've been packing ever since I woke up this morning."

As Ketch looked down, it was not at the baggage, but the charred rock alongside it, apparently doing duty as a doorstop. A rock that had melted-down metal fused through it. *A rock from his place.*

Sight of the rock triggered anew the errant notion he'd almost cornered a few moments ago. A rapid-fire chain of thoughts shocked through his mind, one after another.

The bits and pieces that had tormented his fitful sleep last night suddenly began bunching up, herding together, stampeding into a vague but not yet identifiable whole.

He dropped the britches he'd offered Revel and picked up the rock, his senses reeling as if he were on a spinning bronc about to buck off the edge of a precipice. Humility, apology flew from his mind. As he stared at the rock, his eyes became as hard and glinting as the metal that ran through it.

He crossed the threshold and shut the door behind him.

"Mrs. Bentsen, you and I are going to have a talk."

Chapter Eighteen

"Have a seat," Ketch ordered Revel.

At Revel's hesitation, Ketch pulled around the straight-backed chair she had wedged against her front door during the night.

"Have a seat," he repeated.

Because his voice, like the expression on his face, appeared more bemused than threatening, Revel obeyed.

In thoughtful silence, Ketch dragged up another chair in front of her. He needed time to think, a minute to pull together all the abstractions that darted in and out of his mind. He tried to focus on her earlier comment that first touched off the elusive round of thoughts — what she'd said to him about appropriating a *real* name, any name but "Ketch."

As he caught hold of the thought, Revel's comment made connection with the mental image of Annie's note:

Ketch
I cant take it no more
Cindianne

KETCH! Cindianne? *Dear Lord.*

Like an echo from the grave Cindianne's words vibrated through his very being: *Just like you said I'd always be your "Annie," you'll always be Tom — Tom Jackson — to me.*

He gritted his teeth against a sudden sharp spasm of pain. Whether Annie had learned from Nora or taught herself to read and write as he had done, whether she had slashed her own wrists or not, he might never know for sure. But one thing he'd stake his life on—Annie had never written that goddam "suicide" note.

His fist tightened over the silvery extrusions of the rock hanging pendulum-like between his knees. Because he'd never heard of silver in sandstone didn't mean it couldn't exist. Maybe it wasn't silver. Maybe it was some other less precious metal, but in concentrations heavy enough to make mining worthwhile. *Or killing a woman to drive a man off his property?* Unthinkable. But possible?

Pieces continued to fall into place, just not enough yet to assemble the whole picture. But what he'd pieced together so far started to make a weird kind of sense. He'd figure it out, just like he would figure out who had raped Annie and who had murdered her or driven her to suicide. The same person? The process would take time, but hell, time was all he had.

Revel had been studying Ketch as intently as he had been studying the rock. She sat mesmerized by the range of emotions that altered his face from thoughtfulness to pain, understanding to anger, acceptance to determination. The bemused look returned, and then metamorphosed into one of wry cynicism.

Ketch raised his eyes to Revel. What had been her part in all this?

"Suppose you tell me about this rock," he said.

"That rock?" Revel's forehead puckered. "What do you want to know? I found it out at your place the day the marshal...when you first agreed to work for me."

He nodded. "I know where you found it. Why did you bring it here?"

"I thought it was pretty and I put it in my pocket. I didn't know until you came back from washing up that you were so sensitive about your place. I had no knowledge about you or your problems."

"You mean Wykle didn't tell you?"

"Why should Mr. Wykle tell me anything about you?"

He regarded her steadily, "I was hoping you'd tell me. Guess it doesn't make much of a difference now what you do or don't know. Like Wykle said, 'You've done your part and you got your money.'"

Revel gave a guilty start, quickly regained her composure. "I don't know what you mean."

Ketch glanced down at the rock, then back at her, a fierce light in his eyes. "Lady, the hell you don't."

"Yes, Lady, the heck I don't! All I know is that *something* is going on between you and Charlie Wykle and I'm the one stuck in the middle. I wish to God I'd never heard of either one of you."

Tears filled her eyes, making them luminous. Flinty as Ketch was, he discovered he was not proof against a woman's tears. Dammit, he wanted to believe Revel Bentsen. And, whatever her hand in this deal, he didn't want to see her hurt. God only knew why, but he even found himself wanting to protect her.

"Suppose you tell me what your mix in this is." His voice softened, "I don't blame you for shying off. I know that I have never given you any cause to want to help me. But this is very important to me. I also know that you and Wykle have some kind of arrangement and I fit into it somewhere. Look, all I want is for you to level with me. Tell me what you know. I swear to God, I won't try to drag you into anything. But I *need* to know."

Revel looked at Ketch a long while, held by his steady gaze. She let out a sigh and said at last, "My husband is a consumptive. Do you know what that is?"

"You mean a *lung-er*?"

She nodded. "He's dying of tuberculosis. His physician told me that if I could get him to a high, dry climate, he might have a slim chance of survival. White Reef met those two criteria, but I needed to have some means of support for us. I'd been advised that the best return for the least investment out here would be to sell remounts to the U. S. Cavalry. After I arrived here, I discovered that I didn't have enough money to buy the ranch and do all I needed to, to finish what I had started.

"That's where Mr. Wykle came in," she continued. "He offered to lend me the money I needed, at only three percent interest. But the loan was conditional. And that's where *you* came in. He stipulated that I hire you to break my horses."

"Why me? Did he say?"

She shook her head. "He said you were the best. He also led me to believe you were a friend of his, down on your luck and out of work. He did warn me that you were something of a...a drunk and a troublemaker."

"Well, he didn't lie about that last part, but that's about the only thing he didn't lie about. Did he say anything else to you about me, or my wife? My ranch, maybe?"

"No. I went to see him last night after you — after our *disagreement* out at your place. I practically begged him to release me from our business arrangement. When he wouldn't, I made up my mind to swallow my losses and return home so I can at least be with my husband when he dies."

Ketch stared out in space. Things were back to not making much sense again, unless, of course, Revel Bentsen was lying. He'd heard variations of the dying-husband theme dozens of times from the parlor girls, usually a dying grandmother or aunt back in St. Looie, who desperately needed fifty dollars for a life-saving operation.

But dear God, he wanted to believe her. "You read those notes at my place last night?"

She flushed. "I'm sorry."

"Did Wykle ever mention anything to you or did you ever overhear him say anything about any notes to my wife?"

"I didn't even know you'd had a wife until Woody told me after supper yesterday evening. As for the notes, I did mention them to Mr. Wykle last night...not what was in them, but because there was something about them...I might be wrong, but I don't think your wife wrote that suicide note."

Ketch's eyes narrowed, an unwanted suspicion intruding again. "I'm *sure* she didn't. But what makes *you* say that?"

"Do you have both of those notes with you?"

Ketch pulled them out of his pocket and spread them out on the floor between them while Revel explained her theory.

Mentally Ketch swore at himself. How could he have been so muddleheaded not to have seen that? Maybe not muddleheaded so much as blind...*booze* blind and too full of loss and self-pity to even bother to look.

"This *calligraphy* you mentioned, it's not a word I'm familiar with. What does it mean?"

"Just a very fancy style of penmanship."

"Then a man could have written the notes just as well as a woman?"

"Certainly. For that matter, Nora Peters mentioned when we first met that Charlie Wykle, among his numerous other talents, was a *calligrapher extraordinaire*."

Ketch slammed his fist into his palm. "Damn, I wish I had those other notes that were sent to Annie. If only they hadn't burned up in that house-fire!"

"The charred spot—your house?"

He nodded.

"Ketch, I'm going to ask you something that will probably make you angry—"

"Shoot away."

"Did you burn your own house down?"

He gave her a mirthless grin. "Is that what Wykle told you?"

"No. Woody Vaught."

"Mrs. Bentsen, just how inclined would you be to burn down something you'd built with your own two hands, stone by stone, log by log. What if that *something* was all you had of the only person in the world who ever meant a real damn to you? Would *you* have burned it down?"

"No, of course not."

"Neither would I. A nut or a fool might, but contrary to public opinion, I'm not either."

"I'm beginning to see that." Revel thought for a moment. "Ketch, I owe you an apology."

"Not hardly," Ketch snorted. "Why in the name of all that's holy would you need to apologize to *me* ?"

"Other than some of the scathing thoughts I've had about you, I'm truly sorry about the comment I made last night, about the way your wife died."

He shrugged. "You didn't say anything that wasn't true. The fake suicide note notwithstanding, she may have killed herself. If she did, it would have been because of me, what I am. Sure as sunrise and sunset, I failed her. If she didn't kill herself—and I'd hate to believe she did, what with our baby inside her—it's still my fault for bringing her here to White Reef. Just to show off to a handful of bitches who didn't mean a sh—a doggoned thing to me, that I could get myself a decent woman."

"You were proud of her. It's only natural that you'd want to bring her home and show her off."

"*Home*? What home did I have here? I could just as easily have stayed with her in Kansas, taken the money I'd made on that army sale and invested in her father's farm, gone pardners with him.

Nothing brought me back here except my damnable pride. That cost Annie her life..." his voice fell to a harsh whisper, "...and our baby's."

"You don't know that for sure."

Ketch gave Revel a half-smile. "I *do* know and that's the hell I have to live with every day and every night."

"Don't look back, Ketch."

"How can I not?"

"Looking back won't change a thing, will it?"

He had no answer for that. "Mrs. Bentsen, I'd like to finish the job I started for you. Maybe we can work things out so you can bring your husband out here before it's too late. At some point, I'll have to go in town and settle some things with Wykle, but that can wait. I'll twist broncs for you, every day, before dawn till after dark. I'll bust my gut to meet your deadline or come damn close to it!"

As she rose, Ketch stood.

"Mr. Colt, you have a deal. But like Charlie Wykle, I'm attaching a condition."

"You name it."

"When you go in to see Mister Wykle, I go with you. Deal?" She held out her hand.

A slow grin worked across Ketch's face as he took her hand. "You got it."

Ketch fingered the chunk of rock. Wouldn't hurt anything to send a sample over to Pioche and have it assayed out. It just might provide one answer to many questions.

Ketch moved Revel's bag aside and opened the door. As he stooped down to pick up Vaught's gun, his own chaps, and the britches he'd brought for Revel, all hell broke loose in a single clamor and roar.

Ketch saw Revel slump just a fraction of a second before he heard the decisive crack of a rifle.

Chapter Nineteen

The moment Revel's legs began to crumple, Ketch leaped through the doorway and dropped over her, protecting her body from further harm. He kicked the door shut. All he could hear above the pounding of his heart was his own tense breathing.

Was Revel wounded or *dead*? He swore bitterly under his breath, certain that Revel had taken a shot meant for him.

Ketch had managed to hang onto Vaught's gun, but stillness surrounded them after that single crack. The bushwhacker might still be around, looking for a clear shot at him or, after having shot a woman, he might have panicked and already beat it the hell out of there.

Ketch rose onto his knees and slid his hands under Revel, scooped her up and laid her on the buffalo-hide rug. Crawling to keep below the height of the window, Ketch dragged the rug with Revel on it against the front wall where she'd be out of the shooter's line of vision, just in case the shooter hadn't left.

He crawled back to the door and lodged a chair under the knob as Revel had done the night before. He wanted to keep Revel within his sight, but he needed to rummage through the kitchen to find something to clean her wound and staunch the flow of blood.

In the kitchen, the windowless side door was still latched from the night before. Ketch stood and rapidly began to build a fire in the stove and set a kettle of water on it to boil. That done, he grabbed up some muslin toweling and rushed back to Revel, the hell with caution!

At first he couldn't tell where she'd been hit. So damned much blood! Hard to believe a single bullet could do so much damage. As Ketch handled Revel's blood-spattered body, he had a sickening sense of *déjà vu*.

He ran his hand against suddenly dry lips. *Oh, God, please don't make me go through all this again!*

Steeling himself, fighting down the rush of nausea, he forced himself to examine Revel. Blood on her head, on her chest, on her back.

As Ketch cleaned her, he discovered that the blood on her head was a smear, not a wound. She remained unconscious. For the moment, at least, she wasn't feeling any pain. But her shallow breathing scared the hell out of him.

He stripped away Revel's jacket and blouse and cut the strap of her camisole with his pocket knife. The slug had entered her chest above the right breast near the shoulder and exited below the shoulder blade in back.

His mind began operating as deftly as his hands. The angle of entry was so steep, the shot had to have come from the rise of the mesa that shadowed the southeast corner of her house. Once he got Revel stabilized and someone from town to tend her, he'd ride up onto that tableland and have a look for himself.

Ketch padded pieces of the clean toweling against Revel's wounds to stem the bleeding. Just as he rose to get the boiling water, someone beat on the front door.

Ketch snatched up Vaught's gun and stepped to the side of the room's front window and warily peered out.

It was Nora, her face ashen gray.

He kicked the chair away from the door, yelled, "Come in!" and returned to Revel's side before the other woman had time to step through the doorway.

"Ketch, what happened! I was on my way to visit Mrs. Bentsen when I heard a shot, then someone riding away at full gallop. I thought I'd better...oh, my God!" She stopped abruptly as she took in the scene. "All that blood on you and Mrs. Bentsen! What—?"

"Someone took a potshot at me, hit Mrs. Bentsen by mistake. This is all her blood."

"Is—is she still alive?"

"Barely." He continued to work briskly as he talked. "Nora, you better ride the hell out of here. Women don't seem to be safe around me and one hurt person is already more than I can handle. Send the doc out, will you?"

"Ketch, let me stay. I can take care of her while you ride in. You can make better time on horseback than I could, driving my rig."

"No. I'm not going to leave her until the doc gets here. Besides, the bushwhacker may decide to come back, then what could you do?"

"But, Ketch—"

"Dammit, do as I say!"

Ketch missed the frozen look that passed over Nora's face.

"All right, Ketch, I'll do what you say," then added in a voice too soft for him to hear, "...but that isn't *all* I'll do."

Just short of town, Nora whipped her horse and raced the buggy onto White Reef's main street.

"Help! *Please*! Somebody help!"

Nora's excited screams brought a number of men racing toward her careening buggy.

As soon as the desired audience arrived, Nora stood in her rig and began sawing on the reins to get the horse back under control.

Ever the consummate actress, she folded out of the buggy into the arms of the nearest man. She let the tears roll down her face.

"Oh, God, someone get the marshal—no, get Doc Booth first. It's Mrs. Bentsen. *Ketch shot her*! She's dying...she may already be dead! Oh, so awful...I just can't..." She allowed her body to go slack and become a dead weight in the arms of the man holding her.

"Hey," he yelled, "Miss Nora's fainted. Dammit, someone do like she said. Fetch the doc and Talbert. Hurry!"

The man eased Nora's weight into a more comfortable position, being careful to hold her head and shoulders well above the rain-sprinkled dust of the street.

Talbert was already elbowing his way through the gathering crowd.

"What the hell's all this commotion!"

"Miss Nora come riding into town hell-bent for election. That damn Ketch went and shot Mrs. Bentsen. Miss Nora here seen the whole bloody thing!"

Talbert frowned but didn't respond. That Ketch would shoot a woman was a pretty hard dose for him to swallow. The buster had done some almighty rough things, but something like this...*Damn it!*

Talbert admitted to no one but himself that he'd always been partial to Ketch. Part of that partiality stemmed from the fact that he always had it in the back of his mind that maybe Ketch had been his kid. Back in those days, he'd put in his share of time at the cathouses and he'd been kind of sweet on Ketch's mother. A pretty little thing, half Cherokee. He'd even been tempted to ask her to marry him...till she got in the family way. But hell, there was no telling whose kid it might have been. Yet every time he faced Ketch with eyes so much the color of his own, he had to wonder.

The marshal cussed himself. Maybe he had let that partiality blind him to what Ketch really was. Maybe those outrageous lies Wykle had been spreading about Ketch weren't so outrageous or even lies. Why would Ketch want to slash his own wife or shoot Mrs. Bentsen? Didn't make a lick of sense. But sad experience told him that most killings never did.

Talbert rubbed tiredly at his eyes, then knelt beside Nora. Gently, he lifted her hands between his and began chafing them.

"Miss Peters. Ma'am?"

Nora stirred. Her eyes fluttered open and she looked about her uncertainly. "Wh—oh, I remember now. Oh, Marshal. A terrible thing has happened out at Mrs. Bentsen's place. After last night, I feared something bad might happen. Then this morning when I saw Woody Vaught beaten to a pulp..."

"Whoa, now, slow down, Miss Peters. Just take your time and tell me everything."

She shook her head. "You have to get out there, to Mrs. Bentsen's place. Last night she came to the Newspaper office all upset. She said she had proof that some suicide note Ketch's wife was supposed to have written was a fake. Mr. Wykle and I tried to get her to stay over in town, but she felt she'd be safe at her ranch. Ketch was gone, so she thought, and Woody was there to help her, if she needed it.

"I kept worrying about her, so first thing this morning, I rode out to make sure everything really was all right. That was just an hour or so ago. And that's when I met Mr. Vaught on the outskirts of town, so badly beaten he could barely keep his saddle. He told me he had tried to stop Ketch from bothering Mrs. Bentsen. I gave him directions to my house, told him to go there. Then I drove the team as fast as I could to the Slash R. But when I arrived...dear Lord, it was horrible!"

Nora broke into choking sobs. "Ketch held Mrs. Bentsen down on the floor of her living room. He was all covered with blood—*her* blood. He'd torn her blouse off...she was exposed from the waist up when I broke in on them. Ketch tried to explain it all away. He claimed someone had shot at him and missed, had hit her by mistake. He could see that I didn't believe him and he came after me!" Her sobs crescendoed into a full jolting wail.

Talbert patted her shoulder. "It's all right. Don't take on so, Miss Nora. We'll take care of things in short order. Here, a couple of you fellas help Miss Peters to her home.

"No," she said, thinking of Woody's still being there. She pushed to her feet. "I'll be all right. It's more important that you all get out to Mrs. Bentsen's. She may still be alive and need your help desperately...and she needs a doctor. There's no telling what Ketch—please, go. Hurry!"

Talbert touched her shoulder again then hustled away. "Any of you men want to ride with me, c'mon!"

Nora watched them go. Like rutting sheep after a ewe in season, she thought. She had to force down a smile as she turned and walked haltingly the short distance back to her place at the edge of town, all the time remembering to keep up a brave but appropriately distraught front.

To her surprise, when she reached the house she found Woody awake and dressed. He held a cup of coffee in his hand, well spiked from the smell of it.

Vaught leaned against the wall, a small smile on his face. "What's all the botheration about?"

"You heard?"

"I was watching from your window."

"Ketch shot Mrs. Bentsen."

Woody gave her a crooked grin. "Couldn't of been with *my* rifle, could it?"

Nora tilted her head. Vaught was a bit sharper than she'd credited him. She decided to bluff. "Whatever are you talking about?"

Woody laughed outright. "You know damn good and well. I saw you tippy-toe out of here with my rifle this morning. But I didn't know you was aiming to do a job on the Bentsen woman. How come you decided to throw the blame onto Ketch instead of me? Or am I your ace-in-the-hole in case Ketch doesn't come through for you?"

Nora's startled look gave her away. She never would have connected Woody's third-grade vocabulary with such keen insight.

As if reading Nora's mind, Vaught said, "Sometimes it pays off to act a little beef-brained. Others are more likely to spill their guts to you, 'specially if they think you're drunk. Thanks to you, I know what Ketch has got and what you vultures want and I'm cutting myself in for a chunk. Honey, whether you want it or not, you and Wykle just got yourselves another pardner."

Vaught moved nearer to Nora, towering over her, powerful and threatening.

Fear gripped Nora. She had badly underestimated Woody Vaught.

Instead of having him as either a help or a scapegoat, depending on the circumstances, she now had to contend with him as well as with Wykle.

"I can cut you in," she said at last, "but Wykle may have something to say about that."

"He might."

"That will be *your* problem, Woody."

"No problem, Miss Nora...unless he makes it one."

Chapter Twenty

What started as a chill drizzle gained momentum, now coming down in pelting, driving sheets of mixed sleet and rain. Over the racket, Ketch felt, rather than heard, the thrum of pounding hooves. He left Revel's side and hustled to the door.

Through the downpour he descried a slew of riders and one covered buggy heading toward the house. As the buggy drew nearer, Ketch identified the driver as Doc Booth.

At the signal of the lead rider, the other riders stopped a hundred yards short of the big house and ringed out. The buggy came on, closely followed by the man who'd raised the hand signal. *Marshal Talbert.*

As the marshal and the barber/physician cautiously mounted the porch, Ketch yanked the door open.

"I'm glad Nora didn't spare the horses in getting you out here, Doc. Mrs. Bentsen's right over here."

Ketch gestured to Revel, still lying on the rug in the living room, a couple of blankets piled over her.

"I didn't move her to the couch for fear of starting up the bleeding all over again. I did what I could for her, Doc, but I don't know enough…"

Booth nodded then shoved past Ketch to make his own examination. Ketch made to follow.

"Hold it, Ketch. Stand where you are." Talbert's order hauled Ketch up short—that and the gun he'd jammed into Ketch's ribs. The marshal reached around and carefully extracted Vaught's gun from the waist of Ketch's jeans.

"You spin a fair yarn," Talbert said to him, "but this time it's no go, Ketch."

Ketch shot him a bewildered look. "What the hell is this?"

Talbert sighed. "Seems as how you should know that better than anyone. But, just to make it formal, Ketch, you're under arrest—attempted murder, or murder, depending on whether Mrs. Bentsen makes it or not. For more reasons than one, you better hope to God the lady don't die."

Ketch was aghast. "My God, Talbert! You aren't thinking that *I* shot Mrs. Bentsen!"

"Looks that way, don't it?"

"If I wanted her dead, why would I send for Doc Booth? Nora Peters can tell you—"

"She did. What else could you do, caught in the act."

"What the hell reason would I have to hurt Mrs. Bentsen? For cripe's sake, Talbert, look where she's been shot, the angle. Near as I can calculate, the shot came from back up there, on the hill." He pointed over his shoulder with his thumb. "Sounded like a rifle."

Talbert didn't look convinced.

"Dammit, Talbert, if Mrs. Bentsen could talk..."

"Right. *If*. But she can't. Maybe she never will. You can be damn good and sure I'll check out all the particulars. Only thing is, I have to make certain you're safely tucked away while I do it."

"You mean to put me in jail? But what about Mrs. Bentsen's horses? Who'll take care of them? And what about Mrs. Bentsen herself? I figured the bushwhacker intended the slug for me, but suppose he didn't? What if it was meant for her and he decides to come back and finish the job? Talbert, Mrs. Bentsen needs me here."

"The shape she's in, looks like she don't need no one but the doc and God. And truth to tell, Ketch, I'm thinking you're about the last person she needs. Things have a way of happening to women around you. When we get back to town, I'll be wanting to have another look at that *suicide* note of your wife's, too."

"Jesus, Talbert. Look, whatever you think of me, don't leave Mrs. Bentsen here unprotected."

Talbert chewed the end of his mustache. "I'll leave a couple of men here with Doc to take care of Mrs. Bentsen, at least until I can get someone out from town to stay with her. Maybe Nora Peters will come. But far as you're concerned, I've got to take you in and lock you up. And Ketch, I'm warning you—much as I've tolerated you in the past, you try anything now, so help me God, I'll shoot you where you stand."

Ketch turned and looked helplessly at Revel's inert form. "How is she, Doc? Will she be all right?"

Doc Booth shrugged. "She's been bad hurt, but how bad, I don't know for sure. Not too much I can do for her beyond what you've already done. You're right about one thing though, Ketch—she needs someone here to nurse her 'round the clock."

Talbert nudged Ketch with his gun. "Let's go. Outside. Remember what I told you."

Talbert waved his men in. The posse comprised an indistinguishable huddle of slicker-covered men. The marshal called out the names of the two he considered most reliable.

"Ed. Buck. You two stay here with the doc. Buck, you set right at that front door. Ed, you guard the other door. Don't let no one in but what I sent them, understand? Here, one of you other men fetch me a rope and hog-tie Ketch. Jase, saddle a horse for Ketch."

"You oughta let the bastard walk, Marshal. Better still, drag him in on a rope."

"Why take him in at all?" shouted another.

Another agreeing, yelled, "Sure! Be a lot easier and a lot more permanent to bring him in across his saddle."

"Cut that kind of talk," Talbert growled. "You men just go on and do like you been told."

Nueces brought his *reata* up onto the porch and, at Talbert's direction, secured Ketch's hands behind the back. Nueces gave the rawhide rope an extra jerk and bind until it cut into Ketch's flesh.

"Jus' like one of my horses, eh, *hijo de puta*?" The mestizo smiled wickedly, expecting, hoping for Ketch to complain.

But Ketch had said to the marshal all he had to say. Expressionless, he stared through Nueces, out into the storm.

Jase caught up the bay from Revel's remuda, saddled it, and brought it around for Ketch. Talbert boarded his mount and reached down and took the trailing end of the reata from Nueces. He hitched a couple of dallies around his own saddle horn like a rawhide umbilicus tethering Talbert's saddle to Ketch's arms.

"Give Ketch a hand up, Jase," Talbert ordered.

Jase gave Talbert a sour look before muttering, "Yeah." Making a stirrup of his hands, he said, "C'mon, lady-killer. Get up."

As Ketch awkwardly stepped into Jase's hands, Jase hefted with way more force than necessary, catapulting Ketch headfirst over the horse. Ketch arched his body to break his fall as he overshot the seat of the saddle by a foot. His face hit the ground, but his right shoulder took the worst of the impact.

Ketch stood up, spit mud at Jase's feet.

"Damn you, Jase!" Talbert yelled. "Don't start none of that rough stuff."

"Why the hell not!" one of the other men took up for Jase. "Jase has the right idea. Gawdsakes, Talbert, any man that'd shoot down a woman! Damn his eyes!"

"Just hang on to your suspenders, Brewster. We don't know for sure that Ketch done this thing," said Talbert.

"Hell we don't. You heard what Miss Nora said."

Ketch had lifted his shoulder to smear the mud from the side of his face. He stopped in mid-motion and looked up at Talbert. "What does he mean, *what Miss Nora said*?"

"Never mind that now. I told you we'd hash over all this and a lot of other things once we get to town and you're locked up secure behind bars."

"Hell, Talbert," Jase said, "putting that bastard behind bars is a waste of our tax money."

Talbert muttered, "When did you ever pay taxes?"

But shouts of agreement followed Jase's words. Talbert tensed at the developing mob mentality. The turn in the men's temper made Talbert regret bringing the makeshift posse with him. Ketch had never given him any trouble before when he'd carted him off to jail. But this time, with Nora hysterical and all, he didn't know what he might have to face.

Talbert looked at each man, staring them down one at a time. No single member of this crowd was a real leader. The marshal made a decision.

"You men hightail it back to town. I'll bring in Ketch my ownself after I have a chance to check out a few things around here and up on the mesa."

When the men hesitated, Talbert dragged his sawed-off Greener out of its saddle boot and said a single word. "*Now!*"

None of the men cared enough about the situation to go up against the marshal, especially not for the likes of Ketch. One by one they turned their horses and headed back toward town.

Nueces was the last to leave. He looked down from the height of his horse at Ketch and spit in the bronc buster's face.

Talbert's temper blew. He rammed his horse against Nueces' and kicked its soft underbelly sending it into a buckjump across the yard. For added measure, he lowered the shotgun and set a blast of shot at the animal's heels. Nueces unnecessarily spurred his spooked horse the hell out of there. On hearing the shot, the rest of the posse did, too.

Talbert watched them fade into the veil of sleet and frozen rain and breathed a huge sigh of relief. *Now, if they just don't collect their nerve and jump us somewhere along the way back to town.*

He looked at Ketch. The bronc snapper was shivering in his shirtsleeves, but stood straight and uncomplaining. *By hell,* Talbert thought, *Ketch was more 'hombre' than that whole damn crew thrown together.* He felt an eerie admixture of pity, pride, admiration, and guilt.

"You got a slicker somewhere, son?"

Ketch dipped his head. "Behind my saddle."

Talbert draped the slicker over Ketch's shoulders and latched the top buckle so the wind wouldn't carry it away. The marshal noticed how tightly bound Ketch's wrists were behind his back and debated loosening them a little, but decided not to. Taking Ketch in by himself, he just could not risk it.

"Marshal," Ketch said, "were you serious when you told those men you were going to check out some of those things I told you about? I'm sure we can find the slug that shot Mrs. Bentsen near the doorway either inside or on the porch. It went clear through her just as we came out the door."

Talbert nodded. "All right. Let's have a look."

Talbert unwound the reata from his saddle horn, dismounted, and followed Ketch up the steps, holding the braided leather like a leash on a dog.

Ketch's hands had already begun to swell.

"Dammit," Talbert muttered to himself. He *had* to loosen that rope a little. "Hold up, Ketch. I'm gonna ease up that leather around your wrists. Just don't try nothing funny. I honest to God don't want to have to shoot you."

Ketch nodded, distracted, his eyes searching, intent on finding the slug.

"What's this, Marshal...down there, by the door frame."

Ketch knelt down and pointed with his elbow to a splintering where a chunk of wood had been gouged out in the shadowed juncture where porch board met clapboard.

"Step over there to the end of the porch, Ketch." Talbert wasn't about to chance the buster kicking his head in while he bent to look.

Reaching into a hip pocket, the marshal pulled out a jackknife, then got down on all fours, looking closely. He brushed away some dirt, looked closer. He prodded with the tip of the knife, stood up, shook his head.

"Nope," he said. "Just a nick. Maybe a spur or something gouged it out."

"How about inside?"

"We'll look. Buck!" he yelled, "you at the front door?"

"You bet. That you, Marshal?"

"Yeah. Open up. I want to take a look, see if I can find the slug that caught Mrs. Bentsen."

"Where's Ketch?"

"Right here on the porch with me."

"Ketch! Let me see you," Buck ordered.

Ketch stepped in front of the window.

"I want to see your hands. Turn around. Marshal, move that slicker." Buck wasn't taking any chances. He wanted to make sure Ketch wasn't faking his hands being tied behind his back and maybe holding a gun on the marshal.

Talbert smiled and said in an aside to Ketch, "Buck's a damn good man."

The same thought had crossed Ketch's mind and he felt a little less apprehensive about leaving Revel Bentsen to the man's care.

Only after Ketch turned and revealed his tightly bound hands did Buck unlock the door. As an added note of caution, Buck quickly stepped back into the room to have a clear shot at Ketch as he entered, should it be necessary.

After Talbert explained specifically to him what they were looking for, Buck helped Talbert and Ketch visually scour the wooden floor.

"Don't see nothing," said Buck.

"Neither do I," Talbert agreed.

"There's got to be a slug somewhere," Ketch said. "The damn thing went clean through Mrs. Bentsen." He explained what he had found when he'd tried to stop her bleeding. "The bullet hit her in front just below her right shoulder, came out in back under her shoulder blade. It exited at such a damn steep angle, that's what makes me so sure the shot came from up on that ridge."

"Where was she standing, Ketch?"

"I don't know for sure. My back was to her. I was already out on the porch. We were going down to start working with the horses. I'd stooped to pick up my chaps and some other gear. That shot probably was intended for me."

Talbert peered at the ridge through the storm, held his hand out at what he guessed to be Revel's height.

Catching on to the marshal's intent, Ketch said, "She's a little shorter than that. Drop another ten, twelve inches and your hand will be about the height of where she got hit."

Accordingly, Talbert tilted the plane of his hand to an angle that would match Ketch's description of the bullet's path. Their eyes followed the imaginary line down to just inside the door. Their sight fell on a threadbare rug, a relic from the ranch's previous owner.

Ketch kicked the rug aside.

They found the slug imbedded in the floor.

Talbert again got on his knees. After a little prodding he pulled out the lead slug and held it up in the gray light.

"Looks like a .44."

That told them nothing. In this neck of the woods, every other man and his nephew owned a .44 rifle and/or handgun, since the ammunition was interchangeable. Ketch's rifle was a .44; so was Vaught's appropriated pistol.

"Marshal," Ketch said, "picture the angle the slug must have traveled. For me to have shot her, I'd damn near have to be hanging over the edge of the roof to do it."

Talbert looked up. "Difficult but not impossible."

Ketch swore in frustration. "Then what about up on the mesa? Will you ride up there and have a look?"

"Later. I'll come back by myself and take a *pasear* up on top."

"Marshal, if you wait, any sign that might be up there'll be washed to hellangone." He regarded the older man steadily.

"Oh, what the hell," Talbert said. "C'mon. We'll take a look now. What can it hurt?" He turned to Buck, "You lock up good now and keep close watch. It's nasty out here, but I'd rather you park yourself outside this door where you have a wider range of vision. And remember — don't let *nobody* in to see Mrs. Bentsen without I'm with them."

"You bet, Marshal," Buck said. He immediately removed the skeleton key from the keyhole, followed them out onto the porch, closed and fastened the door from the outside, then pocketed the key.

Ketch nodded his gratitude to Talbert on both scores — for the precautions he was taking to ensure Revel's safety and for his willingness to traipse up onto the mesa in this storm. At least the older man didn't have him convicted and hanged in his mind…*yet*.

Talbert gave Ketch a hand-up onto the bay, then again tethered Ketch's "leash" to his saddle horn.

They rode, heads bowed against the driving sleet. A short distance along the road, they vee-ed back toward the house on a rising switchback that paralleled the road.

With the foul weather limiting visibility, they had to pick their way cautiously along the narrow trail that edged the side of the cliff wall.

As they topped out onto the brush-covered table, two indistinct slicker-covered shapes reared up before them. A flash of fire, an explosion.

Gunfire. Ketch dug his spurs into his horse. As the animal lunged forward, Ketch slid off its near side, toward Talbert. Still tied to the marshal's saddle, Ketch rolled over and scrambled to his feet behind Talbert's horse. The bay Ketch had been riding bulled straight ahead into their assailants. One of the attackers triggered off a couple of futile shots before the riderless bay knocked him and his gun in opposite directions.

Things happened too fast for Ketch to keep track of the second attacker. The commotion had panicked Talbert's horse into a full and uncontrolled run. Talbert had been hit. The marshal kept his saddle, but leaned far over its neck, clinging awkwardly. Without any guidance, the buckskin thrashed into the thickest part of the brushy growth.

Hard as he tried, Ketch could not maintain his footing. The wet reata stretched, but didn't break. The leather snapped tight taking all the slack up, and spinning Ketch around so that he had to run backward. That lasted less than two steps before the taut line jerked him off his feet and slammed him to the ground with his arms stretched out agonizingly behind him.

Everything happened in a matter of seconds that seemed an eternity to Ketch as the frenzied horse dragged him through the pygmy forest of piñon pine, juniper, and sage. The marshal's saddle on one end, Ketch on the other, and the leather rope in the middle formed a kind of bola. When Talbert's horse veered sharply to avoid a tree, the reata hung up on a large juniper. Ketch's momentum flung him into the lower branches against the trunk of the tree. The wedged weight of Ketch's body jerked the big buckskin to a dead stop.

Even with the clamor of the storm all about them and the labored panting of the spooked horse, silence hung heavy in the air.

Like some artist's bleak conception of death, Talbert and Ketch hung motionless, one draped across the horse's neck, the other across the broken branches of the tree.

Chapter Twenty-One

Veins popped out along the side of Charlie Wykle's forehead. The fury-inspired rush of blood darkened his face as he glared first at Nora, then at Woody Vaught.

"All right, Nora, you opened the door and let Vaught in on this. But it's no three-way deal. It's still fifty-fifty and it's up to you to divvy up your share with him any way you want. Your game's pretty clear to me now — I can see all the sides you've been playing. But this is the last time! Next time you do anything, Nora, *any* thing on your own hook, I damn well guarantee it'll be your *last* anything. Now trot that fancy little ass of yours up onto that butte and show Woody where you dropped his rifle before somebody else tracks it down and finds it."

Nora nodded miserably, her confidence shaken. Greed far outstripped any desire either Charlie or Woody might have for her as a woman. Each had made the point that he was just as capable of taking her life as he was of taking her favors.

"You two get going," Wykle said. "I have some other matters to tend to right now, but I'll follow you out as soon as I can. I want to see first-hand what kind of hell you busted loose out at the Slash R."

Nora and Vaught pulled their slickers on and left. Wykle watched them go, his eyes slitted in anger. If anyone tagged them up there on the mesa collecting Woody's rifle, he didn't intend to be with them.

Damn that stupid bitch anyway! If she were only as smart as she thought she was, they'd already be sitting on Ketch's silver pockets. Couldn't she see that the more people involved in this deal, the more opportunities for things to go wrong?

Well, he didn't aim to get hung up in a noose of *her* making.

Wykle waited a full fifteen minutes before donning his slicker and trailing after them. He'd reached the second fork in the road when he met the returning posse. He looked them over carefully, eyes squinted against the sleet's sharp sting. His own insides turned to ice.

"Where's Ketch and Talbert!" he shouted to be heard above the storm.

Appointing himself spokesman for the group, Jase answered, "Talbert's hell-bent and determined to bring Ketch in on his lonesome. Election's coming up, you know. He was goosey that we'd take Ketch off his hands and lynch the bastard."

Wykle cocked an eyebrow. "Would you have?"

"We all sure as hell talked about it."

"Then why didn't you? Did the rain melt your guts?"

Jase shifted uneasily in his saddle, unable to meet Wykle's gaze squarely. "Ah, that damn Talbert..."

"You mean the lot of you let *one* man back you down!"

"Well, hell, Wykle, he's the *law*."

"That's where you're wrong, my friend. The people are the law and *we* are the people. When a miscarriage of justice is about to take place, it's not just our right to act, it's our responsibility."

Jase's shoulders slouched under his slicker. He was a cowhand used to taking orders. Grabbing the initiative lay beyond his ken or capability—that went for the rest of the makeshift posse even more so.

Talbert had recognized that fact. So did Wykle. But Wykle intended to parlay that knowledge to full advantage.

"I'm not too yellow to take on my civic obligations," Wykle said. "How about the rest of you men?"

"Señor Wykle speaks true," Nueces readily agreed in his accented speech. "We should do *something* about that woman-killing *puto*."

Jase still demurred. "I ain't going against no damn law."

Wykle snorted. "I thought you were a man, not a scared little plop of chicken shit."

Jase laid his hand on his holstered gun. "I ain't scared of no man and you better know it. But what if something happens to Talbert? I ain't about to spend no time in the pen on account of the likes of Ketch."

"Nothing's going to happen to Talbert, not if we handle things right."

As he spoke, Wykle contrived a hastily made plan. He laid it out to the posse in half a minute and hardly took any longer to convince them of the need for immediate action as well as the rightness of it.

"All right, then, let's go!" Wykle raised his arm and the men turned to follow his lead back toward the Slash R.

When the lynch mob reached the vee leading up onto the mesa, a volley of shots from above scattered them like a covey of flushed quail. The moisture in the air amplified the sound as the cracks echoed off the cliff wall. They all scrambled for cover, including Wykle.

Long moments passed before they realized that whoever was shooting was not shooting at them.

Wykle swore aloud. Nora Peters and Woody Vaught were somewhere up on that ridge. *What in the name of hell could have gone wrong this time?* The need to know twanged his nerve-strings.

Not bothering to hide his concern, Wykle said, "Do you think that could be Talbert up there in trouble with Ketch?"

"Hey," Jase said, "come to think of it, Talbert did mention wanting to go up on the ridge to have a look-see."

"We'd better go have a *look-see* ourselves," Wykle said.

The group climbed the slick grade with care. When they topped out, they found Nora Peters standing alongside Woody Vaught. Added to the cowpuncher's blackened eyes from the night before was a bloody gash along his cheek where a swinging stirrup from Ketch's runaway horse had clipped him.

"Hellfire, Woody, you're a mess! What happened up here?" Wykle looked at Nora while apparently directing his question to Vaught. The one thing he trusted about her was her innate ability to improvise. Prompting, he said, "We heard shooting and thought maybe Talbert got into a tight with that mongrel Ketch."

Without missing a beat, Nora picked up on Wykle's lead. "Yes. That's exactly what happened. Mr. Vaught was escorting me to Mrs. Bentsen's place. I hoped to be of some help to her. Ketch and Talbert rode toward us from the Slash R. We couldn't make out at first who they were because of the storm. They gave no indication of seeing us…actually, they rode right past us. When the marshal didn't even nod his head and they started riding up this way, we feared something might be wrong. We followed at a safe distance. Too safe, I'm sorry to say, to help the Marshal when Ketch turned on him.

"Woody tried to catch hold of Ketch as he made his escape and got kicked in the face for his efforts. Ketch had shot Talbert, how badly we don't know. For some reason he took the marshal with him...and, uh..." She trailed off, running out of a plausible story line. With a helpless shrug, she looked at Wykle, tossing the ball back into his court.

"Probably," Wykle said, "so he could have an extra horse or, if Talbert's not dead, maybe Ketch is even holding Talbert hostage, hoping to use him as a bargaining chip. Hell, who knows the way Ketch's mind works."

Nora caught her mental second-breath and took up her story again. "As injured as poor Mr. Vaught was, he wanted to follow after them. But I thought we should go for help. We were debating what to do when you all rode up."

Flaws abounded in Nora's story, but Wykle doubted that any of the men bunched around, listening with their jaws hanging open, would fault anything "Miss Nora" said. Besides, she was, if nothing else, a most convincing liar.

Moments later, Jase bolstered Wykle's confidence in Nora's abilities when he said, "Looks like you was right, Mr. Wykle. Good thing we come back with you. Let's go get that devil before he guns down somebody else."

Ice spicules beating against Ketch's upturned face helped him work his way back to consciousness. He hung unmoving, spending precious moments trying to orient himself as to where he was and what had happened.

Oh my God, Talbert!

Not realizing he was strung out over a tree, Ketch tried to get his feet under him. The branches of the gnarled juniper cracked under the motion and Ketch jolted to the ground. An involuntary cry leaped from his throat. Ketch felt as if his shoulders had been wrenched from their sockets.

Stiffly Ketch rolled onto his side and pushed up into a sitting position, then just sat there, unable to move...not wanting to move. Thick blood in his mouth gagged him. He fell back to his side, retching.

He lay in a near stupor until the distant sound of voices stirred him. Not so damn distant! The fact that the storm-muted speech hit him with sudden urgency. Could mean help, but more likely their assailants were searching for them to finish the job.

Clenching his jaws against the pain, Ketch willed himself to move, only to be sharply reminded that Nueces' reata bound his arms behind his back. He drew his arms close against his body and forced his wrists under his lean buttocks. Digging in his heels, he inched backward into the hoop his tied wrists formed behind his back.

He churned his hips back and through the loop as far as his knees. His arms were long, but his legs were even longer. *Lord*, he thought, *this is going to take a traveling-show contortionist.*

The steady pressure he exerted against the leather bonds cut into his wrists, but the same pressure stretched the rain-soaked rawhide. Desperation lent speed and he soon had his bound hands in front of his body. He lifted his wrists to his mouth, tugged at the knots with his teeth.

At that moment and all too nearby, Ketch heard the universal signal of three shots closely spaced. A shout followed the signal.

"This way! They're over this way!"

Another voice ordered, "Remember, that bastard's no more than a locoed animal now. Shoot him on sight!"

Ketch struggled to his feet, a moan escaping at the pain the motion cost his battered body. Not a square inch of his flesh wasn't torn or bruised. Yet he had no choice but to move, to get himself and Talbert the hell out of there and out of sight.

Talbert's horse shied as Ketch approached, but the reata still tethered them together.

"Talbert," he whispered harshly into the marshal's ear, "can you understand me?"

The marshal's head moved a fraction. Ketch hoped that was a response.

"Hang on the best you can."

Another weak nod. *He did understand.* One thing Ketch knew for certain—the older man wouldn't give up. He'd listen and do what he could as long as he had his senses about him.

Ketch said, "Where we're heading the going's pretty rough. No quick or easy way to get there, but once we do, we should be safe. Whoever's after us is out for blood. Do you understand?" he asked again.

Talbert mouthed a voiceless "Yes."

Gathering the slack of the reata, Ketch took hold of the horse's reins, and led the burdened animal across the mesa. He concentrated fiercely on each step he took, trying to numb his mind to his own pain.

Past wild-horse hunting expeditions frequently brought Ketch through this territory. He knew the area as well as anyone and better than most. He directed his steps toward the northernmost end of the mesa where a cleft led into a deep narrow canyon that in turn leveled out onto the floor of a little valley. Numerous smaller side canyons feathered out from the cleft. Ketch had in mind one of these narrows, deep in the bowels of the mesa.

If they gained enough time on their pursuers to reach the main cleft, Ketch believed they could hole up in safety. Vaught and whoever else had joined the search would need a full-sized army to explore all of the canyon's little offshoots.

Ketch glanced over his shoulder at regular intervals, watching for sign of pursuit. He never saw anyone but caught the occasional echo of a steel-shod hoof against rock or a voice calling out, attesting that Vaught and some others were still trailing him and Talbert.

Ketch wondered how much help Vaught picked up and where they had come from. Had some of the posse circled back and joined Vaught and his partner? Ketch found the thought that Nueces might still be with the posse discouraging. Not only did the mestizo nurse a grudge worse than an Apache, he could read sign and track as well as one.

Ketch used his long legs to advantage and picked up the pace. Nevertheless, he was a rider not a walker and he hurt in at least a hundred different places. On the plus side, the people tracking him were either town folks or cowboys as unused to walking any great distance as he was. But they were on horseback, unless...

He led Talbert's horse deep into the worst of the thicket. The heavy cedar and sage growth slowed him considerably, but his pursuers would have to dismount to read their tracks. Even Nueces couldn't read sign through the thicket fast enough to keep up with Ketch on foot.

All things being equal, Ketch figured he could outlast them. He left occasional broken branches in his wake, enough to keep them on his trail, but not enough to make the tracking too easy as he drew them on an apparently random course. Once his deliberate meanders brought his stalkers back onto their original tracks, Ketch hoped more than a few of them would be discouraged enough to drop out of the chase.

By the time the posse could retrace the trail and find out just where he and Talbert had cut off, Ketch expected to be long gone, even if a good tracker like Nueces was with them. At the least, Ketch hoped the group might split up and leave fewer for him to contend with, should they, by some accident, catch up with him and the marshal.

Still leading the buckskin, Ketch continued his circuitous route until, for the second time, he came to an area of boulder-strewn hardpan. He hoped to cross that bare rock, leaving virtually no sign to follow when he cut off to the cleft. The big risk lay in that they would be totally exposed as they crossed the open space. Ketch sent up a brief prayer that they had already gained enough time and distance on their pursuers to slip from one side to the other, unseen.

Taking a deep breath, Ketch clicked to the horse, tugged on the reins and led the burdened horse at a lope across the open space. *No shots or outcry, thank God.*

With a huge sigh of relief, Ketch turned and headed due north. His sense of direction proved true as they came directly onto the rent in the face of the butte.

He leaned over to look down into the chasm. A faint trail clung to the canyon's inner wall like a mud-dauber's nest plastered to the side of a barn. Ketch ran the back of his hand across a mouth suddenly turned dry. By himself, on foot, he could easily make it. But he wasn't so sure about a horse, especially one carrying the dead weight of an unconscious man on its back.

It meant losing valuable time, but before they could attempt going down into the canyon, Ketch had to use up valuable time and finish freeing his wrists of the water-soaked reata.

Finally unleashed, Ketch tapped the marshal's face, trying to get a response. "Talbert. Talbert, can you hear me?"

"Yeah. I'm still with you."

"I've got to tie you to the saddle. This trail is so damn steep I can't take the chance of you slacking out of your saddle at the wrong moment."

"All right, son. Do what you have to do."

Talbert's trust in him humbled Ketch. He marveled, too, at how the old marshal had managed to keep his senses about him as bad hurt as he was. Whatever their differences past or present, one thing was certain—the marshal was a man to tie to and, the thought slipped in, to emulate.

They navigated the negligible trail to mid-point where it seemed to vanish, taken out by a slide. It looked as if they couldn't go ahead. But neither could they turn back—a man could barely turn around, much less the twelve hundred-pound buckskin.

Ketch dropped the reins and got down on his hands and knees. He crept forward, brushing the loose rocks over the edge as he advanced, trying to ensure safe footing for Talbert's horse when the time came. And the time would come, because no way could they stay perched where they were.

At the break, Ketch stood and gauged the distance across the rift. He backtracked to the horse and with that short running start leaped the gap. The balls of his feet hit loose rubble on the other side when he landed. As his feet skidded under him, Ketch dropped flat to the ground. He clawed and scraped to counteract the strong pull of gravity on the leg that dangled a hundred feet above empty space.

He spurred the ground like he never had on a horse until he worked the errant part of his body back up onto the lip. When Ketch tried to stand, he discovered his legs had turned into some kind of barely controllable rubber substance.

He leaned against the sheer wall, fighting reaction. He lifted his eyes and whispered what could only be construed as prayer—"Sweet Jesus." In the past twenty-four hours, he seemed to be making up for all the preceding decades of neglected prayer.

He lingered another scant moment, until legs and nerves returned to normal. He got back down on all fours and cleared the loose shale off that side of the breach. He returned to Talbert with less difficulty and more confidence.

"Marshal, getting you, me, *and* the buckskin across might prove a mite tricky. But we have to try. Even if no one was waiting on top to gun us down, we don't have the room to turn the horse around. And God knows, there's no way the critter can back all the way up that stingy trail."

Talbert forced himself to talk over his pain. "Ketch, if you see that me and my old horse can't make it across, let go. Save yourself."

Ketch regarded him steadily. "You must have a damn low opinion of me to suggest that."

"No," Talbert managed a grin, "a damn high opinion. I happen to think you're worth saving."

Ketch shrugged. "Well, Marshal, we've given each other enough hell in our lifetime…might as well go to Hell together."

He turned away from Talbert and took a short hold on the reins, murmuring over his shoulder, "Just hang on best you can and pray hard."

He backed the buckskin as far as he safely could, not more than a few strides. Then, stretching out the length of the reins behind him, he stepped forward a few paces.

"This is it," he warned quietly. He tugged the reins and ran at an easy lope. The obedient horse followed.

Ketch's breath caught in his throat as he made the leap for the third time, but this time with the horse close on his heels. He scrambled to get out of the way of the lunging animal.

The horse landed at an angle, but with Ketch's weight to counteract the over-shift, it kept its footing, even as a hind hoof momentarily flailed over the rift.

Ketch took a shorter hold on the reins, tugging, twisting, pulling the horse forward, directing, shifting its weight away from the edge of the narrow overhang.

"By all that's holy, Talbert, we made it!"

Talbert didn't hear. He was unconscious.

Ketch smiled to himself. *Was it shock from the loss of blood or the leap across the chasm that did the trick on the old gent?*

Chapter Twenty-Two

The little miracle Ketch had prayed for was answered and he, Talbert, and the horse reached the floor of the rent intact. Once there, Ketch bypassed numerous side canyons in search of one particular narrows he had in mind.

When he found the slot canyon, he glanced upward and fought a smothering sensation. He'd experienced "natural claustrophobia" before, particularly in here. On canyon floors, the towering walls frequently appeared to lean toward each other as if about to collapse inward. In this case, though, it was no optical illusion. The dry land strait they were passing through had originated as an underground stream, undercutting the rock at the base, carving swirls, blind arches, and caves, wearing and widening as the water cut a slot canyon. At some point in the far distant past, the waterway dried up leaving this warped and twisted narrows behind.

Rarely since the ancient stream vanished had water flowed through here—except for the occasional flash flood that washed down off the mesa. Given the present bone-chilling storm, Ketch briefly considered that dangerous possibility. But since they had no alternatives, he dropped the thought from his mind.

His search carried them deeply into the narrows where he found a shallow cave-like shelf chiseled out of the rock about seven or eight feet above the floor of the gorge. He dropped the reins of Talbert's horse and scrambled up to investigate.

Sufficient shelter for him and Talbert. Farther inside, he discovered a small seep that should provide more than enough water for the two of them.

Ketch jumped back down, removed the marshal's bedroll from the saddle, and tossed it up onto the shelf. Taking the horse's reins, he climbed back up onto the ledge and bellied down to pull the animal broadside to the cliff wall.

"You damn jughead, stand still!" Ketch growled at the horse. He was afraid he'd kill the marshal before he'd get him up into the cave.

Since the buckskin stood sixteen hands high, Ketch had only to lift the marshal a few feet. But he lost his newfound religion before he even got the animal to stand in one spot long enough for him to drag the marshal off its back.

After much effort, Ketch pulled Talbert up and onto the prepared bedroll. Next, he built a fire of the kindling and driftwood that nature or somebody — hunter, Indian, cowboy, outlaw — had accommodatingly deposited in the cave.

Cindianne, Revel, now Talbert. The smell of blood was beginning to sicken Ketch, but he had to tend the marshal's wound.

Talbert's eyes opened. "Still bleeding?"

The sound of the marshal's voice told Ketch what effort those two words cost the older man.

"Can't tell, yet," Ketch answered.

He spread open the marshal's bloody slicker and saw what he'd most feared.

"Gut shot." Talbert said it for him.

Ketch averted his eyes without answering. Both men knew what a gut shot meant. Little point in lying about it. All he could do for the marshal now was try to stop the bleeding and to keep him as warm, dry, and comfortable as possible, given their current situation.

He gave Talbert a drink of water, then bathed the older man's face with his dampened kerchief. Doc Booth could do little more if he were here. Ketch never had occasion to use the doc himself, but from what he'd heard, the man made a better barber than physician. Still, you never knew.

"Soon as it starts getting dark, I'll head on out for the Slash R and get Doc Booth. Maybe by then Nora or someone will be out there to look after Mrs. Bentsen and I can persuade Doc to come out here for a look." *At gunpoint, no doubt.*

Talbert moved his head, then spoke, his voice coming in thick, uneven waves. "Not Nora."

"What do you mean?"

"You didn't see?...up there...on the mesa?"

Ketch frowned. "Yeah, I saw Vaught, the sonofabitch. Must've been him that plugged Mrs. Bentsen. And now you. I'm not the safest hombre to hang around with."

"No. The other...with the rifle."

"God's own truth, marshal, I was so busy ducking the hell out of the way, I never got a look at the other gunhand."

"Nora Peters."

Ketch gave Talbert an odd look, reached out, and touched the older man's forehead.

"...not the fever talking, Ketch. Saw her."

"Vaught was holding her?"

"Huh-uh. You're not listening, son...said *she* had the rifle."

"That doesn't make sense. Why would Nora be up there? And with Vaught, of all people?"

"...that's what I been trying to figger...just can't hang onto a thought long enough to pin it down sensible...thought maybe you might have some notion..."

"My God!" The truth hit Ketch like a sledge. *Nora was the missing part of the puzzle.* The part his mind had never considered, actually had *refused* to consider. And now the knowledge overwhelmed him.

Nora. Annie's "friend." *His* friend. Even Revel Bentsen's *friend.* That Nora had been part and parcel of Wykle's game, whatever it was, sent ice through his veins.

Who but Nora could have fed back to Wykle the things Cindianne had confided in her? Maybe Nora had even been the one who'd written those evil-minded notes. And just this morning, when Revel was shot, Nora was first on the scene, wanting him to leave so she could "take care of things."

Take care of things *how*?

"Talbert, back there at Mrs. Bentsen's house, one of the men in your posse said something like 'you heard what Miss Nora said' in reference to me. Just what the hell did she say?"

Slowly, with great effort, Talbert repeated the gist of his brief conversation with Nora Peters in town.

That cinched it! Nora had to be in deep with Wykle clear up to her pretty eyebrows. But why? For what purpose? Somehow, it all centered on and around himself. Ketch shook his head. God knew he didn't have anything anybody else could possibly want.

In giving further thought to what Talbert had told him, Ketch realized with a shock that only two living people could clear him of Revel's shooting—Revel herself and the person who had shot her.

"Dear Jesus!" He had to bring Revel here, as well as the doc. And he couldn't wait until tonight to slip in quietly to the Slash R. *Now*. He had to do it now.

Chapter Twenty-Three

Wykle's "posse" balked. They weren't going one step farther and no amount of Wykle's haranguing would budge them. They'd been mucking through sleet and mud, following their own damn tracks, if Nueces could be believed. The storm hadn't let up and after fruitless hours of riding blind, there wasn't a one of them that wasn't soaked to the skin beneath their slickers.

Wykle tried his persuasive best one more time. "The man's a woman-killer, for godsakes. You can't give up, not this easily!"

"The hell we can't," one of them retorted.

Another yelled above the wind, "You tell me how standing around arguing like a bunch of froze-assed ducks is going to do anyone any good. If you or your tracker finds Ketch, just let us know. We'll be only too glad to make that bastard the guest of honor at a necktie social."

"Hey, watch your corral talk," one of the older men said, "you forgetting Miss Nora's still with us?"

"Hell, no. That's just one more reason we ought to turn back and get her safe to town."

Nora did not demur. She itched to leave this bunch and make a dash to the Slash R before Revel Bentsen had an opportunity to contradict any of the stories she'd fabricated.

In her own subtle way, she attempted to get this point across to Wykle. "It will be closer for me to go on to Mrs. Bentsen's, instead of returning to town with you gentlemen. I can borrow some of her clothes and stay on to look after her."

"All right," Wykle acquiesced, and then added with a sneer, "you other sisters can prance on back to town."

The party split with Nora and most of the original members of the marshal's posse riding back down the mesa trail. When they reached the town road below, Nora separated herself from the men.

"I'll ride with you," Jase offered, but Nora shook her head.

"Thank you just the same, but I'll be all right. Ketch certainly won't be heading back this way now that you men have him on the run."

Jase nodded, touching the brim of his hat. The men sat their horses watching Nora until the storm swallowed her up.

"Now there's one hell of a woman," Jase said, and not a man among them disagreed.

As the other men and Nora turned to leave the mesa, Wykle said to Vaught while the others were still in hearing distance, "I guess you'll be wanting to stay since it was your boss Ketch tried to kill."

"Damn straight," Vaught said, but his thoughts centered on Talbert not Revel Bentsen. He'd panicked when the marshal and Ketch had come right toward him and Nora. He hadn't meant to shoot Talbert, but since he had, and the marshal had seen who'd triggered the shot, he damn well needed to finish what he'd started. Gut shots were most often as fatal as you could get, but sometimes the victim lingered on. And, like Nora with Revel, he had to make sure Talbert didn't get a chance to shoot off his mouth to anyone.

"Let's go, then," Wykle ordered. "Nueces, you lead out."

"Hey, 'migo, where'd you get the idea *I* was staying?"

"You didn't go with the others."

Nueces shrugged. "No reason to stay unless—" he rubbed his thumb and forefinger together, "—you seem so very anxious to get Ketch, maybe anxious enough to uh—"

"Don't give the greaser shit," Vaught said. "He's as hot as the next guy to nail Ketch's hide to the wall. You want me to blab what Ketch done to you out to the Slash R?"

Nueces' face darkened, but Wykle intervened. "It's all right, Woody. We can work something out with Nueces later. But first," he said to Nueces, "let's see if you can find Ketch."

An hour or so later, Nueces pulled up his horse.

"Jus' too damn hard. The storm is washing everything out. It will take more time than that *puto* is worth."

"Is he worth a hundred dollars?" Wykle asked.

That perked Nueces' interest. "Come again?"

It's worth a hundred dollars gold, if you find Ketch for me."

Nueces rubbed his chin. "And all I got to do is find him?"

"That's right," Wykle answered, "unless you want two hundred gold."

"How's that?"

"Why, then you find him *dead*."

Talbert was in bad shape. Ketch alternated between swearing aloud and praying silently. The marshal was just too fine a man to buck out with a bushwhacker's bullet in his gut. He hated worse than sin to leave the man, but he didn't know anything else to do for him beyond what he'd already done — staunched the bleeding and tucked the ends of the marshal's tarp and blanket around Talbert to keep him warm. But the urgency to get Revel Bentsen to safety, somewhere away from the Slash R, drove him with an unrelenting dread that he never before had experienced.

Ketch checked Talbert one more time, before dropping down from the cave's shelf. He caught up the marshal's horse and led it through the narrows. Rather than backtracking along his earlier trail, Ketch followed a shorter, but much rougher, path along the canyon floor. Parts of the strait lay flat and sandy, but rocks, boulders, and driftwood choked others. He rode the horse when feasible, led when necessary, constantly pushed by his need to reach Revel Bentsen before Nora or Wykle did.

The protective confines of first the narrows, then the main canyon, dissipated much of the storm's power. But when he entered the open valley, the full strength of the wind-driven sleet blasted him. Recklessly, he spurred Talbert's horse into a ground-eating run.

Once Ketch reached the Slash R, he knew *what* he had to do — get past the two guards, transport Revel Bentsen, and persuade or force

Doc Booth to accompany them. But until that moment, he hadn't given a thought as to *how* to do it.

God help me. An earnest prayer, because it would sure enough take a miracle. Make that a whole slew of miracles. *All right, one step at a time. Take out the guards first.*

Working on the assumption—and hope—that the guards still stood watch at their assigned posts at the front and side doors, Ketch approached the big house from the rear where there was no door, just a couple of windows.

Now, which room might be Revel's? And would the doc be there with her? He'd have to risk the possibility of Doc Booth spotting him through one of the windows as he approached and sounding the alarm.

He tied Talbert's horse to a bush and crossed the clearing faster than caution allowed.

The house had a raised stone foundation. And even as tall as Ketch was, he had to raise up on his toes to be eye-level with the nearest window. He ran his sleeve across his face, clearing the sleet from his eyes, and peered over the sill. The darkened room seemed as good a place as any to slip inside.

The window hung from leather hinges rather than a sash and swung inward to open. *Damn.* Just his luck that the window was fastened on the inside. Ketch wrapped the tail of his shredded slicker over the muzzle of Talbert's gun and rapped sharply against the pane. The fragile glass cracked out. He reached through, rotated the rectangular block of wood that held the window shut.

Dampness had caused the frame to drag against the sill, but the pelting sleet's clitter drowned out what little noise it made. Ketch grabbed hold of the sill and levered himself over the frame into the room into a tangle of rough cloth.

As a safety precaution, someone had hung a blanket over the window.

As he touched the floor, hands first, then knees, Ketch heard the unmistakable snick of a gun going on cock.

"Hold it right there, you damn worthless bastard."

Caught in that awkward position, his vision masked by the blanket, Ketch realized he didn't have a chance in hell.

The hell he didn't!

He sprang toward the disembodied voice. A thud and loud whoosh of air followed as he hit his unseen target square in the middle. They struck the floor together, a snarl of blanket, arms, legs. The cocked gun bounced away without triggering off a shot. The first of Ketch's hoped-for miracles.

Ketch threw off the blanket and flung it over the other man's face. Holding nothing back, Ketch swung his balled fist at the draped figure. Bone crunched against his knuckles and the man flopped to the uncarpeted floor.

Ketch leaned over and pulled away the blanket.

"Oh for hell's sake." He'd knocked out Doc Booth. He hoped he hadn't broken the man's damn jaw.

Ketch saw Revel's rusty pistol on the floor across the room where it had landed. That explained why the gun hadn't gone off. Probably not even loaded.

Ketch picked it up and checked. It wasn't.

Revel lay in the single bed at the other side of the room. So pale and still that Ketch's breath caught. For a moment he feared she was dead. But then he saw the slow, steady rise and fall of her breasts under the covers. He felt the same kind of weak relief in his knees that he'd experienced when he'd regained his lost footing up on the canyon's ledge.

Ketch tore strips from the blanket and quickly bound and gagged Doc Booth before the man regained consciousness. He jammed the extra strips in his hip pocket.

Warily, Ketch tugged open the hall door a notch and peered down the darkened corridor. Little of the storm-dreary day's fading light reached back to him, but his eyes adapted quickly and he didn't see any shadows that didn't belong in the hallway.

Ketch *injuned* noiselessly into the living room, checked out the closer guard first, the one at the front door.

Buck sat just where Talbert had told him to, hunkered down on the porch, his back to the wall and too far from the door for Ketch to reach out and grab him by surprise.

Ketch sighed. *Didn't anything ever come easy?*

He opened the front door six inches and in a harsh whisper that could have passed for any man's voice, hissed, "Sssst—Buck! Come here, quick!"

Buck snapped up the bait. He jumped to his feet and stuck his head through the opening, speaking in a similar harsh whisper, "What is it, Ed? What's—"

That was as far as Buck got before Ketch clubbed the side of the deputy's head with the gun barrel, knocking the man senseless.

Pulling some of the blanket strips from his hip pocket, Ketch quickly bound and gagged Buck as he had Doc.

Two down, one to go.

Ketch padded into the kitchen, but did not see Ed through the window. He had to take a chance and open the solid wood side door. He cracked the door an inch or so, but still didn't catch sight of the guard. The man must have taken a stroll to the outhouse.

Oh shit. Talbert's horse!

If Ed had gone to the privy, he'd have to be blind or thoroughly stupid to miss the buckskin tied out back. A chill ran down Ketch's back. Ed was now warned and only God knew where he might be.

Ketch sidled through the doorway, wiping clammy hands on his rain-soaked britches. He didn't want to have to shoot anyone, but he damn well didn't want to be shot, either.

He stole along the side of the house, eyes toward the hill. The privy door hung open, empty. Hugging the house, he continued across the muddy back yard, around to the back of the house where he'd "busted out" the window.

Ed's legs dangled from the window. Ketch's hands darted out and clamped Ed by the ankles before the man could slither all the way into Revel's room. A hard jerk and the tall cowboy tumbled back out, landing face down in the mud.

Like Doc before him, Ed held a cocked gun. Unlike Revel's rusty relic, this one worked. As Ed landed, he twisted onto one elbow and triggered off a shot. The bullet sliced a neat little furrow off Ketch's shoulder as Ketch dove under the shot.

Ketch belly-whopped into the sludge, rolled over and flung a fistful of mud into Ed's face. Ed fired off a second shot blind as he clawed the suffocating muck out of his face with his free hand.

Ketch drove three quick lefts deep into the cowboy's well-conditioned gut.

Both men levered up onto their knees, swinging savagely, throwing their whole bodies behind each punch, trading off blow for blow as they slipped and slid in the wet clay.

Ketch had already taken more than his share of punishment for one day. He was already operating more on will than strength. If he kept slugging it out, trying to match punches with Ed, he didn't stand a Chinaman's chance.

Sensing this, Ed picked up the tempo. His steady barrage drove Ketch down into the mud.

Under Ed's merciless battering, Ketch's weary muscles slackened. God, he just wanted to quit. But the stubborn horse-breaker part of his mind forced him to hang on, to think of Revel inside and of Talbert back in the canyon. If he went down, they'd go down with him.

Drawing deep into reserves he didn't know existed, Ketch fell back and flipped his long legs up around Ed's throat and twisted his hips, locking Ed's neck in a scissors hold. Strengthened by years of breaking broncs, his powerful legs tightened their grip. He swiveled again, snapping Ed's head against the side of the house with a sodden thump. Ed's body slacked and folded bonelessly into the mud.

Ketch lay in the mud, drained of energy. He knew he should be doing something, but *what*? He rose up on the points of his elbows. Steadying himself with a hand against the house, he pushed the rest of the way to his feet, sucking in great gulps of air.

As Ed began stirring, Ketch remembered — he took the remaining blanket strips and hog-tied Ed, then dragged the cowboy into the house.

After the beating Ed had given him, he very briefly considered letting the cowboy lie out there in the weather. But hell, the cowboy was only trying to protect Revel, so he half-carried, half-dragged the man into the house.

Inside, Ketch ransacked the kitchen, dumping matches, utensils, and foodstuffs into a couple of flour sacks. Before he carried the filled sacks outside, he caught up and saddled one of the guards' horses for Doc. He tied the sacks behind the saddle on Talbert's horse and Doc Booth's satchel on the "borrowed" horse.

By the time Ketch retraced his steps to Revel's room, Doc Booth had nearly worked himself free.

"Sorry I took you out so hard, Doc," Ketch said. "I didn't know it was you."

Unable to talk for the gag in his mouth, Booth just glowered at him.

Ketch leaned over and removed the gag from the older man's mouth and finished untying his hands.

"Doc, we've got to spur it and get you and Mrs. Bentsen out of here."

"Just do the job here and get it over with."

"What job?"

"Kill us. That's your intent, isn't it?"

"By all that's holy! If that's what I had in mind, I sure as hell wouldn't have gone to the trouble of hog-tying you. Listen here, Doc, someone is out to kill Mrs. Bentsen, but it's not me. We have to take her someplace safe."

"You very likely will kill her, if you move her."

"Maybe," Ketch said, "but with you along she stands a chance. If she stays here, she has none. Besides, Talbert needs you. He's bad hurt, too...been shot. I've got him holed up back in the canyon. You'll have to tend him and her both."

Doc Booth eyed him skeptically.

Ketch flushed. "Look, I know I haven't given you or anyone else in these parts cause to hold a lot of faith in me, but dammit, you know my word is good. Don't give me any trouble on this, Doc."

"And if I do?"

"You're still going."

"Yeah," Doc answered wryly, "I reckoned as much."

Ketch collected the guards' slickers, donning one himself and wrapping Revel in the other. Doc put on his own oilskin duster.

Then, with a gentleness that surprised the watching barber-cum-doctor, Ketch lifted Revel, blankets and all, revealing a side of the horse-breaker he never before had seen. Maybe, he admitted to himself, that was a side of Ketch he never had tried to see, or even *wanted* to see.

"C'mon, Doc, the horses are out front, saddled," Ketch said.

With Doc Booth's help, Ketch lifted Revel onto the saddle in front of him, across his lap. No sooner had they mounted their horses than the storm-blurred shape of a rider galloped into view.

Ketch squinted against the pelting sleet.

Damn. Nora Peters.

Didn't matter much now who it was. The little advantage he'd hoped for evaporated with her appearance. In a matter of minutes, the guards would be freed and on their trail.

Ketch put the spurs to Talbert's buckskin, yelling over his shoulder, "C'mon, Doc! Don't' spare the horses!"

Doc Booth hesitated only a fraction of a second, then without examining his own motivation, dug his heels into the flanks of his horse and followed Ketch at a reckless clip.

Chapter Twenty-Four

Ketch shifted Revel's weight in his tiring arm and she winced. Either the movement or the pain had jarred her awake. Ketch looked down at her bundled form, concern in his voice.

"Are you hurting bad?"

She shook her head. Then, "Where are we going?"

"To where I hope you'll be safe. Do you remember being shot?"

"Is that what happened?" she asked groggily.

He nodded. "I'm not sure whether it was intended for you or for me."

Ketch didn't want to alarm her unnecessarily, but for her own protection, she ought to have some idea of what had been happening. He sketched out for her what little he and Talbert had pieced together.

Doc Booth, riding alongside, mulled over what he heard of Ketch and Revel's exchange, but offered no comments of his own.

As for Revel, Ketch doubted that she really understood the severity of their situation. She said nothing, smiled weakly, closed her eyes, and fell back to sleep. Ketch tightened his arm protectively about her, so helpless, so totally dependent upon him for her safety.

He prayed as earnestly as he ever had in his life. *If I never accomplish another thing, God, just let me pull her out of this deal without further harm.*

When the trio reached the grotto, they found Marshal Talbert in a bad way, but still hanging on. Whether his imagination or wishful thinking, Ketch thought the older man's voice sounded a little stronger as he talked.

"Doc," Ketch said, "if you'll tend the marshal, I'll see what I can do to fix up a pallet for Mrs. Bentsen."

"Yeah."

Talbert raised his head and whispered to Booth as soon as Ketch turned away. "Pretty bad, ain't it?"

"Don't look too good," Booth answered honestly, "but there's always a chance."

Ketch attended to Revel the best he could, given the merciless conditions. He returned to Talbert while Doc was still working on the marshal's wound.

"I've got to go picket the horses where they can get grass and water," Ketch said. "There's a sinkhole back in the main canyon that might do. Doc, will you be able to hold down the fort while I'm gone? May take me an hour or more to ride out there and walk back, but I'll hustle."

"Guess I can make out," Doc grunted. "How come you're favoring that one side?"

Ketch shrugged. "Ed creased me back to Mrs. Bentsen's. Stings some, but it's nothing that can't wait till I get back."

He laid several pistols on the ground. For a man who favored a rifle, he was acquiring quite an arsenal of handguns. Ketch laid Talbert's gun alongside the older man and handed one of those procured from the guards to Doc Booth.

"Don't let anybody get to Mrs. Bentsen, Doc. Nobody—*male or female.*"

Doc accepted the gun from Ketch and hefted it. From the steady look Doc laid on him, Ketch sensed the man's ambivalence and guessed that he was debating whether or not to use it on him.

As he turned his back on the medico, Ketch said "I'm trusting you, Doc. It's up to you whether or not to trust me."

Doc hesitated, then slipped the gun into his own slicker pocket.

Talbert, watching, closed his eyes and eased his head back. "You know," he said to Booth, "folks hasn't done right by that boy, least of all, me."

"Are you meaning Ketch?"

"Yeah."

"I take it then, that he was telling the truth...wasn't him that shot you?"

"Hell, no! Was him that saved my life, or what I've got left of it."

"Here now, none of that talk. I told you there's always a chance."

Talbert lay silent a long while, not speaking again until the doc finished his ministrations.

"Doc," he said, "when Ketch gets back, tell him I got to talk to him. Wake me up if I'm sleeping. Will you do that?"

"Sure. Rest now."

Ketch had made a fair estimate. In little over an hour, he had put up the horses and returned to the grotto.

Doc motioned him over with a tilt of his head.

"What is it? Is Talbert—?

Doc shook his head. Touch and go, but he's a fighter. He wants a word with you.

Since the cave lacked any great breadth or depth, Doc stepped over by Revel to give Ketch and Talbert what little privacy the cramped space afforded.

Ketch hunkered down on his boot heels by Talbert's side. "How's it going, Marshal?"

"Tolerable, for the shape I'm in."

Ketch studied his hands, avoiding the marshal's eyes.

"Ketch, I'm obliged to you."

"*Me?*" Ketch raised his head. "What the hell for? Getting you shot in the gut?"

"What you've tried to do for me."

"Hell, Talbert, outside of Duerson, you're the only one around here who's ever treated me half-way white, and that for all the trouble I caused you."

"Ever stop to wonder why I might be partial to you?"

"How do you mean?"

"There's somethin'...hell, this ain't easy, but there's somethin' I ought to tell you before I check out—I think that maybe I could be your father, Ketch. No, by hell, I'm *sure* of it."

Ketch accepted that in stunned silence and took a full minute to collect himself.

Ketch spoke at last with a half-way laugh, "Talbert, you don't know what you're saying."

"I know exactly what I'm saying."

"Oh, hell," Ketch said as he grasped the marshal's intent. "You don't owe me nothing, Marshal, least of all to go sullying up your own name just to give me one."

"No, listen, son. I mean it. Ketch what do you know about your ma?"

Ketch's face shadowed. "Just what folks around town have been *kind* enough to tell me — that she was a cathouse whore who took one look at me then went out in the alley and took an overdose of laudanum. Seems my wife wasn't the first woman to commit suicide because of me," he added bitterly.

"Ketch, about your mother...she was a...a parlor-house girl, I won't try to lie to you about that. But she wasn't like the others. There was a sweetness about her, a fineness. I guess you'd call it class. I think this was her first job like that. I...I saw quite a bit of her. Thought quite a bit of her, too. There were other men, of course; it was part of her job. But we had something special between us. I wanted to marry her. Asked her, honest to God. Thought I had her talked into it. I didn't know she was pregnant. Anyhow, she kept on...well, *working*, but she cut off seeing me. When she birthed you, she wrapped you up nice and neat, left you on Doc's doorstep figuring a medical man could take care of you, see you lived, I guess. I should have claimed you then. To my eternal damnation, I didn't. But I want to right things with you now. I want you to take my name, Ketch."

Ketch's thoughts tumbled over one another as he considered what it would mean to have a name, to be legitimized even that much, what it could have meant to Annie, what it might mean to his future.

"Will you do that, Ketch?" Talbert persisted.

"Marshal, nothing could make me prouder, but no. I sure as hell won't."

Talbert's pale face sagged with disappointment. "Can't say I blame you. Me taking this long to own up—"

Ketch cut off the marshal with a sharp gesture. "It's not that. You've been damned decent to me over the years. I'm not about to pay you back by dirtying up your good name and reputation. Anyway, like you said what my ma was, well hell, any of a dozen men could've been my pa. Why should *you* take the blame?"

"Dammit, Ketch, it's what I should've done twenty-five, thirty years ago, whenever it was. I want people to know now and that goes, whether I make it back or not."

Ketch grinned, "If you want to claim me, you damn well better make it back. Nobody would believe me otherwise."

"They would with Doc Booth and Mrs. Bentsen backing up your story."

Ketch looked over his shoulder. Both Revel and Doc Booth were watching them. In these close quarters, they couldn't help but overhear everything.

"Tell him, Doc," Talbert insisted.

Booth hesitated in answering. Moved by Talbert's generosity, he had a fleeting urge to make a clean breast of it. Ketch's mother didn't leave Ketch on his doorstep because he was a doctor, but because *he* was Ketch's father. And there was no guessing about it. He'd impregnated Ketch's mother before he came here, before she followed him here. Booth quickly swallowed that sudden urge to confess all. His late wife and four legitimate sons were his primary concern now.

Doc Booth shook himself free of his reverie. "Yes, Talbert," he said, "I'll tell them. I'll back Ketch up. And who knows but what you may be right," he lied. Then he added sincerely, "Ketch is like you, I'm finding out, in all the finest respects. Any *real* man," he said, knowingly excluding himself, "would be proud to have him as a son. If you don't make it back, Talbert, I'll tell the whole damn town what you've said here."

"Hey, Doc, you won't be telling nobody nothing about the bastard except that he's dead," a sibilant, accented voice startled them all.

Nueces Pecado had back-trailed Ketch from the canyon. Back-trailed him and found him.

Chapter Twenty-Five

Astride his horse, Nueces Pecado came chin level to the floor of the grotto shelf. Though he sat twisted in the saddle, his horse hot-footing under him, his gun hand looked plenty steady resting on the ledge.

The light from the small fire inside the recess glinted off Nueces' wild black eyes, giving him a demoniacal look. Not one of them doubted he would use the least excuse to shoot, even though his gaze focused solely on Ketch.

"Come on, big man," he said to Ketch, "a lynch party's waiting for you back in White Reef and you've got a long walk back to where you staked out the horses."

"Hold on," Doc said. "You're making a mistake. Ketch didn't—"

"*Callate*, pill-roller! Nobody didn't ask you."

"Booth's right, Pecado," Talbert's voice rasped.

"I said shut up, all of you." Nueces swung his gun in a nervous arc, covering them all.

When Doc and Talbert's hands tensed, Ketch quickly interjected, "Don't. Anybody. This's between Nueces and me."

Ketch feared the older men might make a play with the guns he'd given them. It wouldn't take much to set off the hot-headed little breed. Any move on the part of the others might precipitate action that would endanger not just the both of them, but would also put Revel in harm's way. Too many people had already been hurt because of him.

"Simmer down, Nueces. I'm coming with you. No trouble here."

"Now you're acting sensible, *puerco*. Drop your gun."

Gingerly Ketch removed the borrowed gun from his chaps pocket and laid it on the floor of the cave.

"*Bien*. Now get down here." Nueces backed his prancing horse away from the lip of the shelf to give Ketch clearance.

Ketch did as told and swung down onto the narrows trail.

Nueces motioned with his gun for Ketch to lead out, but he set the pace by nudging his horse against Ketch's back.

Ketch called over his shoulder, "Better lead your horse through here, Nueces. You don't want him to break a leg."

"You jus' worry about your own damn legs, eh?"

Ketch slowed imperceptibly, allowing Nueces' horse to crowd even closer. He recognized the animal as the same head-shy horse Nueces had ridden out to Revel's place the other day. Fate had dealt him an ace-in-the-hole. Now, if only that same fate would give him a chance to play it...

When they reached the crossing of the narrows at the main cleft, well out of earshot of the others, Nueces stopped his horse.

"This is as far as you go, *hijo de perra*."

Ketch heard a barely audible click behind him as Nueces thumbed back the hammer of his revolver. Ketch had anticipated that the vengeful little bugger wouldn't chance hauling him all the way back to White Reef with a no-risk out like this presenting itself.

The breed will claim he shot me down while I was trying to escape. And who would care enough to question even Nueces Pecado?

Rather than answer or beg as Nueces expected him to, Ketch ducked under the high-strung horse's arching neck and slapped it alongside the head.

Terror-stricken, the horse reared back then lunged forward, flinging its head wildly from side to side. Nueces lost a stirrup and hung half out of his saddle. As he tilted toward the ground, he triggered off a shot in Ketch's direction. But with the horse lunging forward, Ketch had already moved behind the shot.

Nueces kicked free of the other stirrup and landed on the horse's offside, putting the skittish beast between him and Ketch, presenting the additional risk of one of them getting crushed within the narrows' steep-walled confines.

Nueces moved back and forth with the horse, using it as a shield as he looked for a clear shot at Ketch. He soon discovered that the horse shielded Ketch as much as it did him.

Ketch braced one leg against the wall and pressured the horse sideways toward Nueces. Nueces punched the horse in the eye with his fisted gun, gouging out the animal's eye from its socket. The eyeball dangled by its optic nerve, like a sprung jack-in-the-box.

The crazed animal barged ahead blindly, knocking both men against the opposing narrows' walls, leaving nothing between them but daylight.

Ketch recovered his footing first and as Nueces raised his gun, he took a giant step with his right foot and lashed out with his left. Nueces ducked away from the arc-ing boot, and threw off a wild shot. The slug ricocheted low off the wall behind Ketch and slammed him in the shoulder.

Ketch stumbled forward from the impact, barely keeping his balance and fighting to keep his senses. Nueces still had three or four shots left, but Ketch had only fists and feet for weapons. Ketch kicked again, putting all the strength of his powerful legs behind it. The pointed toe of his boot caught Nueces under the chin.

Nueces' head snapped back with a loud pop.

Ketch ripped the gun from Nueces' limp hand as the man dropped to the ground. Covering the breed with the pistol, Ketch toed the smaller man's unmoving figure. No fight left in Nueces...no life, either. His head flopped at an odd angle to his body.

"Slither down a hole to hell, you greasy little snake," Ketch whispered, both relieved and repulsed. He'd never killed anyone before and to do it this way...

He swallowed hard against the rising gorge even while acknowledging that given the same set of circumstances, he'd again do exactly what he had done. Before this deal was over, he might have to.

A sudden lethargy engulfed Ketch and he leaned back against the narrows wall. He knew the ricochet had caught him, but he didn't feel pain, just a throbbing kind of numbness.

Fighting the stupor of exhaustion, he considered what he must do before returning to the others — get rid of Nueces' body, maybe cover it with rocks right here in the narrows; catch the breed's horse, lead it out of here, and put it out of its misery.

Ketch continued to think about it, but couldn't stir up the will to move away from the wall. When at last he did try, he discovered he just could not.

He loosed a low steady stream of profanity. In his whole life he'd never known a day of sickness and God knew he must have had one hell of a constitution just to survive into adulthood.

Nevertheless, the past week had taken its toll: the drugging, the fights, whatever blood he lost earlier when Ed's bullet sliced a strip of flesh off his shoulder, and now this.

He must have lost more blood than he realized. Hard telling now what was blood and what was rain or melting sleet running down his back.

Slowly he sank to the ground. He'd just sit there for a while...rest...just for a little while.

Ketch opened his eyes. It was dark. The storm had passed. Bracing himself against the slot canyon's wall, he dragged himself to his feet. Lead slug grated against bone and searing pain replaced the numbness in his shoulder. His legs had become inordinately flexible and he had little control over them.

In a brief burst of mental clarity, he remembered Nueces' body and the man's injured horse. And not a damn thing he could do about either one of them. Just to make it back to the grotto and Doc Booth, he'd have to be like the guy who fell in a privy and came up with a saddlebag of gold.

Once Doc digs the slug out of me, everything will be all right.

That was Ketch's last conscious thought.

Chapter Twenty-Six

From his perch atop the sandstone ridge, Charlie Wykle watched the panoramic scene below. An exhilaration, a never-before-experienced enthusiasm vibrated through him. Mentally he proclaimed himself king of all he surveyed. What a great feeling!

Below, to his left and east of where he stood, he could see White Reef, now re-named "Silver Ridge." The past month had brought radical changes to the town, its configuration, its temper and tempo and, most of all, to its population both in size and makeup.

Two new saloons and a couple of hash-houses had been built. A merchant from Pioche had dismantled his store in sections, transported it and all his merchandise from Nevada to set up the whole shebang right here in Silver Ridge.

On the other side of the deadline, tent whorehouses, dugouts, sagebrush shelters, slab shacks had, like mushrooms, sprouted overnight. A church was under construction that would do extra duty as a school and its basement as a hospital. Day and night, traffic rumbled through the town as teamsters hauled ore in and silver out. Even a daily stage had been added.

The eastern slope of the ridge, already criss-crossed with new roads, had been denuded as people scrabbled for the meager timber available for building, for fuel, for flumes and shafts and drifts.

For himself, Wykle had started construction on a house in town, the biggest and finest as befitted a person of his growing wealth and social stature. He'd already remodeled the house at Slash R which, as Revel's "partner," he'd legally absorbed.

He'd tripled the size of his newspaper office along with its staff and output. He no longer needed the newspaper either as a source of income or as a cover. But the business had served him too well to abandon. The newspaper had given and continued to give him power—power to influence public opinion. It had been that significant power that gave him direct access to what lay under this ridge. Silver!

In the preceding weeks, he'd also discovered something about himself. He craved power more than money. That burning desire for power inflamed political ambitions in him. Ambitions the newspaper would continue to serve well.

Wykle changed his focus from the view of the town's flurry and bustle to the other side of the ridge where the actual excavation and extraction were going on at the silver mine. *His* mine.

Tailings started to pile up where the miners had begun going underground. The skeletal frame of a three-stamp mill had been built, where he would refine his own ore.

The surface vein ran a healthy eight hundred fifty dollars to the ton. One petrified log alone had yielded 17,000 ounces of silver, which was selling at a dollar-seventeen an ounce. The most modest estimates predicted the strike would produce three hundred thousand dollars in silver bullion within the first year of operation...not an inconsequential sum when you considered that the annual income of cowhands ran about three hundred dollars a year.

"Three hundred thousand dollars," Wykle said aloud, letting the words roll off his tongue, "and it's all mine." At least to his way of thinking it was, with Ketch no longer a factor.

Two full months had passed since Ketch, Revel Bentsen, Marshal Talbert, and Doc Booth had all seemingly vanished from the face of the earth. And thanks to the influence of his—Wykle's—articles on the subject, the general population accepted as fact that Ketch had killed off the latter three for whatever purposes of his own and that the bronc snapper himself was either dead or had fled north to one of the outlaw holes in Wyoming.

No one paid particular heed to Nueces Pecado's disappearance along with the others or, if they had, hadn't deemed the happenstance worth mentioning. The breed's vanishing had troubled Wykle at first.

But when Ketch didn't show up, either, conjecture turned to hope and hope led Wykle to acceptance that the breed had accomplished what he'd set out to do, but likely got himself killed in the process.

Wykle smiled. The way things now stood, even if Ketch should, by some miracle, reappear, nothing would be changed. Wykle not only had everything under control, but also tied up legally. Working through the local Justice of the Peace, he had Ketch declared dead so that the property reverted to the territory. And since Wykle was the only one in the area with any money to speak of, he picked up the property for a song.

He'd handled things so smoothly, that no one even raised an eyebrow when silver was "discovered" on the place.

All very neat for him, except...

Two flies in the ointment—Nora Peters and Woody Vaught.

Wykle had the J.P. appoint Vaught in Talbert's vacated marshal's job, placing the law in his hip pocket. But he had to pay Nora and Woody a percentage of the mine's take, a condition he did not anticipate lasting much longer.

With all the toughs moving in, as they were wont to any time or any place ore was discovered, Wykle figured to have any number of gunnies at his disposal to do the dirty work when the right time beckoned.

But for now, he, Nora, and Woody maintained a tenuous alliance with one another. They each possessed damaging knowledge of the other. Nora had killed Ketch's wife Cindianne and, in all probability, Revel Bentsen, too. Vaught had done for Marshal Talbert. And the albatross around his own neck was, of course, the killing of Murphy the assayer. Nora, damn her eyes, had in her infinite wisdom shared that tidbit with Vaught when she first cut him in.

The fate of Doc Booth had to be a matter of conjecture, but a fairly safe bet that either Nueces or Ketch had punched that worthy's ticket.

Wykle lit a cigar, sucked deeply, euphoric. He felt a joyous sense of impending climax. Before long, he'd remove those two flies from the salve of his contentment. If the removal did not occur naturally, then by god, he would make it happen.

He blew out a cloud of smoke and motioned to the two armed guards standing at his side. Yes, indeed, it was a great life and before long it was going to get even greater.

In Pioche, Nevada, the sun barely shot its first rays over the eastern horizon as a bearded, rough-looking man on the door stoop of the assay office stretched and yawned. He'd been waiting most of the night for its owner to come and open up shop. He rose and stretched again before pulling a crumpled, creased, and badly used newspaper from the pocket of his ragged coat. He sat back down to re-read one particular article for the dozenth time since he'd found the paper blowing around the street when he hit town late the night before.

The paper was the Reef Weekly Record, Charlie Wykle's newspaper, dated what the man guessed would have been six or seven weeks ago, give or take a few. The man smiled grimly as he read.

WOMAN-KILLER RUNS AMOK
A local character known only as
"Ketch," suspected of murdering
his wife several months ago, last week
shot and seriously wounded another
woman, his current employer, Mrs.
Revel Bentsen, formerly of Forty-Fort,
Pennsylvania.
The killer, after first wounding
Mrs. Bentsen, made a successful
escape, shooting and killing town
Marshal A. D. Talbert in the process.
In an eerie and inexplicable
turn of events, the murderer returned
to the scene of his heinous crime and
made off with the severely wounded
Mrs. Bentsen and her attending physician
John Austin Booth. Both of the latter are now presumed to be dead.

The article went on at length from there, closing the story with a detailed description of the "woman-killer." In addition, a full quarter of the front page was taken up with a hand-sketched facsimile of the wanted man. Under the devastatingly accurate reproduction appeared a notice advertising a small bounty followed by the words *Dead or Alive*.

"You waiting for something, mister?"

The bearded man stood up and stuffed the newspaper back into his pocket before responding, "Yeah. The assayer."

"Well, pardner, you're going to have to go over to Silver Ridge to see him. You know where Silver Ridge is, over to Utah?"

"Afraid not."

"Used to be not even a dot on a map, little town called 'White Reef.'"

"Ah. And why would he be gone there, do you know?"

"Man, where you been hiding! Half the town of Pioche joined the stampede over into that country. Ain't you heard? They had a big silver strike and if you know mining a'tall, you won't believe this — the lode was discovered in a *sandstone* ridge!"

The bearded man nodded without answering.

"Sorry I can't be of no more help to you," the other said.

The bearded man spoke through his preoccupation. "That's all right. You told me just what I was looking to find out." Almost as an afterthought, he asked, "There a telegraph office in this town?"

"You bet. Right over there, in the stagecoach office."

The bearded man nodded his thanks and crossed the street and entered the small office indicated by the other man.

A crane-like man with wire-rimmed spectacles, green eyeshade, and gartered sleeves moved to the counter.

"Yes, sir, what can I do for you?" He spoke in a slow southern Virginia drawl.

"I'd like to send a wire. Ed Duerson, St. James Hotel, Denver."

The telegrapher cleared his throat. "No offense, mister, but have you got the money to pay for this wire?"

The bearded man reached into one of his pockets and pulled out a charred sandstone rock with silvery extrusions.

"Will you take this?"

Ketch had no memory of how he had made it back to the cave. But even in a near stupor, his subconscious goaded him on with the knowledge that he had to help Doc Booth tend Revel Bentsen and Marshal Talbert, that the little group needed him to provide food and firewood. With his good health, strong constitution, and even stronger will, he had recuperated faster than the others.

After his trip to Pioche, Ketch returned to the grotto where he and the others had been holed up for only God knew how long. What Revel and Talbert had suffered during that time showed in their pale faces and languid movements. He now gave Doc an apologetic look. "Sorry I can't let you go, yet, Doc. Until I get a better grip on what's going on, I'll need you to stay here with us."

"Hell," Doc Booth said, "Wouldn't go if you sent me. I want to see how this hand plays out. You dealt me in, but I'm throwing a few chips of my own into the pot."

Ketch looked at the barber-cum-doctor with admiration. "Wish I could be more like you, Doc."

Booth hesitated, muttered, "Son, you're already a better man than I'll ever be," and then changed the subject. "What were you able to find out over to Pioche?"

With a half smile, Ketch handed him the torn newspaper and answered, "Most of the rest of the puzzle pieces."

Chapter Twenty-Seven

Charlie Wykle stretched lazily, started to swing out of his bed, then halted mid-motion. A fierce anger hit him as he slowly rose the rest of the way to his feet. On the washstand beside his bed, propped up against the bowl stood a folded piece of quality vellum.

He snatched up the note, lifted it to his nose. The fragrance twitched his nose. Faint, but unmistakable. He ripped open the note and read it. A blinding fury bolted through him. He crossed his hotel room in two steps and jerked the door open.

Two men lazed in the narrow hall — one slouched in a chair facing Wykle's room, the other in a straight-backed chair beside the door. Both men jumped to their feet. Both shouted at the same time.

"What's the matter, Boss?"

"What's wrong?"

"Where the hell did you two slope off to during the night?" Wykle screamed at them.

The guards, Kiel and Jase, gave each other befuddled glances. Jase spoke first.

"We didn't go nowhere, Mr. Wykle. We both been here all night, ever since we took over from Smitty and Tex about two o'clock."

"Closer to two-thirty," Kiel corrected. "But Jase's right, Mr. Wykle. We both neither one of us even stepped down the hall to take a leak."

"Then you must have let someone into my room on purpose. Who the hell was it?"

"No one, boss!"

"Not even Nora Peters?"

"Never saw the woman." Again Kiel and Jase glanced uncomfortably at the other, wondering if their boss had lost his mind.

"Well, dammit, someone got into my room some time during the night!" Wykle ran a nervous hand through his thinning hair. He'd worked past midnight himself. He double-checked with Smitty and Tex just before he went to bed around one-thirty. Both men had been wide-awake then. How the hell could...?

Had someone sneaked in through his window off the hotel's balcony?

Wykle shuddered involuntarily. That someone not only had slipped past his guards and had been that close to him while he was sleeping sent cold chills through him. Hell, if the nocturnal visitor hadn't left the note, no one would have known that he—*or she*—had been there.

"What time is it now?" he snapped.

Kiel pulled out his pocket watch and looked at it. "Just shy of noon, boss."

Wykle blew out his breath. "Jase, go fetch Woody Vaught. No, never mind. Stay with me. The three of us will stick together and all go to see him." Wykle wasn't sure how far he could trust anyone, not even his hired bodyguards.

Foregoing his usual meticulous daily grooming, Wykle reached the acting marshal's office five minutes later. Leaving the two guards standing outside the door, Wykle entered the jail.

Vaught lay sleeping on a cot in the front office portion of the jail. A bunch of miners nursing drunks and aching heads crammed the two open-barred cells at the back of the room. Apparently they'd had themselves a real donnybrook the night before. From the smells emanating from Vaught, the new marshal had been hitting the bottle himself.

"Wake up, goddammit, it's the middle of the day," Wykle snarled as he kicked the side of Woody's cot with his foot.

Woody seemed a little woozy and was slow getting his wits about him. Wykle leaned over, shook him roughly.

Quicker than a shot, Vaught clamped an iron hand around Wykle's wrist. He squeezed Wykle's wrist tightly as he rose to a sitting position on the bunk.

"Don't ever try manhandling me, Charlie," his voice barely a whisper, but heavy with threat.

Vaught's violent and unexpected reaction caught Wykle unwary. More than any other trait of the man, Wykle hated this inconsistency in Woody. Usually subservient, a follower—but with a couple of drinks under his belt, Woody turned nasty, thin-skinned, aggressive. Not being able to anticipate which way he would jump made Vaught all the more dangerous.

Wykle wrenched his arm free. "We don't have time to squabble among ourselves. Something's come up. Here, look at this. During the night someone slipped into my room at the hotel and left this." He held out the note.

Vaught stretched and yawned. "Can't see past the end of my nose this morning. Was up most of the night busting the heads of those damn hooch hounds." He tilted his head in the direction of the packed cells. "What's it say?"

Wykle read the brief note aloud:

I'm on to what you did.
For $20,000 I can forget it.

Woody snapped to attention.

"For hell's sake! Who do you think—"

"How the hell should I know! What I want to know is, did you get one or anything like it, too?"

Vaught repeated Wykle's exclamation, "How the hell should *I* know! I told you, I just got to sleep, well hell, not more'n a couple of hours ago. Here, let's look around."

Vaught rose from his bunk and walked around the room, his eyes half closed.

"Yeah, here's something," Wykle said, "right on your desk, under your ring of keys." He held it out to Woody.

"Read it, huh?"

Wykle ran his thumb under the seal and unfolded the paper. "Same damn thing as mine, word for word. Ask if any of those men back there in the cells saw anyone come in here during the night."

Vaught squinted in the direction of the hung-over miners. "Hell, that bunch wouldn't of known if their own mothers come in here. Do you have any ideas?"

"Before I say anything, take a whiff of this paper."

Vaught lifted the paper to his nose, cocked one eyebrow at Wykle. "I think we ought to pay Miss Nora a visit."

"Damn right."

The two men walked shoulder to shoulder in dead silence, each steeped in his own thoughts. Wykle's two bodyguards tagged closely behind.

"Wait out here for me," Wykle said to them when they reached the newly named *The "Silver Ridge" Weekly Record* office. Although it was lunchtime, Nora sat at her desk working alone. She looked up as Wykle and Vaught walked in.

Without wasting words, Wykle shoved the notes in her face. "All right, Bitch, what kind of double-crossing are you up to now?"

Charily, Nora took the notes from Wykle, read them. She glanced up at him, then at Woody Vaught, then back at the notes.

"What are you suggesting, Charlie? That I wrote these? Is that what you're trying to put into Woody's head? You probably know better than anyone that *I* didn't write them."

She saw the open skepticism in both men's faces and, remembering the last time either man hurt or threatened her, she blurted, "I didn't. So help me God, I didn't."

"It'll take more than God to help you if you're lying to me again, Nora," Wykle said.

As long as he had known her, as intimate as they had been, Wykle still never could tell when Nora was lying or when she was telling the truth. He had no certainty whether her frantic bewilderment at the moment was real or feigned.

His lips thinned. "All right. *Whoever* wrote this note claims to know what we did. If that's the case, you must have gotten one, too, Nora. Did you?"

"Well no, I didn't—" Nora stopped abruptly, the expression on her face clearing into one of understanding. A sardonic grin twisted her lips. "I see. Divide and conquer. That's what this is all about, isn't it, Charlie? Is this the beginning of the freeze-out? I knew it was coming. So this is where you start working Woody and me against each other and out of the picture!"

"You lying, conniving slut!" Wykle reached across the desk and backhanded her, his diamond ring cutting her lip.

Nora did not react. She opted for discretion over valor.

But Vaught warned, "Hey, Wykle, none of that stuff."

Wykle said, "When it comes to Nora, mind your own damn business. Don't forget, Woody, I made you sheriff and I can just as easily make sure you are not re-elected. I have the power to sway public opinion."

Vaught smiled grimly, "Only if you're still alive, *Mister* Wykle."

Wykle controlled himself with difficulty. He knew that Vaught retained an ambivalent kind of respect for Nora, a wedge she wouldn't hesitate to drive between him and Vaught. That was a major problem he had with Woody. At times the man came dangerously close to having a conscience. Vaught's more serious problem was that he was a "mean drunk." Tolerable when sober, edgy after a drink or two, and poisonous as a scorpion when primed with more booze than that. Less malleable at that stage, but at his most useful for Wykle's purposes. Another problem Woody had that could go either way — useful or harmful — drunk or sober, the man nursed a grudge the way a dog licks a sore.

"Don't be stupid, Woody," Charlie said. "Can't you see what she's up to? Exactly what she just said — 'Divide and conquer.' What could better suit her ends than to have the two of us at each other's throats?"

Vaught gave that a moment's careful thought before replying. "Could be. That sure as hell smells like your perfume on the paper, Nora. But it was you, Wykle, who *found* the note on my desk. Fact is, I don't trust neither one of you any farther than I could spit against the wind in a sand storm. Just don't neither one of you think you're smart enough or tough enough to cut me out."

"What you're saying, Woody, is that maybe Nora and I have been underestimating you, that you are as smart and tough as we are."

Vaught gave him a scornful look. "Smarter. And a hell of a lot tougher."

"Smart enough to put Nora and me at cross purposes?" Wykle suggested.

"No, Wykle, too smart for that. Ain't my style to coyote around the rim like you two. When I think, I think direct. And when I act, I act direct. Do well for you two double-dealers to keep that in mind before trying any of your shenanigans on me."

With that warning, Woody Vaught turned and stomped out, slamming the door behind him.

Wykle's guard Kiel immediately shaded his eyes and pressed his face against the window, looking into the office's darker interior.

Seeing Wykle was okay, he turned to Jase, shrugged, and resumed his indifferent watch.

Swearing under his breath, Wykle stalked out of the newspaper office moments after Vaught had. He crossed the street, heading for his hotel room to attend to his missed ablutions. Wouldn't do for the citizenry to see him unkempt. He had an image to uphold.

As he mounted the steps and crossed the porch, he stumbled over a protruding foot. In anger he kicked at the disheveled heap that lay sprawled out on the porch.

Wykle swore again, aloud this time. He muttered to the two men trailing at his heels, "Damn drunk. Town is getting filled with them. Woody better see to it that all these bums and whores stay on their side of that deadline set up south of town."

The "drunk," a rough-looking bearded man, rose and with exaggerated dignity brushed off his filthy duster, punched into a vague shape a hat scrounged off someone's scrap heap, and settled down into one of the dazzling white wicker chairs lining the front porch of Silver Ridge's newest and finest hotel.

This was the same shabby wretch who'd been to the assayer's office in Pioche, Nevada, a couple of weeks ago. And, if he were drunk, it didn't show in the alert eyes hidden by the disreputable hat. Rather, they shone clear and, at the moment, crinkled slightly at the corners in wry amusement.

From his vantage point on the hotel gallery, directly across from the Silver Ridge Weekly Record office, Ketch had observed the late morning's activities. And while he could only conjecture what had taken place inside that office, what he had seen from the outside was enough to curve his lips into a faint smile.

He raised his feet to the gallery rail and tipped the old hat over his slitted eyes, content for the moment to absorb the smells of the newly sawn wood, the sounds of the continual flow of foot and horse traffic on the rutted main street, the crisp breeze hinting of winter fast coming on.

Things were beginning to hum.

Chapter Twenty-Eight

That evening, Nora Peters, Charlie Wykle, and Woody Vaught met again, a virtual reprise of their mid-day conference—except that Nora had called this one. The men forced her to wait more than an hour before they showed up, with Wykle arriving last. As soon as he appeared, Nora waved a piece of the readily identifiable vellum stationery at them, her voice edged with scorn.

"Now what do you fools have to say for yourselves? I received one of those threatening blackmail notes, too. Now you can stop blaming me for sending the ones you two got."

"How convenient," Wykle said. "And no doubt you have some good reason why yours arrived seven, eight hours after we found ours. No doubt the Pony Express was late—something like seventeen years too late."

"Cut the sarcasm, Charlie. I found the note right here on my desk when I got back from supper tonight."

At Wykle's derisive smirk, she exploded. "Dammit, Charlie, I didn't write those notes but I'm sure wondering about you! And why are you so quick to take Woody's word after all the time you and I have been together. Just because he *says* he didn't send these notes doesn't mean he didn't."

"You know, Nora," Vaught said, "Wykle's right—you are one conniving bitch. And maybe we just aren't the fools you take us for." As Woody spoke, whiskey fumes scented the air. "Besides, I thought we hashed all this shit out this morning or this afternoon, whenever the hell it was we got together today.

"I know I didn't write any damn notes for the simple reason I *can't* write any damn notes. I can't *read* any damn notes neither," an admission Vaught never would have made sober or in his earliest stages of drunkenness. "Now, does that satisfy you two?"

"Well," said Wykle, "somebody sure as hell wrote them."

"Who besides one of us?" Vaught asked.

"Good question." There couldn't be anyone else unless...His forehead wrinkled as thought of Ketch leaped to his mind. He shook his head. Couldn't be. But then, Nueces Pecado never came back. Wykle dismissed the notion. He said to Vaught, "You've been hitting the bottle pretty hard. Sure you didn't let something slip to one of those jades you been laying over to Katie's?"

"Just as sure as you, Wykle, that you didn't drop anything to those gundogs you hired to run at your heels."

Wykle shook his head impatiently. "Don't be stupid. The only one besides us..."

Vaught grabbed Wykle by the lapels before the editor could complete his thought. "Listen good, you ruffle-cuffed four-flush. You call me 'stupid' one more time and you'll be spitting out teeth into the middle of next week."

Wykle flicked his wrist and a derringer snapped into his hand.

At the same moment, a violent crash reverberated, followed by the collapse of the large ornately painted window at the front of the building. Wykle tore loose from Vaught and slapped the kerosene lamp off the desk before he dove under it. The room disappeared, swallowed in sudden darkness.

Nora and Vaught dropped to the floor in the same instant. All three lay in breath-holding silence, waiting for the next shot to come.

Moments slipped by, then minutes.

Finally Wykle whispered, "Nora?"

"I'm all right, I think." Her voice shook out through fear-clenched teeth.

"Woody, what about you?"

No answer. Nothing but the soft whisper of rough cloth slithering across the wooden floor.

"By damn, Woody, if that's you, answer, because I'm sure as hell going to shoot."

"Yeah. It's me," Vaught answered shortly, as the slithering sound continued. Vaught kept shifting position, not wanting to give his location away to anyone, not even to Wykle.

Maybe especially me, Wykle thought ironically. He also thought that maybe Woody didn't have such a bad idea and followed suit, moving before he spoke again. He called softly to the relief guns who were supposed to be standing watch outside.

"Smitty. Tex!"

No answer. Wykle began swearing in that same harsh whisper, quit when he realized he was broadcasting his location. He changed his position before calling a second time to the guards, a little louder this turn. He drew a response of sorts—a dull thump, thump against the alley side of the building.

Wykle was curious, but not curious enough to step outside to investigate. Could be some kind of ruse to draw him out into the open.

"Woody. Slip outside, see if you can find out what the hell that banging is."

Vaught laughed. "Go to hell." He wasn't afraid, but as he told Wykle, he wasn't stupid, either.

The three stayed curled into inconspicuous balls at various points around the office floor for the next fifteen minutes while the mysterious thumping on the side wall became more persistent, then gradually diminished.

Patience never was one of Wykle's few established virtues. He scratched a sulphur match into flame, shading it with his hands.

"For crissakes, Wykle!" Vaught stretched out to slap the match away, knelt on something sharp and yelped. He felt for it with his hand. "Hold that match over here a minute," he said.

Wykle edged toward him on knees and fists, the derringer still in one hand, the match in the other. "Damn!" He dropped the match as it burned down to his thumb and forefinger. He fumbled in his vest pocket for another and lit it. "What have you got, Woody?"

"Look here." Vaught held out a large rock with a piece of brown grocer's paper tied around it. "Wasn't no damn gunshot spooked us."

Wykle took the rock from him just as the second match burned down. He swore again. "Nora, where's another lamp?"

"If you hadn't broken my good one...there's a candle up on the wooden file cabinet," she said, but she wasn't about to make a target of herself by standing up to get it.

This time Vaught swore. Least familiar of the three with the office, glass crunched under his knees as he groped his way to the file. He reached up, felt around the top and found the candlestick. He hunkered down on the floor beside Wykle and lit it.

Nora slipped over to them. The three crowded around the dim light, somewhat sheltering the glow as Wykle undid the paper from the rock. As they had supposed, the paper had a message hand printed on it, a large bold hand.

Vaught said, "Read it...aloud."

Wykle spit out the words sour as last week's coffee in his mouth. "It says 'Midnight at Ketch's shack, any or all of you. NO ONE ELSE. Be sure to bring the $60,000 with you.' Yeah. That'll be the day."

The thumping at the side of the building started up again.

Somewhat sobered by the excitement, Vaught said, "Miss Nora, you stay here. Stay down on the floor. Wykle, you come with me. Let's see where those hired hollowhorns of yours run off to."

Nora doused the candle as the two men, each with gun in hand, crept out the front door of the darkened office.

In a town where, over the past few months, guns shooting off at odd hours, fistfights, and hell-raising had become commonplace, the small commotion at the newspaper office had gone unnoticed.

Vaught and Wykle stood at the corner of the enlarged building, holding their breaths as they tried to listen above the street's noise. Again, the thump, thump, thump.

Vaught jumped off the boardwalk into the alley, dropped and rolled to his left into the shadows of the building at the opposite corner. Moonlight filtered down between the structures. Wykle stood rooted to the walk, his back against the front wall of The Silver Ridge Weekly Record office. Breathing as shallowly as possible, he waited for some signal or word from Woody.

"It's all right, Wykle," Vaught said aloud. "It's just your watchdogs, trussed up like calves for the branding."

Smitty and Tex lay in the alley bound hand and foot, tied back to back at chest level. Their bodies formed an odd triangle with Smitty's feet out in the middle of the alley and Tex's propped up against the building. The thumping had been Tex trying to catch the attention of those inside. Both men were tightly gagged with their own neckerchiefs.

The air turned three shades of blue as Wykle reamed the men out. Vaught grinned as he cut the guards free. Wykle had gotten his second wind and launched a new tirade, using cusswords that hadn't even been invented yet.

"Why in hell am I paying you idiots anyhow? What the hell use are you! What happened?"

Smitty rose, rubbing life into his numbed hands. "I was standing at the corner of your office so I could look in your office window from time to time and keep tabs on the alley, too. Matter of fact, I'd just got through checking the alley—wasn't no one there. Turned my head and next thing I knew, someone grabbed me around the throat and another hand covered my mouth. You won't believe this, Boss, but it was like they was Apaches. First, wasn't no one there, then all of a sudden, maybe a dozen. I didn't never have a show."

"You're right about one thing, Smitty...I don't believe you. And what's your goddam excuse?" Wykle demanded of Tex.

"No excuse. Just fact. I thought maybe Smitty stepped into the shadows to take a leak. When he didn't come back after a minute or so, I went to check on him." He rubbed at the knot on his head. "Last thing I remember was a flash of light, just about the same time something exploded like a Sharps .50 inside my head. I didn't know another thing till I woke up hog-tied to Smitty. And Mr. Wykle," he warned icily, "don't you be calling *me* no gaddang liar."

"All right. What's done is done. Go round up Kiel and Jase. I want you all back here in fifteen minutes. We're going to take a ride over into the valley on the other side of the reef. Check your guns. Make sure they're loaded and take extra ammunition, 'cause you're all going to earn your wages before tonight is over."

Chapter Twenty-Nine

Ketch shoved aside the cowhide covering the doorway and stepped into his darkened shack's interior.

"How'd it go?" one of the men inside asked.

"No problems. They'll be coming. I stayed long enough to hear Wykle order two of his hired guns to round up his other two gunnies for a confab with him. We can expect Woody Vaught to ride with them, too. That makes at least six hardcases for us to deal with. Mr. Duerson," Ketch said softly, "I'm sorry as hell I had to drag you all the way back here from Denver. I'm even sorrier you brought Kelley along with you. No offense, Marshal," the last to Morgan Kelley, Deputy U. S. Territorial Marshal.

"Figure this is something I should be handling myself. I had to let Mr. Duerson in on what was going on because this deal most concerns him. But I wasn't counting on any outside...*help*." Ketch almost said *interference*.

Kelley said, "It's my job. Besides, from the sound of things, Ketch, you're going to need all the help you can get outside or no."

"No lie there," Ketch agreed. "Doc, Mrs. Bentsen, I'd like for you both to sit tight right here." He looked at Revel. "Wish there was someplace safer I could tuck you away, but the town's changed so damned much that I just flat out don't know anybody I'd trust leaving you with, except Doc here. Doc, I can't ever repay you for all you've done, sticking with us, tending Mrs. Bentsen and Talbert, for pulling me through. I'll always owe you one more."

"Ketch," Doc said, "believe me...you don't owe me a single damn thing. I'm glad—well, I'm glad I had this chance to get to know you and by something other than reputation."

Ketch touched the older man's shoulder, a simple gesture that said a good deal more than words.

"Marshal," this time Ketch was addressing town marshal Talbert whose wan face expressed volumes about his recent brush with death. "Now that Doc Booth got you back into the land of the living, I honest-to-God would rather you stay right here with him and Mrs. Bentsen. Especially after what you told me about us...I don't want anything...so damn many things could go wrong tonight."

"You're forgetting, this here's my job, too. The man who shot me is wearing my badge. That just don't go. And listen, son, all your life you've had to stomp your own snakes. It's about time someone gave you a hand...and it's time you let them."

Ketch nodded, even though there were still a lot of things he'd have liked to say, a lifetime of things that could never be made up. But, one way or another, time was running short.

"Guess it's all over but the shooting. My thinking is that Wykle will likely come by buggy through the valley with Vaught and maybe one or two of his gun toughs hanging back far enough to make me think Wykle and Vaught are on their lonesome. The rest of his outfit will probably come horseback over the ridge from town. Whichever way they come, Wykle will be looking to catch me in a crossfire, should it come to a fight. And I figure it will—a hell of a fight at that, with the odds two-to-one against us."

"Well hell, boy, you figured wrong," Duerson objected. "They's four of us ready to fight. Like you said, this rooking concerns me more so than you. Don't you be forgetting I was off fighting injuns, outlaws, and grizzlies long 'fore you ever seen the light of day."

Ketch grinned in the darkness. Neither age nor wealth would change this banty rooster any.

"Be glad for your help. That drops the odds considerable," Ketch said without mentioning the fact that of the four on their side, Duerson was an old fellow who'd never see the near side of seventy again; Kelley, although already a federal deputy, was just a green kid not much past twenty and probably on his first independent assignment. That passed the bulk of the real fighting on to Talbert who, in his mid-fifties, had passed his prime, and himself. *And I sure ain't no pistolero*, Ketch thought grimly.

Confident with a rifle, Ketch felt less sure of his prowess with a handgun. *Prowess, hell!* He'd be lucky to hit a barrel shooting from inside it with the lid on top. The odds may be three-to-two, but outside bets would be more like a hundred-to-one. *Well, maybe the outside bettors never heard of David and Goliath.* Ketch let out a huge breath of air.

"Ketch, you got any notions as to how we should go about this?" Kelley asked, acknowledging the bronc buster's better grasp of the total situation.

Ketch lit a candle and hunkered down on his heels. With a stick he drew a series of marks in the dirt floor of the shack. "Here's what I was thinking — Kelley, if you dig in up here…"

In front of the sorry shack Ketch used to occupy, a campfire flickered, sending off a deceptively warm glow of welcome. No one appeared within the circle of light and the night held an eerie silence. No hoots of night owls, no "scritching" sound of nocturnal rodents. Even the crickets and other night insects seemed to hush.

Wykle halted his buggy just at the fringe of the park that surrounded the windowless shack. He'd given his four hired guns time enough to ride over the ridge and position themselves at the north end of the valley just beyond the far side of the shack. Once Ketch showed himself — if it was Ketch — they could circle the bastard and close in on him.

Vaught had been pacing his horse just off the big rear wheel of Wykle's buggy. When Wykle pulled his rig to a halt, Vaught rode up alongside the editor so they could speak quietly. Nora, hidden under a tarp on the luggage carrier behind the buggy's folded down calash-top clutched a rifle. She poked aside the canvas cover with the gun's barrel. Her voice, though muffled, held a sharp edge to it.

"I don't see why the hell you had to drag *me* along."

"Insurance, my dear. I'm not entirely convinced that this isn't something you…" *or you and Vaught together*, he thought, "…cooked up to eliminate me from the equation." He thought again of Ketch. "If it is that horse-buster back, you're in as deep as we are. Deeper. Besides, you handle a rifle as well as any man and we need the extra gun."

Her voice rich with disdain, Nora said, "Right, we need seven guns to handle one man."

"According to Smitty, at least a dozen men waylaid him and Tex in the alley."

Nora laughed. "If you really believed that, Charlie, you'd have three dozen men along to back you up. Admit it—you're scared of Ketch. You always have been…both of you," she added, including Woody in the statement.

"Hell," Vaught said, "we don't even know for sure it is Ketch."

"If it's not either of you two, who else could it be?" Wykle proposed the possibility as a question, but his intonation stated it as a fact.

"I dunno," Vaught said. "When Ketch didn't come helling back here after a couple, three, weeks, I figured him to be done for or at least clear hellangone out of this country. Nora's right, Wykle. Ketch has you boogered. We don't know crap about who we're tangling spurs with tonight. We just might need more men."

"Now don't *you* try backing off from this deal," Wykle warned.

"*Me* back out? With *all* that's at stake, why would I?"

"Because Nora may be right about you. Everybody knows Ketch has had you hoodooed from day one. He's beat the hell out of you every time you two butted heads."

"Mister, you couldn't keep me out of this mix with a spiked corral. I just hope to hell it is Ketch. I have a score of my own to settle with him. Always wanted a chance to tell that long-legged bastard what a sorry lay that whore of his made."

Wykle gave Vaught a sidelong glance. Every time the man opened his mouth, alcohol fumes spewed out. *If the damn fool lit a cigarette, he'd burst into flames.* Wykle flicked the reins and put the team into a slow walk toward the shack and pulled up just short of the ring of light. Chewing nervously on his lower lip, Wykle looked over his shoulder at Vaught and shrugged.

"Come on in," a voice invited, breaking the stillness. In spite of his best efforts to appear in control, Wykle jumped at the unexpected sound. Echoes bounced around in the valley's bowl making it impossible to tell where the voice had come from.

"You don't have to spook," the voice said softly. "You're safe for the time being. You too, Woody, but nice and easy. You're both covered. And before you take any foolish notions into your heads, be warned of two things—you'll be wanting to hear what I've got to say and...there *are* others backing me up." He laughed then, a soft laugh that carried in the still air. "Though there aren't quite a dozen of us like Smitty claimed."

Wykle winced. *So it was Ketch*. The damned horse-breaker had to have been standing right there in the alley while Smitty was spinning his windy or, worse still, close enough minutes ago to overhear him and Vaught talking...and Nora, too. Damn the luck! Nora was one of his hole cards, but if Ketch knew she was hiding in the back of the buggy, the advantage was lost. The good thing was that Ketch seemed to want to parley. If he'd intended to kill them, he'd already have opened fire.

"All right, Ketch, I've always heard your word was good. Now we'll find out. We're coming in, but we aren't coming in naked."

"Bring a cannon with you, for all I care."

Wykle inched the team forward, his eyes trying to penetrate the darkness. He urged the team clockwise around the fire, stopping between it and the hide-covered doorway of Ketch's shack. If shooting started, he could jump from the buggy into the shack for cover, or, if worse came to worst, he could hightail it out of there and leave the others behind. The horses were pointed in the right direction for a dash back to town.

Keeping his hands in plain view, Wykle loosely draped the reins around the whip socket.

"All right, horse-breaker, it's your game. We're here...where are you?" He had to get Ketch out into the open where his men could see the buster.

But Ketch said, "Get down from the rig, Wykle. Huh-uh...this side, toward the fire."

Wykle swore under his breath as he complied. This wasn't going at all the way he had planned.

He tried to peer beyond the fire, hoping to locate his hired guns, but the light blinded him to any vision beyond the fire's glow.

"Now you, Woody. You get down, too, easy," Ketch continued in the same soft voice.

Vaught moved as warily as Wykle had, but when his feet touched ground, he hitched his gun belt around putting his revolver in easy reach. The firelight glinted off his town marshal's badge.

Not for long, you sonofabitch, Ketch thought. Talbert's train of thought ran along the same lines.

Ketch stepped out into the open then, walking in from the general direction Wykle and Vaught had come, but off to the side. Vaught and Wykle stared across the fire, trying to see the horse-breaker. But Ketch made his entrance so that the campfire's glare shone only in the periphery of his vision. His position also kept the cabin out of the line of fire. He loosely cradled a rifle in his left arm and for backup had crammed a revolver into his chaps' pocket.

Standing in the shadows when Wykle and Vaught arrived, Ketch had overheard their entire confab and was aware of Nora in the back of the rig. He was taking a calculated risk exposing himself this way, but he figured that to get a clear shot at him, she'd have to twist her body and lean over between the luggage carrier and big rear wheels. He worried more that he had no chance to warn the others about her. But he wanted justice here, not a bloodbath. As cold-blooded as she was, she'd likely start shooting the minute he exposed her presence.

"All right, Ketch," Wykle said. "You're calling the shots. Say what you've got to say and get this damned palaver over with."

"Did you bring the sixty thousand dollars?"

Wykle laughed out loud. "Hell, no. Why would we? Whatever you know or think you know—no one would take your word against mine and the *marshal's* here..." Wykle said, referring to Vaught, and thought...*or the word of the very respectable 'Miss Nora.'*

"Never can tell what might wash up after a storm," Ketch countered.

"That all you got to say?"

"No."

"What then? You going to tell us you've got some deposition written down somewhere telling all you know, to be opened and read in case of your untimely demise or some such shit?"

That brought a smile to Ketch's face. "That's more your style than mine."

"Wouldn't matter. Nobody would believe that, either. It still comes down to your word against mine."

"You said it yourself. I have a reputation for my word being good."

"Not any more," Wykle scoffed. "If I say so myself, the Silver Ridge Weekly Record did a damn fine job of slashing that reputation into microscopic bits and pieces. Not even your own mother would believe anything you'd say now — if you had a mother."

Ketch shrugged. "We can get back to that argument later. But before I lay my cards on the table, how about clearing up a couple of things for me."

Wykle looked past the fire and saw one of his men — Kiel — slowly advancing on Ketch. "Sure, why not?" he encouraged Ketch, buying time for his man to get into a sure-shot position.

"You worked it through the local J.P. to move my property over into your name."

"Yeah. Ironclad, all done legal. Not a thing in the world you can do to change it, especially with your being wanted for murdering two women."

"Uh-huh. But what's been needling me, what I can't figure, why did you kill my wife? Why didn't you just go ahead and kill me then work your 'legal' dodge on her to get the place. Hell, for all that, the poor kid would probably have sold out for a song. She had no ties here. She'd have been glad to get back to her family in Kansas."

"That was a dumb play, Ketch. That should tell you right there that I didn't do it. Your *friend* Nora pulled that little trick. For a brief spell, Nora tried operating on her own hook. She figured she could cut both your wife and me out of the picture and work her charms on you. You weren't as susceptible to her wiles as she had anticipated. When that plan fell apart, she fell back into line with me but not before she dragged Vaught into it."

"Nora, huh?" Ketch held his silence for a long time, getting his emotions under control. He learned two things tonight — Nora had killed Annie, and Woody had assaulted her. But at the moment, he had other people with him that he had to consider. With that in mind, he said, "Woody, this is between Wykle and me. If you back out of this now, you can back out peaceable."

"Sure, like hell I can. You *saw* me gun down Talbert."

"Talbert's alive, Woody."

"Don't bullshit me. I know where I shot him. Gut shot men don't survive."

"Whoever said that must be the same smart bastard that figured you couldn't get silver out of sandstone, either," a disembodied voice echoed from the other side of Wykle and Vaught. "But that ridge over yonder and me put the lie to both those notions. But I'll tell you this for fact—the sonofabitch who's coming up behind Ketch's left shoulder takes one more step, he'll find himself considerable more than gut shot."

"That ain't really you, Talbert?" Vaught asked, disbelief evident in his voice.

"It's me all right and I want my badge back. Drop it on the ground and take on out of here."

"Not yet. I'm playing this hand out."

"It's not work the risk, Vaught," said Ketch. "Wykle doesn't own one little stitch of that silver mine. The sixty thousand is just to pay up for whatever he's already taken out. And since he didn't kill anyone, far as I'm concerned, he can clear out, too...unless it was him that shot Revel Bentsen."

"No," Wykle stated emphatically. "That was another of our little Nora's didoes."

"Easy enough to blame her for things when she's not around to say different," Ketch suggested, hoping to flush Nora out, maybe even take a potshot at Wykle instead of him, but she didn't bite. Nora Peters may have been a damned sight icier than he believed possible in any woman, but nevertheless, she had just convicted herself.

"Well," Wykle asserted, "whatever Nora did is done and it's not going any farther than right here. Nor does it in any way alter the fact that the mine does belong to me...like I said, all done up legal."

"No, Wykle, you've got *my* property tied up. That's what comes of being so damn cocksure of yourself and believing you're smarter than you really are. And if Nora did kill Annie, she did it for nothing. You see, Wykle, what you're mining never did belong to me. You found out that I bought my place from Ed Duerson and like everybody else around White Reef—excuse me, *Silver Ridge*—you assumed I bought the whole damn piece. What possible use would a horse-breaker like me have for a sandstone ridge? I bought just what I needed and what I could afford. *The valley*. Ed Duerson owns that mine. *He always did.*"

"You bastard! You'll never live to tell him about it."

"Why Charlie boy, I already did. Him and a U. S. Marshal."

Heedless of Talbert's earlier warning, Wykle exploded in fury, "Cut Ketch down, Kiel!"

At Wykle's yell, three kinds of hell broke loose. But Ketch trusted Talbert to put the hired gun behind him out of commission and kept his sights on Wykle. Even if the editor hadn't wielded the razor that slashed Annie's wrists, his lies and greed had provoked her senseless murder.

To Ketch the run of things seemed to take place in exaggerated slow motion. Wykle sidestepped to the right, a gun flipped out of his sleeve into his hand. Ketch swung his cradled rifle at hip level, led Wykle, and fired.

Wykle's leg chopped out from under him. The editor hit the ground, spun, turned toward Ketch. He triggered the cheat gun and something plucked at Ketch's coat sleeve as Ketch levered another shell into his rifle. Slowly he raised the rifle and sighted down it. Ketch and Wykle fired their second shots at the same moment.

Wykle missed. Ketch didn't.

A miniature fountain of blood spurted out of the artery between Wykle's eyes and before the shot stopped echoing, Ketch pivoted and dropped to one knee. A slug tore the shabby hat from his head. *Vaught*.

Ketch returned the man's fire, certain he cropped the former Slash R foreman's ear. But before he could get another shot off at Vaught, Ketch saw one of Wykle's gundogs coming up the blind-side of Talbert. Ketch levered and fired until the gun heated his hands.

Then, as quickly as the havoc began, it stopped.

In a daze, Ketch looked about him. He couldn't tell who was hit or who wasn't. He yelled, "You, Wykle's men! Wykle's dead. Anything you do now, you're coming up against a Territorial Marshal as well as the local law…and you won't be getting paid one red cent to do it. If you're able, back off and clear out. We have no squabble with you. As far as we're concerned, you hired on blind and didn't know what you were getting into."

A murmured exchange followed Ketch's offer. "Fair enough. Give me a minute to get my pardner onto his horse. He's been hit."

Ketch waited, unmoving, until he heard three horses ride out. He dreaded his next chore—taking stock of his own people.

With a shock he saw Revel standing pale-faced and trembling alongside Wykle and Nora's buggy. Her white-knuckled hands clutched his out-sized cast iron skillet.

"What the hell—"

"Nora Peters," she forced out through chattering teeth.

Good God! He'd forgotten about *her*.

Nora's rifle lay on the ground by the buggy, but Nora lay still under the tarp. Ketch threw back the canvas, reached in and grabbed Nora's hair with one hand, her throat with the other. This was the bitch who had slashed the life out of Annie, who had killed their baby, who had tried to kill Revel.

He jerked back her head and gave a startled gasp.

Again, he said, "What...the...hell—"

Revel explained in a shaky voice, "Doc and I pulled the cowhide aside to see what was going on when Charlie Wykle yelled. I saw someone rise up there on the luggage carrier. I didn't know who it was, but I saw the rifle aiming right at you. I—I grabbed up the first thing at hand." She looked at the skillet still in her hands. "I ran around the tail of the buggy and swung as hard as I could."

Ketch looked again at Nora's face. Her nose had disappeared, mangled beyond identification, her top lip was split completely in two, all her front teeth, top and bottom, gone, knocked out.

"Wow." Ketch stared, his fingers twitching on her throat, wanting to squeeze the life out of the woman. But she was no longer Nora Peters, just a thing. Besides, he couldn't be what Wykle had painted him to be—a woman-killer.

As he released Nora, she opened her eyes. Ketch said to her, "With your new looks and by the time you get out of prison, you won't be able to buy yourself a job whoring at the cheapest crib south of the border."

He called out, "How did everyone else fare?"

Doc Booth said, "That damn Talbert's done gone and put me to work again. But he'll survive and with a lot less work than the last time. He took a clean shot through the upper arm."

They found that Kelley had taken a slug through the thigh. Ketch had a few scratches, but he'd suffered worse any number of times just snapping broncs. Duerson came through unscathed.

As for Wykle's forces, the one Ketch caught coming up on Talbert was dead and the one who had come up behind Ketch was badly wounded, but Doc "allowed as how the bustard would survive." Doc didn't figure to do a damn thing for Nora, not even to ease her pain.

The same clinical detachment that had permitted him to let another man claim his son manifested itself as he handed Nora a needle and thread. If she wanted her lip sewn together, she could damn well do it herself.

Ketch looked around for Woody Vaught but found no sign of him. That must have accounted for the third horse he'd heard ride out. Just as well. He'd settle with him later. Enough mayhem had been committed for one night.

Ketch leaned back against the buggy.

Thank God it was all over.

Chapter Thirty

As Ketch left Talbert's office, Revel stepped out of the mercantile/post office across the street. Ketch angled toward her, chaps flung over one shoulder, his face beaming.

When he reached Revel, he said, "Everything's squared away. LeCompte, the Justice of the Peace who set things up for Wykle, swore on a Bible he didn't know what Wykle was up to or that there was any 'skulduggery' involved. The man practically tripped over himself trying to right things, to prove he didn't have any of Wykle's dust on his coat tails."

None of Ketch's usual taciturnity evidenced itself as he shared his good news with Revel. "Ed Duerson's decided that since Denver isn't all it's cracked up to be and things have livened up around here, he's going to stay on and supervise his own mining operation.

"Best of all, I can let you have the money you need to send for your husband. Ed Duerson's insisting on giving me twenty-five percent of the take until his mine peters out. In the meantime, I'll finish busting out your broncs for you and drive the finished herd to wherever that dam—daggone cavalry buyer is. I'll go clear to Fort Hays, Kansas, to deliver them, if I have to. We'll get you and your husband set up so you'll never have to worry about another thing."

Revel listened patiently until Ketch finished his euphoric and uncharacteristically long speech.

Ketch waited for a similar response from her, but it didn't come. Hadn't she understood?

"Mrs. Bentsen, did you—"

"Ketch, there's no need for you to do anything for my husband or me."

"Why not? I sure won't be attaching any strings."

"I just picked this up at the Post Office." Revel handed Ketch a torn envelope. "Apparently this *missive* had followed me all over the country and arrived here while we were holed up in that canyon."

He looked at the return address written on the back: *Glen Haven Sanatorium, Glen Haven, Pennsylvania.*

"You can read it," she said.

He pulled the contents from the envelope—a bill. No letter, no message, just a statement of charges due:

July 14, 1877
For services rendered in re Andrew R. Bentsen:
Hospital room 3 months $180.00
Medications 68.00
Burial plot and
related expenses 45.00
Total due $293.00
Please Remit Immediately

Ketch's hand shook in anger. *What a brutal way for a woman to learn her husband had died!*

Revel put her small fists to her bowed head. "He was dead, Ketch, before I ever even set foot in Utah. I should have stayed with him. Those last days I should have been there, with him." She shuddered, and then began crying soundlessly.

"Aw, Revel, don't." He started to reach out to her, drew back his hand. "Listen, you had no way of knowing how things would work out. You said yourself his doc told you that bringing your husband here was his last—his *only hope*, for God's sake."

She lifted her head, trying to blink back the tears. "Yes, he did. But, Ketch, I'm not sure that's the real reason I left to come here. I didn't want to stay nearby and watch him die. When he needed me most, I wasn't there. He died alone, God forgive me."

This time Ketch gently folded her to his chest. "You did what you believed best at the time. That's all anyone can ask of you. That's all you can ask of yourself."

"I can't help it," she sobbed. "If only—"

Ketch shook her gently. "Hey, come on." He held her out from him and spoke without his usual cynicism. "So what are you going to do now? Go the Ketch Colt route? Dive into a bottle and pull the cork in after you? Revel, Honey,"—the endearment slipped out—"life's filled with *if onlys*. If only I'd shown half the understanding with people that I did with horses, my life and half the town's would have been less miserable...if only Wykle and Nora weren't so greedy, my wife and baby might still be alive. Not too awfully long ago, a beautiful lady I truly admire laid me out seven ways to Sunday, persuaded me to stop looking back—that looking back doesn't change a thing. I believed you when you told me that, Revel. You weren't just stringing me, were you?

"Just stop and think. You still have your ranch here and thanks to Wykle's free spending of Ed's mining money, it's fixed up royal. You've made some damn good, loyal friends. And the time you and I spent together the past couple of months—in a sudden country like this, two months' acquaintance is like two years of friendship...or...or *courtship*, back East. Even with Doc and Talbert chaperoning, I was hard put to remind myself that you had a husband. Do you understand what I'm saying?" His calloused hand brushed the tears from her cheek.

She looked up into his eyes and in case she didn't understand his meaning, he cut the deck a little deeper by adding, "This probably isn't the right time or place to declare myself, but you must have figured out by now that I love you. I think I did from the first time I saw you, when you walked into Katie's, with that little green hat on your head."

Woody Vaught's harsh voice shattered the tender moment.

"Step aside, whore. Stand clear of your bastard boyfriend!"

Ketch turned. "Man, you're drunk. Rent yourself a room at the hotel and sleep it off."

"I been drinking, but I ain't drunk."

Vaught stood legs spread, arm crooked with his hand brushing the grip of his holstered revolver.

Caught unarmed, Ketch shoved Revel to his right and stepped to the left, putting as much distance between her and himself as possible.

It took Revel only a second to size up Ketch's precarious situation. "Mr. Vaught," she said, "that nasty business with Charlie Wykle is over and done with. Count yourself lucky that you got off as easily as you did."

"That ain't why I'm here and Ketch knows it."

Revel turned to look at Ketch, and even though Ketch's full concentration centered on Vaught, he answered her unspoken question. "This son of a bitch raped my wife when she was four months pregnant."

"I sure did. Gave the little bitch just what she was looking for. And I ain't going to spend the rest of my life looking over my shoulder wondering when you're gonna come after me."

Ketch felt the blood drain from his face at Vaught's open admission. But strangely, instead of flying into a senseless rage, Ketch felt himself at peace — cooler, calmer, clearer thinking than at any time in recent memory.

Wordlessly Ketch walked toward the man who'd violated his wife, the man he'd sworn, over the grave of his wife and baby, to find and kill. The day of reckoning had come. All that Ketch asked of God as he doggedly paced off the distance between himself and Vaught was that He allow him to get his hands on Vaught. He might get killed himself, but he determined that Vaught would go down to hell with him.

Forgotten by both men, Revel reached down and unlaced her thick-heeled shoe.

Ketch's calm, insistent, and unexpected advance toward an armed man rattled Vaught. Just as Woody Vaught jerked for his gun, Revel flung her shoe at him with all her might and hit him in the neck. The shoe didn't so much as startle Vaught and the front sight of his gun hung up in his holster.

All that distraction gave Ketch the break he needed. He whipped the leather chaps from his shoulder and swung as Vaught's gun jerked free. The heavy hide rocked Vaught and sent his shot wild. Ketch leaped the two strides' distance separating him from Vaught, just as Vaught triggered a second wild shot. Ketch tackled him high, pinning his arms to his sides. As they wrestled to the ground, Woody loosed a third shot that ripped off a chunk of flesh down the length of Ketch's calf.

But God had answered Ketch's prayers. He had Woody Vaught in his hands and this would be a fight to the finish.

Ketch tore the gun from Vaught's hand, breaking the man's trigger finger as he twisted it. Another shot fired off wildly, smashing a window somewhere. Ketch tossed the gun into the street. One of the rapidly gathering gawkers snatched it up and tucked it inside his own waistband.

Shouts of "Fight! Fight!" rang up and down the street as the townspeople sensed something more momentous than the usual drunken brawl.

As soon as Vaught became aware that one of his shots found its mark in Ketch's leg, he zeroed in on that vulnerable spot. He wrapped his leg around Ketch's injured one and raked the sharpened rowel of his spur over Ketch's wound.

The expected scream of agony never materialized. Emotion lifted the horse-breaker above feeling. His powerful hands took hold of Vaught's throat and squeezed until Woody's eyes bulged with the pressure. In desperation, Vaught jammed both his arms between Ketch's and broke Ketch's hold. Vaught rolled away and jumped to his feet.

Favoring his injured leg, Ketch rose more slowly. Both men stood tall, circling each other, the one huge and beefy, the other lithe, wiry, and limping. With his lighter weight, Ketch had depended on his agility to offset Vaught's greater bulk. But now that he lost that mobility along with its advantage, Ketch turned to his lightning hands and quicker mind to dull the plodding foreman's edge.

As Vaught charged in, Ketch ducked under him, then straightened with all the force left in his legs, lifting and pitching the bigger man ass over teakettle.

Like a stunned grizzly, Vaught shook himself, and then turned to face Ketch. Ketch half-knelt on the ground—the counterforce of the foreman's body had buckled the bronc-buster's bleeding leg. Vaught drove his massive shoulder into him before Ketch could get all the way back onto his feet. They landed with Vaught on top. Ketch felt a rib crack. *His own.*

Ketch twisted and jerked his elbow up into the other man's jaw, and again into Woody's teeth, cracking a few. Vaught rolled away from the punishing elbow. Ketch used his one good leg to painfully jack to his feet.

The thought bounced around in his mind, *Let Woody come to you — just don't let him get his hands on you.*

Vaught obliged by rushing Ketch. With a quick hop-step off his injured leg, Ketch sidestepped as the other lunged. As Vaught swept into the space Ketch had just vacated, Ketch swung his clasped hands upward, like a lumberman with an ax on the upswing. The low blow to the gut, along with Vaught's own impetus, lifted the bigger man half a foot into the air. Vaught grunted, spewing a flux of undigested food from his lips. He swiped at his mouth with his coat-sleeve and inhaled a huge draught of air to let the wave of nausea pass.

Ketch's strategy flew to the wind as he sensed an opportunity. He began to press. Hobbling forward, he threw two short right jabs, followed by a hard left to Vaught's gut, setting off another round of gagging in the bigger man. Vaught clumsily retreated as Ketch continued to crowd him.

They moved slowly, soddenly, south along the street, the eager onlookers following. Past Katie's. Past the old hotel, the new buildings, the abandoned Silver Ridge Weekly Record office, the new hotel, and all the way to the livery stable at the edge of town.

The crowd circled-in tightly as they neared the corrals. Someone moved in too close and tripped up Ketch. He fell heavily on his wounded leg. High adrenaline made him oblivious to the pain, but the damn leg refused to function the way he wanted it to.

Vaught grabbed the moment and belly-flopped on top of Ketch. The ends of Ketch's fractured rib grated against each under the heavier man's weight, and Ketch lacked the strength to throw him off.

With Ketch pinned down, Vaught reached down to his boot and pulled off a spur. He swiped at Ketch with the knife-edged rowel. Ketch twisted his head away, jammed the heel of his hand under Vaught's jaw. Vaught slashed again. Ketch's forearm absorbed the worst of Vaught's strike, which left a track of bloody beads across the side of Ketch's neck.

Sure now of his advantage, Woody levered himself to his feet. In seconds he'd turned from prey to predator. Sure of his kill, a vicious smile crossed Vaught's face as he stalked Ketch.

Hampered by the uncooperative leg, Ketch did his best to dodge the slicing, slashing spur, but the steel cut tracks in everything it hit. Vaught started aiming for Ketch's eyes.

The sonofabitch aims to blind me!

Frantically, Ketch grabbed hold of the lowest corral rail and scuttled himself backward under it into the pen. The horses, alarmed by the shouts and the sudden intrusion, bolted in every direction, whipping up a cloud of dust. As Vaught climbed over the top rail in pursuit, Ketch's hand sprang out of the dust cloud, grabbed onto a lapel of the beefy foreman's short coat and hauled him headfirst into the corral dirt.

Vaught's fall broke Ketch's hold and the big man jumped to his feet, once more on the offensive. Latching on to a fence rail, Ketch hoisted himself up. Now on his feet, Ketch awkwardly backpedaled, trying to avoid the fist-encased spur, searching for an opening to get past Vaught's defenses.

Ketch moved behind a darting horse, evaded Vaught by clambering through the rails into the breeding pen, the one with Peady's stud in it. The startled black whistled shrilly, kicked wildly. Ketch ducked away from the flailing hooves, his attention momentarily diverted from Vaught who vaulted over the railing to come into the pen after him.

With the big stallion behind him and Vaught attacking from the front, Ketch had no choice but to stand his ground.

But Vaught, in his over-eagerness to finish Ketch, dropped his guard. He swung his spurred fist in a reckless roundhouse — the opening Ketch needed, the one he'd been hoping for.

Ketch put his whole body and all the strength of his muscled torso into a solid left to Vaught's gut that drove the man clear back against the rails. Woody doubled over clutching his stomach, retching dryly. Ketch yanked Vaught's head up by the hair and smashed him in the mouth. As Vaught lifted his guard to protect his face, Ketch rained lefts and rights to the gut. Woody dropped his hands to cover his middle. Whenever Vaught lifted his hands to protect his face, Ketch loosed a flurry of corkscrew chops to the man's exposed gut — driving his knuckles, twisting the wrist, screw-driving each punch deep into Woody's softened belly. Then back to Vaught's face, back and forth, face, gut, over and over.

Crossing his arms over his face, Vaught ran blindly from Ketch's onslaught, headlong into the agitated stud.

Vaught swung at the animal with his spurred fist. The beast reared back onto its haunches, pawing the air with upraised forelegs. In a frenzy of terror or rage, the horse dropped to all fours and thrust Woody to the ground. Again it rose on hind legs, came down, its slashing forehooves hitting Woody's chest with the force of twin sledgehammers.

The stallion reared up once more. Ketch tried to wave off the animal's savage attack, but, as if it had begun something it couldn't stop until it finished, the stud struck again...and again, all too quickly for any of the onlookers to help Ketch intervene, even if they'd been brave enough to try.

Ketch himself seemed stunned as he looked down at Vaught's mutilated body.

A collective gasp went up from the crowd as the stallion lowered its head and bolted toward Ketch.

Peady, moving faster than he ever had in his life, winged his way into the stable, grabbed his *Greener*, and raced back to the breeding pen and shoved his way through the bystanders. He stopped dead as he lifted the shotgun to his shoulder.

The stallion was standing calmly by Ketch, nudging the horse-breaker's shoulder with his muzzle.

Ketch, panting, exhausted, sickened by what had happened, unconsciously looped his arm over the stallion's neck and massaged the muscles under its mane.

As if coming out of a daze, Ketch lifted his head and sought out Revel instinctively knowing exactly where to find her among the throng of onlookers. His eyes locked with hers; he vaulted over the corral and limped as fast as he could, through the crowd, toward her. But as he drew closer, something in her expression made him hesitate. His insides tightened. *What must she be thinking of me now?*

But Revel's thoughts were far from Woody Vaught's battered form lying in the corral. Sight of the big stallion and Ketch in the corral, standing almost as one, brought a rush of past images to mind — Ketch breaking that "widow-maker" out at her ranch, man and animal merging into a single jack-knifing centaur. Woody Vaught's words at Peady's corral — *"Ketch and that devil-horse are two of a kind."*

Continuing to stare at Ketch, the world seemed to halt as Peady's words also echoed stark and clear in her mind — *Ketch and that hoss are two of a kind, but I tell you, in the right hands, either one of them critters, this*

hoss or Ketch, could turn out to be right fine specimens.
   In the right hands...
   As Ketch took another hesitant step toward her, Revel held out her hands.

the end

AUTHOR'S NOTE

Today, Silver Reef, near Leeds, Utah,
is a virtual ghost town. In the 1870s,
however, Silver Reef was a bustling
mining town and site of "the mother
lode." According to one story, the rich
silver deposit was discovered when silver
oozed out of a hot fireplace built of local
sandstone. Another has it that the silver
was discovered as the offshoot of a
practical joke played on "Metalliferous"
Murphy of Pioche, Nevada,
an assayer with a reputation for finding
ore in dubious samples. Some miners
who knew silver could not be found in
sandstone gave Murphy a chunk broken
off a grindstone that had been made from
sandstone quarried from the white reefs west
of Leeds. Murphy's report of rich silver chloride
in the rock cast enough doubt on his veracity
to cause the miners to expel him from camp.
Legend has it that Murphy was never heard
from again. What the miners didn't know was
that hundreds of years earlier, silver had
been found in sandstone in Germany and
that the white sandstone reefs west of Leeds
did indeed contain the mother lode.